EVELYN CONLON was born in 195.  W9-BLS-822
educated there and at St Patrick's College, Maynooth.
taught English and has lived and travelled in Australia and Asia.
Her short stories have appeared in many publications and
anthologies, and have been broadcast on BBC radio. Her first
collection, *My Head is Opening* (Attic Press), was published in
1987, and her first novel, *Stars in the Daytime* (Attic Press and
The Women's Press) was published in 1989. Her second collection of short stories, *Taking Scarlet as a Real Colour*, was published
in 1993 (Blackstaff Press). She was a recipient of Arts Council
Bursaries in 1988 and 1995. She has been writer in residence for
Dublin City Library and counties Kilkenny, Cavan and
Limerick. She lives in Dublin and is a regular commentator on
the arts.

A GLASSFUL OF LETTERS

♦

EVELYN CONLON

THE
BLACKSTAFF
PRESS

BELFAST

• A BLACKSTAFF PRESS PAPERBACK ORIGINAL •

Blackstaff Paperback Originals present new writing, previously
unpublished in Britain and Ireland, at an affordable price.

First published in March 1998 by
The Blackstaff Press Limited
3 Galway Park, Dundonald, Belfast BT16 2AN, Northern Ireland
with the assistance of
The Arts Council of Northern Ireland

Reprinted July 1998

Typeset by Techniset Typesetters, Newton-le-Willows, Merseyside

Printed in Ireland by ColourBooks Limited

A CIP catalogue record for this book
is available from the British Library

ISBN 0-85640-618-X

for
Pat Murphy
Nell McCafferty
Patsy Murphy

ACKNOWLEDGEMENTS

As I put this book to bed I think of the late Lar Cassidy of An Chomhairle Ealaíon and the continuous encouragement that he gave me over the years.

My thanks also to the following people: Patsy Murphy, who gave this book its first diligent reading; Carol Kilbride, ex Aer Lingus; Jim Griffiths, NCAD, Lecturer in Glass; Marina Burke and Niamh Parsons for typing; Paddy O'Brien for playing 'The High Wire'; Anne O'Neill for solicitorial work; Ania Corless of David Higham Associates; all the staff at Blackstaff; Kate O'Callaghan and Patrick Farrelly for hospitality in New York; Ezio Vacari, my first connection with Verona; and as always Fintan Vallely for everything.

I would like to acknowledge the assistance of An Chomhairle Ealaíon who awarded me a Bursary in Creative Literature, and Aer Lingus Art Flights, all of which helped in the completion of this book.

EVELYN CONLON

1

I've never been called upon to be particularly brave. Having said
that, bravery has an indefinable character. It can mostly be
avoided, often without anyone knowing of one's cowardice.
Most people don't see their lives as others see them and consequently, some people mistakenly think they've been brave, and
others, who have shown great courage, see their lives as having been
merely lived. In this latter category, I suppose, you could place a
few of my actions. I put my legs up in stirrups and allowed a most
ignorant-looking specimen of a doctor to rupture my membranes,
in a suspiciously cruel and rough manner. I didn't cry; I even tried
to make him feel at ease, emitting only a few low, refined words,
'Are these things absolutely necessary?' (I tell you this about myself
so that you'll get the full picture of me. It's no use dressing myself
up as if some things had never happened.) But in order for an act to
be brave, does the person about to do it have to know how awful
it's going to be? Or does the action have to be unusual, or does it
have to happen to a man? If any of these three conditions apply, I'm
disqualified.

Once I also behaved extremely calmly (I'm not sure if calmness
can be described as extreme), during an emergency on our plane,
but that was my duty in my line of work, and it could also be called
cowardice that I didn't sit down in a seat and weep copiously. I

didn't let out big gulps followed by the small yelps associated with a bitch whose pups have been taken from her and drowned, which is what I wanted to do, but I was afraid that my co-workers would think me a failure, so fear of being branded unbrave made me behave bravely. I didn't feel it. (I will, of course, eventually be called on to be really brave, on my deathbed, or at my death if I'm not in bed. I presume bravery is called for then, both internally for one's mind and externally for the look of things, if there are people around. I certainly wouldn't want to make an ass of myself screaming the place down. If I've managed to get that far, a few more minutes won't kill me, so to speak.)

But if bravery is not one of my big character traits, well, I have others. I don't know what they are because I have them all in small amounts, sprigs of things, really. But this story is not about me; I have no story without other people. It's about my neighbour, Connie, and other neighbours, and what happened to her and us one year. She was brave.

Although I'm not on the same time as everyone else due to the continuous flying, I keep more or less up to date with the happenings on the street. There are some gaps, of course. Sometimes I ask my husband a question about so-and-so and he looks at me quizzically and then, always gently, says, almost apologetically, 'Did I not tell you, I thought I told you, so-and-so is dead.' We often argue over whether he has told me such and such a thing, he insisting he has, and that I either wasn't paying attention or that I don't remember. I pack my assertions tight up to his, one for one. But about dead neighbours, no, we presume that one doesn't forget that someone has died.

My husband runs a business on Rathmines Road, next door to the crèche where we used to send Ciarán. It's five minutes' walk from the primary school he attends (Kildare Place School which used to be in Kildare Place: a school where the teachers appear to be happy and the children are), and ten minutes from where we live. All the proximities have made our job of rearing Ciarán easier.

My husband is a great father: his own age has not dawned on him yet, so he thinks the child is his younger brother. I envy them occasionally – their knowing about line-outs, the fact that they can bury personal pain because the world is still theirs (well, Ireland certainly; well, no more than any other place, just differently). Ciarán knew what was what on that score by the time he was five years old. I envy them the seriousness with which they are taken and how they get their ball games to be so important. But mostly I treat them as the surprises that they are to me, the separate components to our home. I don't know how they see me – that's the difference between us – they probably don't see me as outside themselves. When I come back from a transatlantic, the electric blanket is on, the house is spotless, but when I've had my sleep, they shy away from the kitchen as if it were mine. I don't know where they could have got that idea. But I get to leave again to New York, London, Paris, Rome, and once to Sydney. I could not live without my job (not any old job, the one that takes me on and off this island, in and out of my street) so that the out-ness and in-ness mean something when I have them. I don't know if my husband or my neighbours know that this is what I'm thinking. Perhaps they feel that I just kept my job in Aer Lingus for a while after the baby was born and then, because things worked out so well, what with how near the house was to the crèche and then to the school, and that to Kevin's job, and the fact that there is only one child and that the father is so good, I drifted into keeping it permanently. They don't realise that firstly, it is no accident that the house is so near the school (I picked it when I was three weeks pregnant, spewing a dozen times a day and in a state of euphoric shock) and that I would not have married any other kind of man, simply not. People know only what they can handle.

It could be said that there is something wrong with me, that my bonding, both times it applied, went wrong. Otherwise why would I choose this job? My parents wanted me to be a teacher, or at least an accountant like both of them, or a lawyer. I had the brains to be a lawyer, they thought. I thought that I had the brains to carve out for myself a small piece of fresh air that would keep me sane, and the most important component of that fresh air was move-ment. Unlike other hostesses (lately also hosts), we in Aer Lingus do not consider this a job, we look on it as a coming and going. We could not spend our lives knowing where we would be every day at whatever time, for years to come, and yet we could not be emigrants because they spend their lives being Irish rather than living a life. In Ireland we do not, naturally, have to be Irish: we are red-haired, perverse, thin, drinkers, pioneers, good in the morning, all-night artists, bad-tempered, gay, tall, theatre-goers, homeless, politicos. I have the best of both and all worlds, and I know when I'm enjoying myself, time doesn't just happen to me.

My parents rather snobbily thought that I could have established a career where the occasional travel was necessary, but I felt that that kind of job would have ruined my hearing. One of them (I can't remember which one as they melted into each other at times of conflict, putting up a united front that was shocking in its immutability) actually said 'glorified waitress' when I told them that I'd got my interview. But as I say, there's a problem with my bonding and I had no intentions of working nine to five (that's eight hours every day, approximately eighty thousand hours in a working lifetime) in a job that one of my parents wanted.

I immediately found that this work gave me everything I needed. I flitted to cities like people visit different streets and I arrived with a fresh confident feeling, in time to go to art galleries and museums (confident because I wasn't a lone tourist; I always had the hotel and the other hostesses to run back to if problems arose). I had a job to back me up. In the beginning when I would describe to my parents the Musée D'Orsay, the Rodin Museum or St Peter's, their eyes clouded over with disappointed dreams. They had been prepared, and could have afforded, to support me in doing whatever would have been necessary to get me to those places in a more suitable manner. Lord help us, they thought, where did we get such a stubborn child? They never heard what I actually said. Eventually I stopped enthusing about connections I'd made, about artists whose names I could now recognise, painters whom I could now match with times and countries. They found Manhattan easier to listen to. It seemed appropriate to them to be an air-hostess there; it didn't seem to cruelly tease them with possible glories that I could have achieved. Poor parents, never realising that you don't get two chances at life, that it's now their child's turn.

But all that was years ago. I acquired a varied education through experience, through seeing and meeting people on and off planes. Air-hostesses enter a strange world; they are in a war zone of sorts, complete with captain. He runs the ship, the show – we even ask him if it is OK to stay away from the hotel at night. And they have this other place, the passenger zone, where people do the oddest of things. In the first and second zones one behaves in a certain manner but can still have oneself to one's own self at the same time. There is a third place (time off in strange cities) and a fourth, home, where everyone assumes, as long as you keep feeding them titbits, that they know you, but they don't. All sufficiently varied to suit me. All disconnected enough to allow me more than one life.

I learned, too, how much I can hate people. Last week there was a man bossing everyone on the flight over, acting as if he were the only passenger in the sky that day and taking out the inadequacies of his childhood, marriage, job, on us. Flying is hard for him; he has to burst out all the prig in him over a few hours whereas usually he lets it out slowly. People are always disappointing me, acting to type. I can hate museum wanderers with a passion, as if I was the only person entitled to be there, a little like my passenger. A tourist, which I have never seen myself as, saying to his girlfriend, 'I like that, but I'm none too keen on the furniture. Drab.' 'Appreciate it for what it is,' she says in a longing voice. I talk to myself, actually saying the words out loud, 'Save your breath, honey. He will have forgotten the furniture by the time you get to the next room, but he'll remember it sometime in New Plymouth or New Something, when you're long gone, and he'll say, "When I was in Europe I saw this great furniture in a museum. In Venice, I think it was."' He's in London. It will be all 'I' then. People will think him more interesting for having done this on his own. You will never have been.

I have learned, and it makes me sad, that people can look alike no matter what the colour, sex, age or clothes. And that they act in the same manner. And that some look like cadavers from a distance, their heads, skulls before death. But those bad thoughts can always be comforted by busy, good moments and filed away in my somatic system.

When I was twenty-six I met my husband, although I didn't

know then that that was what he was. I lived in a constantly warm house in Swords: constantly warm because we four, all air-hostesses, did different shifts, so we boiled kettles and lit fires back-to-back. It was a well-watched house too, by neighbours who seemed like aliens to us, people with marriages, cars and children. Kevin asked a friend of his, who was going out with Betty (Italian route), if he thought he'd have a chance asking me for a date. The friend, a boisterous man with a tinny laugh, told us this as a joke and I disliked it so much, mainly because I didn't know which of us the joke was on, that I found Kevin's number and asked him if he wanted to come to a party with me.

Kevin was nervous and I simply couldn't understand why. I had no interest in him. He's not nervous now. I kept saying 'yes' to his requests for dates, for reasons which were nothing to do with wanting to go out with him; I didn't know what the reasons were. When I met him with friends of his he wasn't nervous at all; he was rather sprightly and confident, actually. The whole thing puzzled me. When people describe, or when I read of, falling in love, it still perplexes me. That's not what happened to us; well, to me anyway. Maybe it did happen to Kevin and that's why he was nervous. I would notice that when we were walking together he would skip to get in step with me, or shuffle to get our feet hitting the ground in tandem, presuming I wouldn't notice. I quite honestly thought it was crackers.

What happened to me was different. Instead of checking my heartbeats, I was busy finding out things about him, being surprised to see that he would fit in with my job perfectly. He's an easygoing man, and he doesn't suffer from jealousy. (Suffer is the word; not like some of the husbands who really have an awful time fighting themselves and their wives.) I found myself engaged: the experience was one that I presume sits on the love Richter midway between an arranged marriage and a union made dizzy, and perhaps dangerous, by lust.

After the engagement party Kevin and I went to bed together. Now I hadn't much experience, much to compare; we didn't in those days. But I knew a good thing when I saw it, even if I didn't know. He was simply unbelievable. I wouldn't have expected it to look at him. It's funny how stupid we are. We really do believe the ads. We think the good-lookers, the suave ones, are the ones who are good in bed. Maybe it's partly true that one needs a little confidence to start kissing and to dare a panoramic lovemaking, but only partly and only sometimes. And often absolutely not, because the handsome are too interested in themselves. And really, we shouldn't have fallen for the guff. Good lovemaking couldn't have been invented in the seventies, the eighties, the fifties, the twenties. Some people have always been able to do it properly, as if it mattered, and those people have not always looked the way we imagined.

Kevin didn't look like Kevin the lover. He was pleasant-looking, with a few minor faults: a nose that bumped a little, the usual sports humps and scars, cheeks that looked flat sometimes, ears a little too big, the usual. I had, of course, seen his bare chest that wasn't bare at all. I was very taken by all that hair; my father's chest was like my own except for the bumps. Kevin's hair seemed like some kind of guarantee to me. But though pleasant-looking, even good-looking, I would never have had him down for the painstaking, all-inventive, all-everything lover that he turned out to be. It was then that the engagement changed its scale; it was then that I knew what I'd got by saying yes. All that taking me out on dates must have cast a subconscious spell on me.

Kevin and I curled up into a place that became time, that became our wedding. We were almost unaware of our guests.

I don't remember much about our first few months – just an overall sense of warmth, a touch of cystitis that seemed worth it, and some songs. A few things did happen that dropped a sense of trauma over me, as if a sheet, without holes for the eyes, nose and mouth, had fallen over me. Notices were posted that my life had changed and couldn't be put back together again. And shock disappointments came ridiculously from nowhere. I say ridiculously, because disappointment has to have had contrary expectation, and why rational grown-ups expect some of the things they do from marriage defies me. But then I wasn't grown up when I married, still amn't. And then I started getting sick in the mornings. Would you believe that for a week I put it down to a change

7

in my brand of tea, or an inexplicable aversion to tea, to strong tea, in the morning, or to the cystitis perhaps? Ha, ha, ha.

I governed our house-searching. I shifted it to streets beside nurseries and schools. It was just as well I was pregnant; all the houses seemed to boast of being near schools. That sort of advertising could force one into getting pregnant so as not to waste the amenities. I paid particular attention to nurseries. I had made up my mind that I would like this child and the only way I could guarantee that was not to let it ruin my flying life. That settled, between it and me, I got down to growing a baby. It's hard and peculiar work and can leave a constant film of tears behind the eyes. It is also powerful work but unfortunately it's a power that mostly frightens rather than attracts. Frankly, the whole process fascinated me. I was daily amazed and also very randy. Lucky, then, I was working on the ground, near Kevin. Airlines are kind to women who are 'expecting'. Oh, I love it, 'expecting'! In the last months my dreams were too weird even for dreamland: giving birth to horses' heads and once, with my mother present, giving birth to my toilet travel bag. I can still hear her screaming, 'It's a bag.'

My day came. With luck, most of us will die with less pain. That's all I have to say on the matter. And it is not true that it is forgotten: it is simply misfiled for the sake of the human race and it lies there below the skin surface of women who sometimes look at each other across crowded rooms, buses, airports, galleries, and say nothing. My little son. My beautiful son. The soft skin of him. The shock of him. The terror of him. The dampness of it all, blood, milk and tears. He got used to being born, the little mite, and began to smile. I healed. And there came a day when I took my flight again. It was hard in the beginning, thinking of him as I had never ever thought of anyone before, but I knew not to give up my job. I just knew and I thank God for wisdom like that which comes from nowhere.

Having a child shifts the central focus of your own life. You see other people in different contexts, you need neighbours. But neighbours spread a long way out and it's hard to see why some of them become more than people who live close by, and others adopt the nodding, beaming stance of people who know they're neighbours and, yes, know that she's an air-hostess and that he's a businessman of some sort, and know that they have one child, or that the other man has been out of work this last six months, and he was married once, and the new woman in the rented house is on the radio sometimes, you wouldn't think it to look at her, but still they're neighbours who are not in. The people with whom you set and you become a single mind, a collective thought process, so that when I'm in Paris or on the corner of Fifth and Eighty-Third I know what Connie would think. And when I'm changing at Charing Cross I have a good idea what Fergal or Bernard would think. Or when I meet an ex-hostess in Edinburgh for breakfast I know which of my neighbours would like this place best.

And they become one (not necessarily out of desire) community for its own sake, being a thing of beauty that lived only in the heads of hippies. Our one consisted of Kevin and I, our neighbour Connie (the greatest blessing that could be bestowed on a street), Connie's husband, Desmond, and it was only because he was her husband that he was in, because God knows I think he hated us all, or rather loved no one but himself. I kept all my feelings about Desmond to myself; I presumed that Connie got something from him, hoped indeed that he gave her everything. This hope was not just the general wishing well for one's friends that a person feels; it was more personal because Connie was, and is, one of the most important people in my life (indeed the most important after my husband and child and, sometimes even more important than them). Then there was Bernard Cunningham, Connie's father-in-law. He is Desmond's father, actually, but funny, we never thought of him as that. And then Fergal, our single man, although technically he wasn't single at all. He had gone to college with Connie, they had shared houses and pasts. She was the only person, I believe, that knew anything about his six-week marriage. Six weeks! Astonishing. Makes one really curious. What could possibly have happened in such a short time, something, obviously, that hadn't happened before, to end a marriage? Had someone got the most extraordinary, I mean out of this world, sexual habits? Had someone got no interest whatsoever? Were they moved to suicide with disgust over the thought of it, the very thought of it? Had someone believed that marriage was the licence for, for WHAT? And which of them was it? Of course it could have been something ordinary. Perhaps. Six weeks though, it's unlikely. Anyway, he's an architect and has been out of work for some months, so he's going to America. On my flight, actually.

Connie says that it will get us all writing again because we can't afford to ring him. Well, the rest of them will have to, I won't, as I'll see him occasionally on my day off. He's going to let his house; in fact, the tenants are moving in a few hours after he leaves. He hopes not to be gone more than a year but I don't know about that. A stretch of time can turn up things and make it impossible to return. Why do I have an odd feeling about him going, as if the fact of it will set events in motion that will change us all? Ridiculous; everything does that anyway. Nothing happens that wouldn't have happened differently if something else had or had not happened.

2

Dear Connie,

My last suitcase has become the centre of my life. I have been
flitting around and peering into it since seven o'clock this morning. It seems that if I check it often enough I'll ensure that I'm
not making a mistake. I think that everything, except this pen
and paper, is packed now. Whatever is not can be left and used
by the tenants. I'll be in touch soon about all the arrangements;
sorry we couldn't sort it out last night, but with so many people
dropping in and out it was impossible to talk. Nice of everyone
to call, but in another way I felt it put a very final pressure on my
leaving. We'll see. After you went home, Patricia and John called
– separately, of course, but guess what? They left together! So
maybe my departure will be of some use to someone – other
than the live register, that is (lovely words those, as if the unem-
ployed might electrocute you if you touched them). I'd better go,
Helena is giving me a lift. She's on the transatlantic route this
week and she'll be on my flight, so there'll be plenty of cham-
pagne and brandy. It will be nice to have her coming and going.
I presume I'll be able to meet her every now and then in New
York; she'll take letters if anyone wants to write me more

urgently than An Post can accommodate. You get my drift, I'm sure.

I really must go, I'll drop this through your letterbox on the way, and thanks again for taking on the minding of the tenants. Please look after yourself and those lovely children of yours – Desmond can look after himself.

Your loving friend,
Fergal

PS. You will make sure that you and your dear father-in-law (I know Bernard hates being called that) write to me. Regularly. I promise to reply promptly. I thought Bernard was very interesting last night talking about positivity and his next move, even though he's obviously extremely upset both about the death of his wife and losing his job. I've never heard anyone describing their job so lovingly, certainly not me. You did when you had the job in the geography encyclopaedia place in London. I wonder, do you ever regret not staying. I shouldn't have said that, it's easy for me on my way out. I know that it's not possible for everyone to go. If they did who would we 'emigrants' have to miss? I really must rush – God, I hate flying!

Dear Connie,

Well, I arrived, as might be expected, took the Carey bus in, really handy. I couldn't believe how easy it was; I expected some nerve-wracking experience. I could have gone with Helena in the Aer Lingus coach but I felt that I had put her to enough trouble on the flight over, what with wanting turbulence continuously explained to me and checking our scheduled landing time over and over again. God, she works hard.

The sun was setting over Manhattan as I came into the city, it was truly beautiful. I haven't seen it since as I've been more or less stuck out here, getting over jet-lag, looking for a job and accommodation and all that. I've sorted the latter and am confident about an interview in the morning so I'm just dropping this to let you know that my new address will be 28 Spring Street, NY, NY1004.

> Lots of love,
> Fergal

Dear Connie,

I feel like a child at boarding-school relaying details of my first week – the boys are all right, the teachers seem to be OK, and I've made two new friends. By the way, my dormitory, the building and the whole surrounds are magnificent. Yes, I got the job, architect's office, which makes me feel part of the world again. I realise now how very depressed I've been being out of work at home (see how quickly I add the 'at home'). The work is reasonably similar to my old job; it's just the names that are different. Sometimes when I'm at my desk I think I'm in Dublin, then I hear some startled street noise firing its way up twenty storeys in through the window, and I feel a twinge of shock. Perhaps people really do stay where they've left for a long time. Look at Bernard, he is certainly still in Waterford, and maybe will be always. My apartment is large, bright, beautiful, but strangely unlived in. I cannot seem to match a history with it, certainly not in the way we could always imagine something about the last tenants in our crummy bedsits; perhaps this is real outsideness.

I love the variety of people and colour at work; people have less struggle proving their uniqueness in an unhomogeneous place. (And doesn't that seem to be what most people's lives are about? I know some are lucky enough to live calmly and gratefully pleased with all offerings. Are you one of those? I think so.) Yet I find myself going to Irish bars because the language there will not merely be the same, I will also know it. I try, mostly unsuccessfully, to avoid our dear friend Philip. If he's not sniffing coke he's bored and boring. His stories get larger every time I meet him. Either they are true, which is horrific, or they're not, which reveals something even more worrying about his mind. I'm afraid I have no desire to walk the road of his past or present with him. I wish I still cared but maybe getting into our thirties in Ireland has made us too easily dismissive of cokeheads; we didn't have to put up with too many of them and, of course, we got good at dismissing many types in order to stay sane. The last time I met him I couldn't stop thinking of the chances he had in comparison to the rest of us but it is often the lucky who make a complete mess of their lives and cannot have them sorted out.

I've joined the NY public library. Ah dear, Connie, you'd love it. There isn't a book in the world not in it, well, give or take. I mustn't begin to exaggerate or you will dismiss me. I remember your pet hates. I'm catching up on quite a few writers. I tend to go out only at weekends because travelling and coping with the noise and the speed, on top of work, makes for an exhausting day. No Slattery's here to nip out to, ten minutes before closing. I feel exhilarated by now in this city, as do most people, but of course we insist on believing that our experience is unique. Manhattan is so mathematically easy, marked out as if these people would always be children, foreign, lost or too busy – it helps the sense of achievement to have the geography under control so soon, to be a walking cartographer. Mind you, the safety factor is apparently not as easily learned. I've decided to give it a miss altogether, otherwise I'd be in a continuous state of apprehension. The place affects me in stages, as if my body and mind sensibly take in only what they can digest each day.

I've been thinking a little of our friendship, not the most common of ones. I wonder if it blossomed out of necessity rather than desire. (I don't mean to trivialise it by saying that.) But have you noticed how male friends invariably disappoint each other? I think you came along just when that had happened to me once too often; so really it was all an accident. Only joking, only joking. God, this letter-writing could be dangerous. I can't flounder back over my sentences or use my hands to draw exactitudes of what I do or don't mean. So let me go back to less dangerous descriptions.

The noise in New York is its most unique sense, I believe. Everything is part of the noise. I like standing and trying to figure out, by a process of elimination, what the components might be. Some lunch times I sit in this small park and try to knock each one off. First the police sirens: it's important to switch them off. Cop shows have made them so familiar that they might hide there, camouflaged as wallpaper. Now does Dublin have a noise? I can't remember anything except the buses squealing like small pigs in the distance, with a microphone close to their mouths, of course. Or perhaps like fresh newspaper squeaking on a newly methylated window, do you think? Does Dublin have a smell? Yes, I know, Bewley's, and Guinness yeast on a certain type of night. Ah, and the noise of foghorns on the same type of night – but what else? Here there is everything, all Europe's, all Asia's, all Africa's, all South America's foods, heats. Different kinds of heats, enclosed, dry, damp, underground, overground, crowd, fear. Why don't I just say that here has all noise, all smell, all sight, all taste if you want it? But the touch is by rote and is insincere. So far. Speaking of which, I haven't thought of Carmel much since I came here. I swat at it when I notice the memory becoming intrusive. I suppose that will eventually give me eczema or horrendous boils. That would be like something she'd do, and boy, would she enjoy it. Enough of that. But honestly, I do feel that I'm entitled to one guilt-free place

– even God couldn't have expected me to stay with her. Actually, He would never have expected me to last even a week; doesn't He see everything?

Lunch is almost over. I'm finishing this in 'my' park, sometimes watching the customers filing in and out of 'my' deli. The weather is beautiful but people keep warning me that the deads of winter and summer will change all that. Don't worry about my house; I expect that there will be some human wear and tear by the time I get over on my holiday next year, and unless the tenants need some immediate attention, you shouldn't have too much to do. I must rush now. I'm looking forward to your letter – I know that with the kids it's not that easy, but really, once you get started, it will be. Sit down now and write.

Love,
Fergal

To Bernard from Fergal

Dear Bernard,

Arrived safely, as no doubt Helena or indeed Connie will have told you. I have got the job and the apartment (sorry, the flat) or the place to live. I've been catching up on some old friends, although I believed before I left that I wouldn't. It's amazing to think of all the older people I know who spent a few years here at some time, my father and mother included. Indeed, I believe you spent six months here also, but you were all so silent about it. I wonder was it regret at coming back that kept my parents quiet? At least I can ask you. Why did you leave?

Already I have that emigrant's interest in those who arrived before them. I think you get it in the first drowning flush of lone-liness after customs clearance at Kennedy. The name of the airport helps with familiarity but you can't stay there, you must go out through that door. Imagine, the airport was not called that when you were here; we do so presume that life begins with us. And what a strange name it did have – Idlewild. In the airport I got terribly embarrassed by the behaviour of three Irish lads in the café where I stopped for a coffee before getting my bus. Why should I have cared? They were only my countrymen, not my bloody children, but our island shrinks so here. Odd, that's not what happens in Australia. Helena always said that. Perhaps it's because Australian cities are hintered by such emptiness that the excitement of arrival turns to awe and moves outward. The country itself is the point of interest, not the people. So here I am, starting a New York life, thinking of the past, and clocking in with you.

Regards,
Fergal

POSTCARD
To Connie from Fergal

Dear Connie,

WHERE are my letters?

NOTE
To Bernard from Connie

Bernard,

When I called you weren't in. We must write to Fergal; his brief postcard this morning suggests to me that he thinks we've forgotten him. Will call around this evening.

Connie

Dear Fergal,

I really am sorry for not writing sooner but I was putting it off because, somehow, starting this correspondence puts a reality on your being in New York. I've been trying to convince myself that you're merely on one of your short holidays, and that you'll drop in for lunch as usual any day now. I didn't know I'd miss you so much (I'm getting the moaning over and done with first). I've been thinking that we really do live our lives as if on a stage; we are actors who hate it when the other actors are missing. We save up lines for specific, different people in our lives and wait until they come on to say them. It's no use saying them to the wrong person, to someone who wouldn't have the context. I think a lot of my lines are for you, so they're being unsaid now.

It is possible, I suppose, to keep our friendship intact by our letters, but somehow it won't be the same: I need to see your eyes, I need some space in my kitchen to be taken up with your blustering and your um-ing and ah-ing, I need to hear your impatient cough as you ring the doorbell at the wrong time. (Your arrival was never really at the wrong time.)

For weeks before you went I was really angry; envy caused that, I suppose. I passed the airport a few times on my way to visit my friend in Swords and I found the intensity of my anger quite debilitating. I can only presume that it came from a desire to be as free as you, although, of course, I must say that I don't wish my children unmade. Or maybe I found the breaking of our years-long friendship just too unbearable; we've known each other an awfully long time. Funny, people never say those things to each other face to face; social dependence is taken so much for granted until it's broken. When I worked in the village shop during school holidays I took for granted people coming in to buy a packet of cigarettes and then coming back ten minutes later for matches, just because they had seen someone else coming in, someone they wanted to see or someone they wanted to have a go at. Now I know how intricate those dependencies were and how honest it was for people to live in admission of them. Going into a pub is different: people can pretend that they're there for the drink rather than the company, which is mostly not true.

But I was talking about your leaving. I don't think I will ever make a friend like you again. Naturally I wasn't thinking of a quick, easy replacement, but even if I was so inclined it would be impossible, because of the years we had together and where those years were in our lives. It's so rare for men and women to be real friends. I think the only way it happens is if they know and like each other, while both are busy eyeing up other people and never each other. In youth all this is possible because there are so many possibilities, but later, if two people like each other as much as you and I do, they complicate it and ruin the whole thing by making uncomfortable sexual passes at each other. I like the friendship of a man; men are so much more unworried than women. Well, I liked your friendship, anyway, regardless of why it started. Perhaps I'll now have to get my consolation from soap operas! Only joking, I hope.

Enough of this. Let me tell you now what I did today (you seem so starved to know, although for what reason I cannot imagine; our lives are so predictable and boring, as you know – well, at least mine is). The weather is awful, awful wet, straight downpours, low-hanging clouds all day, dark mornings, dark afternoons. It's a relief when actual pitch black falls around us, at least we're not being fooled. I read a book once, set in Sweden (I can never remember the name), and the opening stated that the author was a teenager before realising that there was a climate other than Sweden's. It was then she knew that her parents were mad. I think that applies equally here. Did you ever listen to the way we console ourselves – 'But it's beautiful in summer'? There's no guarantee at all that it will be beautiful in summer. When the SAD people really hit shore here they'll make a killing.

Good Lord, I've just re-read this letter. I left it down to collect my brood from school. I also have Helena's Ciarán this week as she's in Rome – she had a number of days off and decided to spend them there. I see that my mood is most downbeat and I'm afraid I will depress you, but I promise to lighten up next time.

I've called in formally on your tenants, Stephen, Liam, Gina, and someone whose name and gender escaped me. Honestly, I felt old. They seem nice – not nice-nice, but a little like what we resembled in our student days – pleasant, but you'd never know what's going on in their/our heads or beds. Not that much went on in mine. I think it's Stephen that's with Gina, although I could be completely wrong; maybe Gina's with Liam or maybe Liam is with Stephen. I told them that I won't be calling often, just occasionally, to see that all is well. I assured them that although I have a key I won't be using it when they're not there; I don't intend to become a snooping proxy landlady. That seemed to cheer them all up.

It's wonderful that you got both job and apartment so quickly; soon you'll have a woman, no doubt. Speaking of which, I bumped into Carmel and we had a quick coffee in the Kylemore. By the way, they're putting a lot of glass in it; I fear the light will destroy its furtive, womb-like quality. Carmel seemed well and was glad that you were settled in. She did strike me as being a little rueful and sad but then she cheered up and told me all about this wonderful new job she's got. She didn't seem in the least desirous that bits of you drop off or swell up; indeed she said that she might write to you and left me her telephone number. Desmond is well, involved in some horrendously difficult process at work; consequently he's slightly vague and nervy but it will pass. Sometimes I sense a remoteness emanating from him like a strong smell, but I'm so busy with the children I have no time to draw him in. I wonder if I've done something intrinsically lacking in understanding to him. How could he get so far away? These questions are much too large and are probably the wrong questions anyway.

Do you realise that this letter-writing could be dangerous in more ways than one? It could be a form of long-distance therapy that opens up safely sealed boxes. For instance, I've got music on while I write this that I haven't listened to in years. That in itself could bring up the sort of memories that overturn the applecart in spectacular, freak ways. We'll see.

>   I do miss you,
>   Connie

To Fergal from Bernard

Dear Fergal,

Connie reminded me to write. I received your letter, thank you. All is well with me, that is if I ignore the rheumatic twinges that are no longer, alas, junior twinges. But at my age, what can I expect? Cod-liver oil can't cure time. The street is unchanged since you left, except for your tenants, of course, an interesting-looking bunch as far as I can see. There are three or four of them, I think. I'd better stop squinting out the window. I'm not that old yet. The weather has been the weather.

You asked why I left New York. I was indeed there for six months. I went over in the early fifties to an old aunt and uncle. I remember them clearly: he worked as a fireman and played the piano accordion in the evenings, at home and at Irish dances. She was a nurse. (What else? All the Irish girls that you met out were nurses; the others who were minding houses didn't get out as much, I suppose.) Why did I leave? Well, you know how things can be described in many ways? We could see the world as it appears to be, all outside sheen and people living good lives, or as good as possible. Then we could see it cynically, people seeming and trying hard to seem different than they actually are; so it depends on how I look at it. I was working in a glass-blowers in Manhattan. The work was precise and I was learning something, but it was all in straight lines; there wasn't room for rounding off. That time a person wouldn't leave Ireland and come back soon afterwards; if you went you went and were expected to stay unless you had a drastic midlife crisis or came home with money, so when a job

21

came up in Waterford Glass I wasn't expected to take it. People presumed that if I wasn't happy in New York I would think it a pity that the job hadn't come up before I left, that I'd live with regret, as was our due as a nation. But it can't have just been the job. I think, if I remember correctly, that there was something about America which I tremendously disliked, a failing of all else except momentary satisfaction, a closing-down of expectations other than material, a self-absorption that was akin to swallowing oneself every day. All this in contradiction to the country's professed image of itself as a free and freeing place. What a laugh. There were still slaves there, for Christ's sake. I went to a few political meetings (this came naturally to me; I had been reared in a Connolly house and my mother had been a suffragette). I've just heard her voice correcting me – 'Suffragist, my dear, the *ette* was substituted to trivialise.' I must say my going to meetings did not go down well with some of my work mates. So no, it wasn't just the job; I preferred my familiar hypocrisies, I preferred as well to be white in Waterford. I wouldn't have used those words then, but the intense self-examination and self-description of recent political movements has given me an understanding of what I felt. Some of the Irish, you know, were far from cherubs when it came to race relations. I presume it's all different now. I hope so.

I sometimes regret having come back when I hear the election results or watch too much of *Questions and Answers*, or see cliques forming around themselves and making the same mistakes. But that's not the place; it's what age does to one, you can see too damn much. It is too difficult now to regret, because the most meaningful part of my life came about as a result of my decision to come back. I met Moira two weeks after coming home, and what would have happened me without that?

Ah, life is a funny old chance, having a cold and staying in, missing a bus and meeting some unknown person, taking a different street home: all can totally change its course. Especially when you're young. Our ability to change diminishes with every new rheumatic twinge or every new inch around the waist, not because we don't want to, but because the combination of possibilities get fewer in our age group.

22

I am indeed very interested in what happened to my generation who stayed away. You and I could start research, you in your public library, me in papers of the time and in my still-functioning memory. We could compare notes. But then what would it tell us? That here we were, a little too blasé about popping out boys and girls to build countries far away from home? That our politicians encourage us to have short memories so they can loot the little power available? That many births were regretted if only because people do not become consumed with missing children whom they have never had?

Enough of this. I am thinking of going down to a glass place near the Coombe or Christchurch to see if they might have a few hours work a day, or even a week, for an old codger. It would keep my hands busy. Or maybe I should ... no, I won't say anything, but I have a few ideas to fill time and prepare some ground for new thoughts.

Good luck, Fergal, and always remember that you can come home.

> Regards,
> Bernard

To Helena from Fergal

Dear Helena,

I really enjoyed our dinner last week. The Hilton certainly lived up to my notion of it; in fact, I'm going there again tonight with two people from work, Jack and Julie. They live out in the sticks and have occasionally stayed over with me. They're going to see *Dancing at Lughnasa* but they're meeting some in-law in the Hilton beforehand and they'll stay with me afterwards. I'm meeting their relative too because he runs some big company in Australia – you never know. I must have imagined that there was a spring day last week when I agreed;

at home one would at least only wish to change one's residence.

I sometimes wonder how that play does so well: most of the people who go haven't a clue what it's about, but they love it anyway. I like having people stay over; it's the only time my apartment resembles a home. I seem to pass through it on my way to breakfast or bed, and seldom potter about, the outside having too big a draw on me, but I enjoy it so much when I do. Although, I must say, I am reading a lot, in bed. However, so much on the outside assails the senses, for good and bad, that I feel as if I spend more time out than I actually do.

It is quite, no, very, interesting for me to meet you in what has been your life for many years. Little did we all know what different influences you have always had. I was disturbed by your niggling doubts about Connie's life but on reflection I wouldn't worry. She is so capable, I believe that she will ride out these few difficult years, and perhaps we're wrong anyway. Just because we wouldn't want to marry Desmond doesn't mean that she isn't having the time of her life. For Christ's sake, don't leave this letter hanging around, I can imagine what would happen if she picked it up on one of your duty-free nights.

I did go to Eamon Doran's on Friday. What a mixture! Everything from ludicrously successful businessmen to flashy rich women to newly-arriveds. All together only because they are Irish. Matt, who is a perfect gossip, pointed out one man who is on the run, sitting at the table next to what he described as a top, top brasser in the NYPD. It would be lovely to be an invisible photographer or a fly. Pity flies can't talk. And I got the book you wanted for Bernard's present. I'll have it read myself before your next visit. So until I see you, happy flying. I can meet you in the Temple Bar if that would be easier for you, or wherever, depending on what you're up to. Give me a ring.

Love,
Fergal

Dear Fergal,

It is one of those godawful Irish days. The wind is deafening and the rain is grey and pitiless; it's no wonder people drink so much here. Helena told me about your wonderful dinner in the Hilton. How I envied both of you. It's OK, don't worry; as you know, I know how to envy constructively.

We had a great night here on Desmond's birthday, starting with drinks in D and N's and ending with more, here in the house. Desmond and Helena sang for hours; it was most instructive for someone like me who cannot remember the words of 'Hey Jude', and who also cannot remember when Desmond was last so relaxed and happy. Good times ahead! Kevin was in top spirits, regaling us with tremendous stories of bachelor days. It must be a great thing to be, a bachelor! I know you're not one technically, but if we ignore the minor few hours that you were in Wonderland, if we airbrush you out of your own marriage and let Milan Kundera put the hat on whomever the hell he likes, then you are. We finished the lovely brandy you sent me, which by an osmotic miracle transformed the children into all-night sleepers.

This is just a short note with some copies of the *Irish Times* and a *Tribune*. Get page five! Now are you sorry that you're missing the gossip? More later as the details emerge.

Your loving friend,
Connie

To Fergal from Desmond

Fergal,

Both my father and my wife have apparently written to you, aren't you lucky? I've been bludgeoned into sending this postcard. I'm not a letter-writer, so don't expect too much communication from me. I suppose I could try to remember to drop the odd line from work, but usually by the time I get there the children have ruined every thought in my head. But of course you wouldn't know anything about that. Weather is holding up.

> Yours,
> Desmond

To Fergal from Connie

Dear Fergal,

It wasn't raining this morning; in fact it was so fresh and crisp and hopeful it felt like a person who had completed a week off cigarettes. I left the children at school and bought the paper on the way back. I hadn't listened to the news for some time; I'd been putting on music instead – Peter Ostrushko, to be exact, Maighread Ní Dhómhnaill or Fran McPhail, great music for an autumn morning, fills the head with ideas. Unfortunately, today I read the paper. The attorney general has made it clear that the aim of the wording for the next abortion referendum is to deal with a life-threatening, not a life-shortening, situation for the mother, and a risk of suicide will not be grounds for an abortion. Why do they have to do things like this to a perfectly acceptable day? I simply cannot bear the thought of all this again, me and how many others? How dare they! I'm also wondering by how little must our lives be shortened in order for it not to be a threat, if you know what I mean. As you know I'm not a 'whatever' but it seems to me so logical. Why don't they just allow us to do the necessary deeds of nasty life here, on our home ground? Then we can get down to normal rows that go on about abortion everywhere, including your new place. If they cannot trust us with a choice, how can they trust us with a child?

I had an aunt who was heavily involved from the start in the American so-called pro-life movement. I'm anti-life, of course, I tried to drown all my babies at birth. I remember being fascinated by her involvement. I could have got hooked by her because she was good-looking, jolly, beautifully dressed, and you know in the end it's the sound and the look of the people who attract us politically, but I held back, for what reason I didn't know. Now I do; I had an uneasy feeling about interfering in the private action of someone else's life. Someone else's, NOT mine. But does that stop anyone here? Oh no. With gusto they get into moral posturing, they get ready for the cockfight; they can't stop women from getting the boat, their attempts failed so far, but by God, will they make them suffer! All so we can boast a pure island. Crap. Who's 'they'? My neighbours, I suppose; some of my friends, most of my relations. And yet did you know that according to the Presley 'who touched someone who touched him' test, you can't move here without bumping into someone who has had a connection with an abortion?

See! They've got me going again and I swore that this time I would pretend that I was somewhere else, listen to a lot of music, read foreign newspapers, magazines, switch off. Actually, that's why I decided to write today, to lift my mind above the mêlée, reclaim my morning mood, but I had to get it off my chest. I hope I didn't drag you down into the muck with me. But of course you'll be able to check out a Manhattan sunset, take a Staten Island ferry, drown yourself in street business – have I got near? That will soon frizzle with the sordid dishonesty of your own country. Oh how I wish I was there. (Mind you, I can do what you can't: switch on Raidio na Gaeltachta and blast it out really loud. They can't take that away; they don't own everything, even though they certainly think they own tradition.)

So, as you see, all continues as usual. Kids are fine.

Connie

To Connie from Fergal

Dear Connie,

Something struck me the other day. In the houses that I visit the women get the telephone messages all the time. Your uncle is dead, ring your mother. Your sister has had a baby girl, ring home. Your brother has got engaged, to Mary, ring Catherine immediately. We never get any. So ring me sometime and leave a message.

> Love,
> Fergal

To Connie from Helena

Albergo Sole Hotel,
Roma

Dear Connie,

I was delighted to get away yesterday; for some reason everything was beginning to crowd in on me. I know I shouldn't be moaning to you, who never gets away, but neither should I not say what I also feel. By the way, next time I'm coming here, you're coming too. The reason I'm writing is that I've been thinking about what you were saying on Monday about us and children and all that. Unlike you, I think I was mostly vague about having become a mother. I was amused when it became clear to me that that was what I had become. I hope that doesn't seem a flippantly tainted way of talking about such an important thing. Why do I hope that? Because I want you to think well of me. There. But honestly, it was a non-action on my part. I suppose that a curiosity consumed part of me and would always have done so, so putting it off seemed pointless. I would have had to face it sooner or later and spend a lot of time agonising. It seemed easier to do nothing about not having a child, and anyway, I think I felt that there was no reason why I shouldn't have a child as well as the next woman. At least I think that's what I felt, but how the hell would I know?

I do know that I am ridiculously lucky having the job I've got, meeting the husband I have, being blessed with a well, trouble-free child and having you as a friend and neighbour.

Weather is beautiful. Looking forward to Kevin and Ciarán coming this evening.

Helena

To Fergal from Bernard

Dear Fergal,

Yesterday Connie asked me to fix a burst waterpipe in your house – first emergency, odd time of year for it to happen. It's a long time since I've done any plumbing. Last time was in Waterford; I remember it, Moira was alive. She hated unexpected things going wrong in the house; Desmond is like her in that way. But the great thing about that for me was that she treated me like a God when I did the fixing.

The tenants have your house done up in an interesting fashion. I think you'd like it. They have posters and postcards everywhere – just as well that the walls are painted and not papered. They burn incense, or whatever that stuff is that reminds me of Benediction – maybe it's not that at all. I could see a few things that need doing, particularly the garden, so if you'd like me to do them, I will. Thanks for the book, it's wonderful so far. I didn't know that so many of our ancestors behaved so badly in the frontier wars, although, of course, I didn't know the names of the good guys either. I've just started it so I wait to see what the exact point is. I'll write again soon.

Bernard

Dear Fergal,

Last night Desmond and I went to *Husbands and Wives* and had a terrible row afterwards, or rather I did a lot of shouting and Desmond ignored me. Imagine not talking after that film! He sat staring into the fire when we came home; it drove me mad. I could see Woody getting bogged down in his own life. I wondered if he was making his excuses prior to the event, if he was dealing with the issue uncomfortably honestly, and then after he'd finished shooting the film life got out of hand and refused to stick to the script. Or was he just dumping on Mia all along? The silence drove me to arguing about the differences between men and women, although I couldn't see much difference between Woody and Mia. Was Liam Neeson supposed to have underarm sweat showing on his shirt? Could incest be an emotional crime? And on and on. But Desmond sat silent. Now what couldn't Woody Allen make out of that? It certainly appears to suggest that the man is either grossly unhappy or unbelievably stupid. Which man, you ask? Sorry for loading all this on you, but honestly, I have to tell someone. I miss you; your absence gives me too much to think about and too much time to do it.

May I remind you, dear busy man, that you owe me a letter. Of that I'm sure.

Connie

To Fergal from Connie

Dear Fergal,

Please ignore my last outburst. It is a horrible and unhelpful thing to complain about one's spouse. I'll write you a letter of your own in a few days. After I've got yours.

> Love,
> Connie

To Fergal from Helena

Albergo Sole Hotel,
Roma

Dear Fergal,

I arrived here last week and am staying in a friend's hotel. The trouble about that is that one can never complain, but the good part is that I always get a lovely room. I met the owner years ago on a flight, he was returning from a business trip in Ireland, and I went for a meal with him in the evening. Nothing romantic, well that is if there can be such a thing as a 'nothing romantic' thing in Rome. The hotel is small, beautifully tiled, and has an internal piazza where the birds fight with the cats for control of the airwaves.

I intended to write after we last met in New York but never seemed to have the time. Anyway, it's more snazzy to get a letter from Rome. Just had my pasta for the night and am contemplating Sunday night Campo di Fiorno life – a pretty lazy affair, but tomorrow will break open all the noise. Crossing the Alps was spectacular, no cloud or mist over them. When I see the Alps I think of how small the world is, but also how much better-looking it is from the air, which is why I keep my job, I suppose.

When Rome was unfamiliar to me it had far more charm but that's the way with everything, with bodies and streets, anyway. I remember, on my first visit, discovering that, unknowingly, I'd slept within walking distance of St Peter's; this seemed to make it all so much more awesome. Now I come for all the normal reasons that we go on holidays, to remove the ordinary and shed all those jobs which need to be done, and give the kitchen table a rest. Still, I'm not complaining. Coming here is so different to going to New York. For Irish people it creates real oddity – when we go to England we know we're not English, and that has as much to do with how they react to us as the way we do to them. When we go to America we know we're not American, but because they react to us so positively, we forgive the things which grate the most because we are relieved. And the things that grate the most are the non-European things – the politics, the age, all of which you can get here.

I don't speak Italian properly, as you know from our peripheral involvement in that worrying little episode in New York. How the hell was I supposed to convince him that you hadn't called him whatever he thought you had? But you know, that's one of the reasons I love it here. Loss of language makes everything stark and novel; it's the nearest to childlikeness we can ever recapture. I can order meals now, which is more than I could do my first time. A spinach omelette and a block of cheese wasn't what I had expected for my dinner; mind you, if I remember, it was gorgeous. Of course, loss of language makes me lonely too, but that's a natural state. We fill up our time with such a lot of needless conversation. I love the way my senses are more finely tuned when I know I won't be able to blather my way out of it. I can follow exact smells of everything from the food I want, to danger. I see clearer, hear voice changes. But then it all deserts me and I throw myself head-long into conversation with the first English-speaking man I bump into, ignorant of the fact that he could be the next ripper doing a good job at being a businessman. Mind you, they don't usually hop countries to get their kicks and the local variety don't usually feel the necessity for such drastic disguise as learning a foreign language well. Enough paranoia, but my nightmares are always different when I'm away from home. And enough of Rome for the minute. Kevin and Ciarán are joining me this evening; we're all taking the opportunity of my extended stay over to have a break. How lucky I am.

I've just written to Connie and thinking about her has brought to mind again our last conversation about her. My God, do we ever talk of anything else? She would be mortified at our gropings to understand what her problem is. That is, if there is a problem. I've turned the whole thing over many times and have now decided to believe optimistically that we are wrong. I've decided that I can't see why you think Connie is so unhappy. I know that Desmond is a bit of a drip, but only a bit, and who of us isn't at times? As I said, I think three children shook him enormously but his withdrawal is surely temporary. Connie appears to be totally engrossed and made happy by her offspring; a fact I envy many times. I couldn't be like her, which is why I envy her. The fact that I was involved in a conversation that concluded by saying that she needed psychotherapy urgently leaves me feeling a little disloyal. We all need psychotherapy in our country, but for what reason? To discover that we're up shit creek? For Christ's sake, we know that anyway. Frankly, I'm sick of people telling me that they need to do 'more work on myself'. Where's this work going to get them? What's the end product going to be? An ever-cheerful mystic, a bloody corpse? Forgive me, I'm sure I may be wrong. Now how's that for prevarication? Yes, perhaps she should have got a job that could have used up some of that snappily organised, endlessly open disposition, but what job? And who is to say that it would have made her any happier? I don't think her look is any more distant than ever it was. I can't see how you imagine her rattling around in her kitchen waiting for stimulation. Maybe I'm blind or maybe the consequences of accepting as correct your fears about her are so immense that I can't bear to think you're right. I must say I find your care touching. I wish I had a friend as concerned as you but maybe then I don't need one; or maybe I'm just a cold bitch.

One way or the other, I've decided to convince her to come with me on my next stopover here, and I'm sure the break will bring back all the smiles. How this can be organised, I do not know, but between us we'll manage somehow. I can't believe that Desmond won't throw his all behind the idea. Well, at least while I'm in Rome I can't.

More later; I must get ready now to battle my way out to the airport to meet the man and boy.

Lots of love,
Helena

3

Connie is medium height and thin. Her red hair has had the same angular style since I've known her, a straight fringe, a swinging drop falling to midway down her neck. Her eyes can hide nothing and have piled her history behind them. But she has control over all that is past; she has it safely regulated, except there in her big eyes. Some people are so transparent that exchanging good morning with them feels like peeptoming. Not Connie, unless you're up close.

Every morning she gets up before her husband, Desmond Cunningham. She washes the twins, two of her three children, dreamily, she loves every one of them, she holds at bay any annoyances they cause her, she hopes the youngest will stay asleep until the rest are handed out to the world. The breakfast is in rotation, the bathroom and bedroom doors are well swung by the time Desmond comes into the kitchen. The children, who up to then have been chipping at the morning, grow sullen from his watching. They are waiting for the excuse of teenage years to start a real row with him. Sometimes he smiles at them and when he does their stomachs loosen in response, jollity threatens.

But most mornings he feels that their manners are appalling, that his wife should be able to have these things – schoolbags, lunches – better organised. Covered up is what he means. He thinks that getting annoyed with her lack of management will in itself right her errors. He doesn't realise that every morning he spends like this is actually adding up to be his life. He is a disappointed man. He has been married for a number of years and the first idea of twins was a delight. They looked beautiful in their blue and pink when they were born and people went on and on about them. But soon he couldn't have a decent conversation if a visitor called, or even with Connie, the noise, the clutter, broke up his thoughts. He secretly blamed Connie for getting pregnant again and that arrival, a red-haired girl, put paid forever to any callers. No one in their right mind would come to a house full of shrieks, smells and exhausted babble. He was not cut out to be a man among babies. He believed that most adults aren't, but women manage to move into it; their currency is love, after all, so it is easy for them. If he still wanted Connie he wanted her alone. He looked at her this morning, viciously thinking that underneath her dress her body had changed more than he could have imagined possible. He had said the right things, but my God, you couldn't actually look at the stretch marks. His mother had probably looked like that too. Had his father also been pretending? By not mentioning them after the three necessary times, he thought they had gone away. He was glad when breakfast was over; the last minutes before freedom were always tempered with civility and, maybe, love.

Desmond, the bright child, had become an art teacher in a first-rate art college. He also managed the department. Some of his students wanted to be artists, real artists. Yesterday that young Cork fellow was in, chattering out his life story in five minutes. Did he not know that he was not quiet enough to be an artist? He talked all the time. How could anyone who made so much noise be any good as an artist? He couldn't hold his breath long enough to think. The sound of his voice drove thought away. Listening visibly annoyed him – when would he be able to interrupt? Manners would finally flee him and he would land his fast talk on the table. There was a wide gossipy look in his eye, and he had a satisfied smile. Desmond could see him sitting in the pram with his hands on the edge, beaming delightedly. He still looked the same. Who did these people think they were? Desmond believed that art was a serious matter.

Why, even his father was quiet with the sense of his work and you wouldn't call cutting, working for Waterford Glass, art. Sometimes the girls came in to him. By mistake, only if they hadn't been warned. He simply didn't know where they thought they were going. He worried at the impossibility of their desires. He brought the conversation home once and Connie uncharacteristically lost her temper – he'd say that for her, she had a calm, reasonable personality.

Connie brought the twins to the door as this week was my turn. She did it week about, when it fitted into my schedule. Often Kevin and I would say that there was no need for Connie to do it when I was not on earlies, but she liked the week on the school – it changed her routine; she got to see morning outside; she got to see her children slipping away from her through the school door, then turning around to wave at her. Sometimes this could be like a stab wound and other days she could glow for hours thinking of it. It was hard, this kind of love, the passionate dreamy kind that she would kill for, if needs be. Easily. If someone were to touch one of hers, she could kill him with her bare hands; she had thought about this and it didn't frighten her; it was different.

Connie woke and fed the baby. Was it love, she wondered. How can it be so different for different people? Is it, in fact, like taste? Caramel is beautiful and so is mustard. That's it, she said aloud to the baby. This baby. Now this baby was a different matter to the rest of the universe. She tried not to think about how much she loved her because it brought too much fear.

On this Thursday I would come after eleven o'clock. We would have coffee and she would hear about New York, what the weather was like, if I went into Manhattan. Where did I eat, did I see any-thing special? Connie took seriously her link with an outside place. She got enough information during these talks to keep her mind working, to place herself in some time, to make pictures for looking forward to. She hated it when I was off work for a week. I, on the other hand, liked my days off the same as anyone else, but loved relating the details of my working days to her. Connie was not envious or petty, she was wide-mouthed for experience and did not feel dissatisfied by my luck and wandering. It was all right by her that I alone had my job; if she had really wanted it for herself she couldn't have loved me. She imposed an order on my stories: I knew the importance of something by whether I thought, I must tell that to Connie. I never told her about the odd bit of flirting that I did. I felt that that would have sullied her, or else I feared her disapproval. Connie did no wandering, she was faithful.

Connie marked her days while growing up. Her background was respectable country. She believed that her parents 'allowed' her to grow up. When first 'allowed' to work in the village shop she was deeply grateful, and still is. It got her clear, she says. I don't know if that means that she learned certain things or that a fence passed below her. She still cannot figure out why they let her take the job. Could it have been the sort of slip-up parents make once in a blue moon: major slip-ups that have lifelong consequences, made because the parents are tired and don't hear the question properly?

'Mammy, could I leave school and set up a night-club?'

'Certainly, dear.'

The consequences of not listening can be so dire that you'd think we'd always be on the alert, but really one would have to be continuously wide-awake and ridiculously clean-eared to catch everything. Or maybe Connie's parents did know what they were doing; maybe they saw the ingrowing of her life and felt that a spell in an outside place would open up her life a little.

Connie has a sprinkling of brothers and sisters somewhere but we know very little about them; she seems to have lost them along the way, or they her. One night we were startled to hear that she had a brother working as a dance instructor in London.

'You kept that quiet,' I said, asking why in the tone of my voice.

'I suppose,' she smiled, no, mischievously beamed, back, hoisting up a black flag against further questions.

Occasionally I think that something odd must have happened for such a distance to have taken hold. When did it happen, I wonder, and why, but I never ask. And then I figure that perhaps it always does happen; perhaps it's normal; perhaps it is only my family relationships that are abnormal. But then I am away so much I can afford intimacy with my parents. It will not catch a hold of me by the throat and strangle me. I must say, my sister who lives beside them gives out personal information sparingly, a little now, a little again, like administering medicine.

Unlike me, Connie did go to university. She came up from the country, opened her eyes and ears wide, and kept her mouth shut for some time. She learned and changed more than she ever knew there was to learn and change. In her first few weeks she met Fergal. They struck up what can only be called an extraordinary friendship. I've seen bits of it. They are inseparable if completely independent. Brother and sister? No. Ordinary friends? Unusual. Settle for friendship of a most fortunate kind. I forgot to say that I did indeed go to Belfield too, but it was for such a short time that I mostly forget. I'm afraid I too opened my ears and eyes and was too fascinated to concentrate. This may not be the whole truth: I think I was also intimidated, lonely, and out of my depth – I couldn't figure out, and wasn't told, which books to buy and which to read in the library, and I have never been able to proceed without a plan. I endured a few weeks of torture and then got a job in the coffee bar. It was the memory of that job that prompted the 'glorified waitress' remark and, indeed, probably made the air-hostessing a little more palpable. Imagine if I'd stayed on the ground working as a waitress! So it is likely that I served Fergal and Connie cups of black coffee which left unusually sloppy stains on the enamel-green crockery. We were surprised late one night to discover that a week or so of ours, at that peculiar time of life, had overlapped.

Connie got a very good degree and then surprised everyone by leaving Ireland for a year. She has told me of this surprise so I believe her and can imagine it. She gave up the one interesting job that she had, writing entries for a geography encyclopaedia, and came back for reasons as inexplicable as those for which she left. That year is buried secretly but must mean something; its very secrecy suggests that it means a lot. But I don't believe in allowing titillation or curiosity to become too intrusive. I've seen hours, journeys, being passed by people in ways I presume to be totally out of character, so I understand the need to leave some of our lives out of our own focus. I never comment on past indiscretions.

On her return to Ireland, Connie punched in her life pleasantly enough. She always had somewhere to go, something to do, someone to meet. She played squash, went to hear music, occasionally went dancing, learned where to have breakfast on Saturday. Twice a year she visited her home place. The following week she drank huge amounts of alcohol and coffee; she left wine bottles scattered all over her flat. Fergal would eventually rescue her, calm her down, and she would then behave as if nothing had happened. And so did everyone else. Imagine a woman, a red-haired, noticeable woman sitting beside you on a bar stool. She falls over, and while you're tuning your reflexes to do whatever might be appropriate, she picks herself up, dusts the collar of her jacket, sits back up on her stool and continues her sentence. You are never quite sure if it happened.

After one of these 'home-bouts', as she called them, Connie went to a party with Fergal. There she met Desmond. She could remember him standing in the room, looking severe. What a challenge! She had liked his difficult distance, in contrast with the last messy, scathing love affair she'd had. Passion like it was good for memory but useless for living. Utterly useless. And some things are lost forever; not through carelessness of your own, they're just lost. You cannot stand there, growing old, waiting for returns that are not going to happen. Her and Desmond's coming together was passionate in its own way; in fact, it would have been astounding for both of them if Connie had not remembered something else. It certainly was for Desmond.

The two of them went out together, stayed in together, and learned their ways around their likes and dislikes. Sometimes, even in the middle of enjoyment, Connie would worry – 'But if I hadn't gone to that party with Fergal I wouldn't even know the fellow's name. But then how do you get to know someone?' 'Oh leave it, Connie,' she'd say to herself, and return to fastidious enjoyment.

Desmond brought Connie to meet his parents in Waterford, Bernard and Moira. Connie had never seen anything like it. Desmond's parents held hands, sitting on the couch after dinner. Bernard washed the dishes and swept the floor, without being asked. They went for walks linked all the way; they looked directly into each other's eyes; they repeated each other's names continuously. It was a stunning panoply of love. After the weekend,

Desmond and Connie spoke about marriage a lot and somehow found themselves checking hotels, booking a chapel, getting a date sorted. In truth, Desmond wasn't completely sure; neither was Connie, but who ever is?

Connie got depressed after the honeymoon. Desmond got irritated, but time filed their corners and brought them closer to, and into, each other. During Connie's down period, which eventually worked itself into a real depression, her doctor suggested that she go into group therapy, for a few sessions.

'Who is in the group?' Connie asked.

'Ordinary people, ordinary people.'

'No thanks,' said Connie. 'I know enough of what they have to offer, haven't I got my family?'

The thought of explaining her feelings to them snapped her out of it. The problem was Desmond – the way he threw himself into closeness and then shrugged his shoulders as if it didn't matter at all. She was pulled into personal depths with him, then ignored, contradicted, abandoned, then brought back around the same circle. In time, because she did not have enough confidence to drag the problem into the open, she trained her emotions to more or less fit Desmond's scheme. They both dumped their difficulties into small, perfect silences, ones so perfectly constructed that they could grunt out of them if need be. If occasionally Connie asked herself what she had done, the part of her that was afraid of the answer, any answer, gathered up her doubts and annulled them.

Connie and Desmond bought a house in which they lived for a year. Many a year has been forgotten, put down to bad judgement, but Connie couldn't totally erase the gloom of that first twelve months. They saw the house on a winter evening and the sitting-room fire, stacked with coal that sprinkled, convinced them to buy. Never trust the messages of a fire on a wet October night. It was too dark to see the state of the pebbledash. The first time they had the key and stepped into the hallway their mistake shocked Connie. Mists of it still blind her but she makes herself believe that she must have stood, surely once, in one of the rooms and felt cheerful; it's just that she can't recall it. She does remember enjoying her office work inordinately and doing a lot of crosswords. Fergal was away, wrote to say that he was getting married and coming home from London, rang to say he was home and that they must meet, rang the following week to say that the marriage was over. He bought a house in Rathmines. His presence in the country dragged Connie, in her dreams, up by the bootstraps and she set about finding a new house. As luck would marvellously have it, there was one for sale six doors from Fergal. She played that down as she, for the first and last time, bullied Desmond by strictly secret manipulation into moving from the disastrous semi-detached wall-gardened limbo. The relief of the move filled in the cracks.

Connie's first pregnancy went according to plan for the first five months; that is, if there can be such a thing as a plan for that particular adventure. She was then informed that she was having twins and her innocence found the revelation interesting. Desmond, too, was pleased, she thought. She was steeped in the ignorance that shrouds all first-time mothers; she even brought a book with her into the labour ward. The new mothers in the beds next to Connie laughed at this and she thought, What a crowd of natural pessimists, begrudgers, martyrs to perceived inevitability. Ha, ha, ooohhh.

Because her baby turned into twins, Connie had to give up her job. For six weeks she breast-fed both, the boy and the girl, at first sometimes forgetting which she had just fed or winded, never which breast had just been sucked. She stopped dressing them in lookalike clothes and that helped. They drew life from her, but getting them weaned and on to mushy bananas gave her an inordinate sense of achievement. Her sense of an outside life returned slowly. Fergal dropped in a few times a week at least, and baby-sat occasionally to allow Desmond and herself go for a drink. These drinks scared Connie because she found that she talked all the time about the babies and couldn't hear what Desmond was saying. So she started buying bottles of wine to have when Fergal called and they gave the pub a miss. But Desmond didn't seem to like Fergal much; he withdrew into a shadowy prickliness and soon the evenings of wine became less. So Fergal would call instead for lunch when Connie and he could behave as they always had. They argued with, supported, agreed with each other. Their conversation was never chronological but did have a beginning and an end.

I first met her in June of her second year on the street. She had, of course, often seen me, she said, 'being taxied off in your pin-neat uniform or taxied back laden with parcels and duty-free'. That's how she put it. Over a bottle of duty-free we tied the beginnings of confidences. It wasn't terribly easy for the housebound Connie because she had almost lost the ability to knit in and out of new people's lives, and so afraid was she that she might vomit her whole life out at the first serious question put to her, that she was over-cautious in the beginning, appearing to be offhand. But in time she calmed down, saw that there was no rush, this would last us, and we eased into a routine that was governed by my flights. She began to help as well with Ciarán, insisting that there really is very little difference between two and three. I'm not sure. Between three and four, yes, but between one and two, or two and three? Next thing, of course, she's pregnant again.

I don't understand this thing of children, even though I have one myself. I consider it a most odd occupation, a ludicrous way to spend a portion of one's life. If I say that to anyone I then have to explain why I had a child, and really it gets too complicated. Firstly, I know why I did. Secondly, I have no idea why, and lastly, I don't know. But one child is one thing; more is decidedly peculiar. And I'm never careless and I cannot see how anyone else could be, about that anyway. Although, of course, I could be wrong, completely wrong, and maybe it's just my training in the air that makes me so. My job also helped me not to get pregnant; many of us have to go on the ground when we find ourselves unable to conceive, due to the gravitational pulls of time, air, seas, and heights.

Anyway, Connie got pregnant again. She seemed to enjoy the experience in an exclusive sort of way. She would wheel the twins in their buggy, down the street, her stomach rounded out in front of her, her back arched precariously to carry the weight, and people would move off our footpath long before it was necessary. One of our neighbours started tipping his cap to her, a habit he still has, others bowed their heads slightly when they said 'good morning'. But Desmond was not happy looking, he grew sulky and offhand. During this pregnancy, it was Fergal, at lunch times, who put his hand on Connie's belly to feel the baby somersault. The skin on Connie's stomach was always hot, parched thin, and the cool of hand through her maternity shift gave it great comfort. Fergal and Connie never touched much, for long anyway, but letting one's hand rest on the stomach of a pregnant woman doesn't count for touching.

I was away the night she had the baby. But next day I visited her. She told me that it was Fergal, not Desmond, who brought in the bottles of Guinness. She said, 'I'm afraid I got no Guinness from Desmond this time', and she laughed. 'But Fergal brought me six bottles. Good old Fergal.'

And she sighed in that trembly way that new mothers, or recently miscarried women, have; on the verge of tears, not for what they have just said, but for something else tremendous and awesome. I had Ciarán and Connie had the twins in the Coombe. I never drive even remotely in the direction of Cork Street or Rialto, since. Christchurch is even a little near for my liking. But this time Connie was in the Rotunda and they had these gorgeous baskets suspended between the bottom posts of the bed. We discussed the difference between the hospitals; how much pubic hair they shaved off, did they give a drink of water in the labour ward or not, what their attitude was to screaming. We came down heavily in favour of the Protestants. Of course, our comparisons couldn't be described as scientifically valid because, well, time moves on and brings developments with it, attitudes change (sometimes for the better) and also this was Connie's second delivery, whereas I was, and would be, permanently stuck on experience number one. We compared bath-time; whether they gave you loads of salt, breast-feeding, night-feed rules. There didn't seem to be anything else to talk about. Anticlimax was written all over Connie, or was it something else that I couldn't fathom? We occasionally glanced, a little furtively, I thought, at the baby. I also thought about how hard second children have to work to get noticed. I was restless to leave; I didn't want all that memory clogging me up and was terribly grateful for the New York route.

After that Connie really did help with Ciarán, even I agreed that there wasn't much difference between three and four. She became embroiled in motherhood. This left her little time to run up questions about Desmond, or rather, about the combination of Desmond and her. Passion was becoming a memory. Her days became a transfer of each other, lifting, feeding, changing nappies, consoling, leaving to and collecting from, and more of the same. She became an expert at apparently useless talk: 'We will go for a walk soon; we're going to go for a nice walk in a minute; a minute is more or less like a moment; now we'll put on your coats; let me show you how to do that; now we're off; look at the birdie; wasn't that a nice walk? No, don't bite your sister because it's not nice.'

Treats became a grabbed half-hour in bed. She waited expectantly for Desmond to come home each evening, as if he might turn out to be a different man to the one who had left this morning. As if he could, by a light touch on her shoulder or cheek perhaps, draw her into another life. She could shiver when she heard his car hit the piece of gravel opposite the kitchen window, with expectation. But Desmond was having different problems and had no notion of what she wanted from him. He played with the children as soon as he came in, trying to catch Connie's attention as he did so, hoping that she would think him a good father. As if she didn't know that he was playing with them, as if she didn't know what they were doing every second of their waking lives. After fifteen minutes of this highly artificial charade, Desmond would tire.

But somehow, when Connie got the children to bed, she could drag a conversation out from somewhere, the news, a thought she had. She tried hard to steer the conversation away from babies. It was always easier if she'd had a visitor during the day, the more recent the better. A visitor brought outside life in the door with them, and Connie could keep it in the air for a remarkably long time. Connie had Fergal, and me a little, as fallbacks; Desmond had work. We didn't know at the time how far apart they were. And we never called at night. Fergal had at one stage but seemed to feel unwanted by Desmond. I thought that I could understand why that was. I thought that Desmond wanted Connie and the children to himself. My dear husband is like that, especially if I've been away for a few days. One should not be congratulated on the desire to be alone with one's partner; one should be congratulated on the luck that makes it so.

But nothing so lucky as this was happening between Connie and Desmond. If feelings have muscles, then the ligaments of their emotions were torn. Connie and Desmond were each accumulating vast amounts of knowledge – he on the running of art and design courses, she on the motor and mouth skills of children. There was no overlap and neither of them wanted to know anything of what the other had learned.

I called one day, back again from New York. I felt that Connie was away somewhere. I made the coffee and she drank it, snapping at the children constantly. I'm not very good in situations like that; I immediately want to be somewhere else. I knew what I should do – offer to take the children off her hands for a bit (an appropriate expression that, because that's where they always are, attached, glued on to one's hands). I prefer to think of the expression rather than do the deed. But I left a letter from Fergal and told myself that that would take her out of her strange mood.

4

Dear Connie,

Apologies. Apologies. Apologies. How could I have let it slip?
Well, the usual excuses, terribly busy and also terribly going
through a distancing stage. Not from you, but from the whole
country. If I don't I'll become halved and end up like a dried grape-
fruit. No, maybe not, maybe just schizophrenic. The busyness
comes from a few rather colossal new jobs at work; I think I'm
now taking part in New York architectural history. And also from
settling into a not unsatisfactory social life. But enough, more of
that some other time. Thanks for the papers; as soon as I'd finished
them I thought, well, now I must go for a daunder down Sandymount beach, maybe even as far as the red lighthouse if the tide's
out, seems like a good enough day; oh dear, where am I? As for
your blood boiling over the abortion issue, no wonder. That's
why people become politically active; it means they don't have to
seethe alone, they get less introverted ulcers. Bet you didn't know
there was any other kind.

Seeing as you asked me to forget your row with Desmond after
seeing *Husbands and Wives* I'll try, but please allow me to be amused,
and please also consider that you got much more from the film than

anyone else. Participatory audience you were. Something similar to what I was myself in my own little flurry with the married state. I'd say Carmel's airbrushing would have been more thorough than anything the Communists could have done; there would have been no stray hats around after she was finished. Well, dear Connie, if I haven't written, that doesn't mean that I haven't been thinking about you.

In fact, I had an extraordinary dream last week; it lasted a whole three days. I was going on holidays to the west of Ireland with you, either Donegal or Clare, the places kept being mixed up. It was such a slow dream. We drove over those roads that look as if they're disappearing right into the middle of the earth, or else petering into a hill that drops off the edge. We went through those small, neat towns where the ice-cream shops all look the same and the chippers have murdered the potato. The rain began to fall heavily, creating a dark, warning feeling in the car. That's right, you were driving the white banger of a Peugeot and clouds scudded noisily around us, actually near the windows; it seemed as if we were in a plane landing. Then eyefuls of blue lit up as far as we could see and the sun came out again. We found the house where we were to collect the key; it was at the end of an industrial estate! How odd. No, wait a minute – it was Údarás na Gaeltachta, so it was Donegal. I would have known that it was Donegal when I met the landlady (matter of fact, immersion, read the meter, where to buy turf); in Clare they would have dithered more, where they are only recently getting seriously used to tourists.

The house smelled damp but through the growing dark we could see what promised to be a panoramic view in the morning. We went to our beds, next door to each other, just like old times. And now here's the strange thing – I had a dream in my dream. About you. I dreamt that you were about forty-five years old and that you were walking down a long corridor where you bumped into a man of about twenty. He was coming out of an exercise joint called JBs. He was walking away but then he turned around and looked at you. He came back. You were laughing. You said, pointing at the sign, 'But what does it mean?' He said, now standing very close to you, 'It means that only people whose surnames begin with

48

J or B can use this fitness club.' 'You're joking,' you said, and then you looked into his face. 'Which are you?' 'B,' he said and kissed your lips. You seemed to shimmer up to him. Then I woke from that dream into my first dream. How decidedly strange. (By the way, what a good idea for a fitness business, a whole string of them, in fact. People would buy houses according to their names in order to be near their club; people's names would decide what town, or even county, they lived in. As soon as I get to work I must do a city plan based on the initials of surnames; it would add a new dimension to marriage. If Mary Mahoney married John Johnson and they wanted to live in the Ms he would have no objections to her keeping her own name; indeed, he would insist on changing his to hers.)

Back to my dream. We made a gorgeous fry-up. Oh please, I'm going to cry: sausages, white pudding, wholemeal bread. We had one of those endless breakfasts where we kept making fresh pots of tea. We talked about many things, mostly about differences between Sarajevo and Belfast. This was sparked off by the incongruity of a Belfast man heading the peacekeeping forces in Sarajevo. We talked about friends of ours, ones who changed for the worse, ones who were alcoholics and didn't know it, ones who weren't but claimed to be, a new phenomenon that. We agreed that we thought it was a way of getting notice. Look, I may not be . . . whatever . . . but I'm an alcoholic. We didn't talk about ourselves at all. Then we went for a walk.

Now let me tell you about that walk. I can smell every inch of it. We went down a narrow road, picking the soft tops off briars and cracking the last foxgloves between our fingers. It wasn't just the skittishly healthy wind, nor the rocks, smooth as bottoms, lying beside each other, nor the beach. When we came to it, it opened up to the sky for miles. It was something else as well. There was no reality. I went into the sea. I know that I didn't take my clothes off in front of you because that would have been improper. I walked into these colossal waves as if I was going into someone's mouth. I was exhilarated beyond belief by the force of the water and was hit, as one usually is on the first Atlantic swim of the year, by the rightness of things. I went under, head first, and cried. I could feel the tears sliding off my eyes into the sea. When I came out I didn't need to dry my clothes, as is the way in dreams. We went home then, I think, or I woke up or something. Connie, what could it mean, do you think? Good Lord, the time, must rush to work; I'll post this on my way from work and no doubt around midnight I'll regret it. Actually, I won't post it; Helena has just rung and I'm meeting her for a coffee at lunchtime so you'll get it tomorrow. Love to Desmond and the kids.

Fergal

To Helena from Fergal

Dear Helena,

Well, sorry about the lunch; the others from work don't usually join me. I know it made for a ridiculous attempt at communication. Isn't the woman Pamela something else, wired to a high-tech generator? Actually, occasionally, she's calmer; I think she just feeds herself intravenously on coffee. One morning I suggested that maybe she should try a little grass on her way into work and she dug me in the ribs and shouted, 'Oh you're a hoot, you Irish.' I was sore for days, so now I keep my mouth shut and avoid her as best as I can, in case I end up stuck to the back wall of the office or, indeed, impaled on the drawing board. One can often see me running back into the jacks when I smell her striding along the corridor. I came down with a case of the dreads because I was convinced that she was trying to make a pass at me, but luckily I never found out if it was true. You need to keep buttoned up when you are beside her.

When I went home that evening I felt strangely lonely, and very annoyed that I hadn't managed to have a conversation, so I re-read my letters – I do this regularly, not in a way to worry about, more like re-reading the good chapters in a book. Hence this scribble to you. By the way, your friends Cathal and Áine stayed here two nights ago. Apparently they had rung the people they were supposed to be staying with and some extraordinary excuse was proffered over the phone: 'My wife exercises in the spare room but I'd be happy to drive you to your hotel!' Of course, your friends had put *them* up and had traipsed around Dublin with them for three days, drove them to Wicklow, the lot. They were quite shocked but it doesn't surprise me any more. I once obligingly agreed to do some work for a colleague at the weekend, but when I called I was told it didn't suit because the husband was filling in the equivalent of an Arts Council form. Perhaps I exaggerate slightly but it didn't look very big to me. The fellow thought he was an artist. Maybe he was but I never saw any signs of it. So after my rather tense coffee, I got to the corner of the street and said in good Irish fashion, 'Well, fuck you too, baby, and don't think I'll forget that.' I still have a superior attitude to them and the work has not yet been done. I know New Yorkers have to protect themselves from becoming hoteliers, but can you imagine how they'd feel if we did that to them when they arrived in Dublin – they'd be in post-trauma for years. Of course, we think there's a great advantage in showing people around our town – I mean, your town. The jizz could be gone. I remember I used to think Dublin such a beautiful place. I loved every day. Then I got to know where everyone would be at every hour and I no longer wanted to be there. But when visitors came, and I was showing them around, I could still enthuse like an uncapped spring. I remember doing things like bringing people into the Shelbourne and saying, 'There's a great social mix here: there's a millionaire builder over there, there's the Irish prime minister's PR man, and there's the famous journalist, and there's so-and-so.' I did too. Imagine pretending that there's a social mix in the Shelbourne!

So it's not always martyrdom for us when we're showing people around. Anyway, I really enjoyed having Cathal and Áine. They saw my view of New York and then headed upstate where they were going to a family wedding. Is Áine bouncy or what! We took a train to where they were connecting with their family; she went to get our coffee and the man behind the bar leaned over to pat her on the shoulder before he realised what he was doing. Her cheerfulness has that effect. You want to get close.

Well, your letter. God, how I do remember Rome! The river like a subconscious stream in the city's head, the shock of old and older things making me as insignificant as a housefly, with even less possibility of arrogance. And Florence – I always think of blue tiles, red tiles, yellow tiles, cold tiles. We still remember first impressions, but unfortunately we try to pile up on top of them as if experience should be valued more than them. Our desire to be sophisticated often erases our best moments. It's like people, really – we want to get to know them, sometimes for no better reason than to control the notion of them in our heads, to have conquered them. 'To know you is to love you.' Like hell! To know you is to have you under control. Which is maybe another reason why you don't want to learn Italian. When I used to go on holidays I would always want to learn the language, but once I wanted to know French, I also wanted to know German, Spanish, Italian, Urdu, Bulgarian. I'd get so depressed by the thought of all that grammar I'd settle for hand signals. Imagine learning English? I taught it once for two weeks to Spaniards. Mostly I read the newspapers and got them talking – great stuff, I thought. On my last day I asked them if there was anything they'd like me to do. 'Please could you do phrasal verbs with us.' What the hell are phrasal verbs, I wondered. 'After tea-break,' I said. Surely some of the old hands could tell me. And sure enough they could, it was a common request. Put any preposition with any verb and you have a new meaning. Go on, do it: go into; go through; go on; go at; run into, through, on, at. Got you.

But knowing a language makes you feel less like a tourist. Did you ever notice how it's all right to be a tourist during the day? You can express your various needs which have to be met on the grounds that you're supporting the local economy; come night-time, you want to be a local. At heart we all despise tourism, the new imperialism.

Ah, about Connie. Indeed you may be right, perhaps she is OK. But the person left at home in relationships spends all their time being in the relationship. And she could get caught trying to please everyone. I once told her that we can get over wanting to be liked. She said that she tried and was surprised to find that I was right but that having found out she went back to normal; like coming off a diet having comfortingly discovered that you can lose weight. No doubt psychotherapy would be of no use. I think we're a nation of people who would not benefit from it. The analysts would, but not the people. But something should happen in a life. I know, I know, what something? What do I know of life, anyway?

Love,
Fergal

To Bernard from Fergal

Dear Bernard,

I'm having a spate of tidying and letter-writing. Something must be going to happen, I suppose it just might. There is a process involved in tidying; not just the process of doing it, but also the stages of awareness as one does it. I think, perhaps, that women enjoy it because no one can get at them when they're tidying. Waffle, I'm sure. Yet I certainly feel that no one can get at me when I'm caught up in the senses of a Hoover. But tidying the place you live in is not the same as tidying a desk. You put the pens and pencils into the pen and pencil holders; you gather up the paper clips, the staples, everything; divide and stack, for all the world a harvester, and then you're ready to work. Of course, as you empty the bin a postcard, a note, falls out and you're somewhere else, picking over your life like a child with chickenpox. But when a house is tidied you sit and think of where you live. And I realised this morning – here is where I live now. I didn't want to admit it, but there it is, a concrete fact. To avoid too much regret, I immersed myself in a recently acquired book on glass. It's actually for you but I'm reading it first. I'm also dipping in and out of a few American history books and my every instinct cries 'appalling'. Wonderful how ignorance can be erased by a little reading! (Not always a comfortable thing if you're finding out what your own ancestors were up to; perhaps I've brought this up with you before.) I'll include a list of my purchases with the next letter – we should start a cross-Atlantic swap library; Helena could be the courier. I'm sure you could always get the ones I'm reading and vice versa, but there's something subversive about swapping books, a feeling of underground education. Because the powers-that-be always select for us, the choosing of one's own books is true anarchic adulthood.

The interesting thing about reading a history of America like Thompson's *Golden Door* is that it paints war in an inevitable light, making our own bloody and awful war, as it plays itself out, seem like an essential paragraph in the future of history books. Plenty of numbers dead or not dead, but no heart. His dubious reluctance to face the Civil War honestly and his sly hint that slavery was, well, you know, not quite as bad as Harriet Beecher Stowe would have us believe, is hard to take; yet I know it is this sort of book I should read, so that I understand where this place came from. Because language and ideas have, happily, changed in the last twenty years, it is necessary to read history from times previous, so that we know why that change was essential. And in those less self-conscious books we get a view, innocent perhaps but valid nonetheless, of the goodness in the desires of this country. I'm working my way through the shelves. I've just taken out Jane Foster's *An un-American Lady* to throw myself into complete turmoil, I'm sure. Next to come is the overturning of everything I've just read; in other words, Native Americans and Latin America and Vietnam. At least I'll know what's what at the end of it.

Reading so many history books makes one think, also, of one's own personal history: a rather confused affair in my own case. I became aware of just how confused a number of years ago. When my father died it took me a long time to get my own history back. In order to feel well, I think we have to know what our past was, what we want our future to be, and how well our present is going, both in overcoming our past and shaping our future. But when my father died I left my past behind. Everything I remembered had him in it. My mother had given me some of his clothes years before, some hats and shirts, and I had photographs. I tried removing the hats from the top of the wardrobe, and putting the photographs in drawers, but that didn't make much difference. The day after I heard about his funeral (we weren't at it, of course) the butcher shivered when I ordered my meat and said, 'Someone's just walked over my grave.' I was confused; I wondered if I should tell him so that he wouldn't be worried about the strange presence that had flittered before him. I think it was that incident which made me believe that I was, in fact, carrying his curse within me. My mother had always been a dark sort of human. When she could forget about herself and what people thought of her, a cheerfulness would fizzle out of her life like a new flower. But after a while her face could change; it was like watching a cloud pass over the sun. Now that her husband was dead she became even stranger. I worried about her a lot, for some time. It was as if, as if, I had to become her and thus save her from her pain. And if I didn't think of her for a few hours I felt choked by guilt and then I'd remember that, yes, he was dead, and something was over for her. I seemed to become very old in the few months after he died. And funny, my mother eventually started to become younger. Then she died and I tried to stop thinking about either of them.

The combination of both deaths had ended something for me. I could never feel comfortable around relatives any more. Bad news was their adrenaline. Mournfulness made them feel comfortable in their collaboration with eternal guilt as a means of keeping themselves, and me, down. I think they particularly enjoyed telling me atrocious stories because I would flinch, so they would know they were getting a reaction. Every time I changed room during my mother's funeral, there was another relative in it with more bad news. I suspected that they wished more awful things on themselves. And mourned the passing of possibilities for disaster. The only cheerful one was my aunt Marnie, who really did have a terrible history, but her job was to hide scars, not pick at them. But violently forgetting your past comes back on you; it wrecked my marriage, I think. Or contributed. I've begun to think of these things here; perhaps I'll reach some conclusion.

I hope these wanderings aren't insensitive or depressing. But this should cheer you up – my local baker actually gave me the recipe for bagels. I think he presumed that the likelihood of me actually baking them was remote and so he risked my custom. Here it is.

You can add spices, raisins, finely chopped nuts etc. to your basic dough.

Recipe: combine one cup scalded milk, quarter cup butter, one tablespoon sugar and one teaspoon of salt. When this mixture is at 105 to 115 degrees, add and dissolve for three minutes one packet of active dried yeast. Blend in one to two eggs, and $3^3/_4$ cups sifted all-purpose flour. Knead this soft dough for about ten minutes, adding more flour if necessary, to make it firm enough to handle. Let rise, covered, in a greased bowl until doubled in bulk. Punch down and divide into eighteen equal pieces. Roll each piece into a rope about seven inches long and taper at the end. Wet the ends to help seal. Form into a doughnut-shaped ring. Let it rise, covered, on a floured board for about fifteen minutes. To help firm the dough, you may chill it for two hours. Drop rings, one at a time, into a solution of four pints' almost boiling water and one tablespoon of sugar. Add the bagels separately, turn them over and cook about three minutes longer. Skim out and place on an ungreased baking sheet. Coat with beaten egg-white. Bake in a preheated oven 300 degrees Fahrenheit for almost twenty to twenty-five minutes until golden brown and crisp

Good luck with it. Regards to all on the street.

Regards,
Fergal

To Fergal from Bernard

Dear Fergal,

Thank you for your delightful letter and I look forward to the book: the New York perspective on glass, I hope. As it happens, I had just finished the archaeology book on glass by Ruth Hurst Vose – an ideal name for a glass museum keeper. I was reminded of the intricacy of the procedure because even I forget and sometimes take the light coming through my window for granted. And thinking about that, I looked around my front room – the light bulb, my mirror, my camera sitting on the table (I don't use it much any more), the table itself, for God's sake (Connie and Desmond bought it for me when I moved here), my spectacles and, of course, my Waterford collection. I was catapulted into memory and action. I had been meaning to try for some work for a while, some small part-time job, because although I've enjoyed my time reading since I came here, my garden too, getting to know the area, my grand-children, I thought there was a little time that needed filling. I've always preferred the idea of filling time rather than killing it. So I took myself to a glass shop that I've been passing on my walks up to Christchurch cathedral. It's at the end of Clanbrassil Street. Myra Glass. Now I must admit I found it odd going to the counter, because it seemed like many a lifetime ago when I would imagine jobs and put myself into them to see if they would suit. As it hap-pened, however, one of their staff had just gone out sick so here I am now with a temporary part-time job selling glass. I will work from nine until one (sort of like Junior Infants).

It's a number of years since I read it, but I remember *An un-American Lady*. I remember at first being struck by Jane Foster's bravery during the war, recounted so matter-of-factly. But then to see what McCarthyism could and did do. The suicides and the sui-cide attempts don't tell the actual story of what precipitated them. She described it so well because she concentrated on the little things. I had a vision of her sister-in-law's house in Chicago. I still have. Jane wanting to pull the curtains at dusk on this goldfish bowl and the sister-in-law shamedly admitting that no one here did, as drawn curtains could signify hidden goings-on. How frightening! And that is not so long ago, the fifties only. No wonder I left. To see such cowardice, such debasement, such fear, and the great bravery of those who left. The creeps came out of the woodwork then; that's the only thing I don't like about being my age. I can periodically see it happening again, but the wise or the mature are never heeded. Such is life. It would appear that goodness and badness must be experienced before being believed. It is sometimes amusing in times like that to realise how the normal events of a past life can make a person appear guilty. Guilty by association. So is America still at the 'love me or leave me' stage? Or have the civilities of sense taken hold?

Your history book sounds daunting. I'm not sure that I could read that view now; I find it hard enough to read some journalists. A radical journalist mostly has to be a misnomer, a contradiction in terms, because they report, or should report, only what happens. A journalist with a radical outlook is, of course, another matter. Some journalists are like writers; they don't know why they were born, and worry. They're the good ones. But seclusion is needed for writing books. The less one talks the more we'll write (look at your own letter-writing) and journalists must, by the nature of their jobs, have less seclusion.

I do not find the talk of life and history depressing. I feel my time speeding past so rapidly that I do not believe it, and so I still feel optimistic. As I said, the only irritating thing is knowing too much at times. I have had a good life; sometimes I live off my stockpile of happiness. Occasionally those moments can catch me in the eyes and the heart when I waken, I walk faster that day, food tastes better, I can feel myself traversing the street, people look at me, there's fresh country air whipping a breeze on my face, people look again at me. All this in a city. And death is not a taboo of mine either. Indeed sometimes . . . never mind.

I've finished this correspondence for the moment. The sun is streaming through the window, hitting my glass. Did you know that crystal can be used as an adjective to describe devotion?

Yours,
Bernard

Dear Fergal,

Well, everyone around here is working now, except me, of course. Looking after three children is just a dawdle. I hear myself telling myself not to complain. The sun came out today on its first new day for a while, making a spanking, fresh, teasey sort of morning. As usual, it made people think of the country and summers past – note how I presume that others think the same thing as me. So everyone stepped out off the footpaths on to the road as if the car had not been invented (me included) and frightened the life out of some unfortunate half-sleeping driver. He then screamed at me and the children watched fascinated, children always being scared, but secretly titillated, by someone shouting at the person who usually shouts at them. I walked home from the school with a woman who was pregnant and I felt the mushy feeling of history that staggers through ages that are punctuated by things like the baby first pointing its finger at you and smiling. This woman, from the next street, is not very happy, I think. Her husband may not be the man she would really have chosen to have her children by, but not all women get that one right. Often by the time they have enough sense to know its importance, they already have them. He must have been all right for courting but how was she, any more than anyone else, to know better and to realise that courting is not child-rearing? Her new baby has started to show so her body is proportioning itself, stretching, plumping, in harmony. Her skin is beginning to tan, her face is transparent and shockingly beautiful. I felt sorry about her shyly expressed complaints and thought, quietly, how hard it is to love someone who always makes you wish that they were different.

But in the meantime, the job has to be got on with. We have to teach the children the truth; but what is the truth and how much of it can a child, an adult indeed, stand? I remember having a real problem about how to teach caution. I remember particularly worrying about the fire. How do you teach a child who doesn't understand words? How do you keep a child safe and yet not petrify them? I remember one of the twins working his flat bottom over to the fire one day (I was washing the dishes in the next room, thinking of nothing, no place, no time, a pleasant nothing). He must have pulled the fireguard away easily; the coals behind it were always dancing, so I suppose he thought that if he lifted away the obstruction he would be able to see more. He got his little hand around the front part and pulled. What is pain? A child must wonder where it is coming from. Let go the firefront but it is still there. Scream, and Mammy will come and she will fix it. But she can't. I remember shoving his hand under the cold water and the pain obviously went. But when I switched off the water it came back. I remember pushing his hand into his bottom cream and it was gone, but then when I took it out, it was back. I suppose he can't remember the whole awful few hours, but I can. So nature does not have caution built in, and fear, unfortunately, has to be learned.

I don't think that mothers can expect to be treated properly by any man. They carry about them a residue of terror. They are symbols of human helplessness. They could leave us with a burning hand, for God's sake, or they could even stick our hand into the fire. But they don't do any of those things, usually. We scream, they do their best. No wonder we hate mothers sometimes; they represent our cavernous helplessness and yet they get us over it. Girls, as well as boys, feel this too, but then they get into training for the job themselves. So in a way all girls and women are tainted by motherhood in men's eyes.

But there are good things; there is the time when remembering and forgetting are the same thing. There are delightful moments, like putting a hand around a child's bottom underneath its nightshirt, its bottom free before the nappy goes on, the stab in your stomach at the softness of it. Your eyes are made by the stab to look into the child's and your two smiles crease into one, lighting up a quick flare over the evening. It's a pity we can't spend more time remembering those moments but one of the major problems about rearing children is wishing that time would pass. If only it was next month and he had those last two troublesome teeth, if only it was next year and she had got over the tantrum stage. Insurance clerks, doctors, gardeners and architects don't actively wish their lives away daily. I'm sure there'll be something to pay for this unnatural wishing when the last of mine reaches sixteen or eighteen. And sometimes I can be blinded by rage too (not really blinded, let's say fogged over) and I'm afraid I'll smash windows or something. Gosh, I must ask Bernard why it is that the sound of smashing, splintering glass seems so cathartic. And I must not become boring; everyone is not interested in children. Maybe should be, but they're not.

Well, when I got home I decided to spring clean, even though it's not spring. And I didn't. Instead, I found the writing-case you gave me the summer I went to London. I don't think I ever used it, but I found, tucked in a pocket, a few of those terrible retreat cards we convent girls used to send each other. 'I hope you enjoy your retreat, pray for me. Love Mary.' God bless her; she was ugly in a bland Dutch kind of way. I remember our class know-all saying that, and me, goody-goody two-shoes that I was, saying: 'Oh no, she has a lovely smile.' 'Oh for God's sake' – I can hear the exasperated retort – 'you only think that because of the relief from seeing the change in her expression.' What horrible little scuts we were. Another one said, 'The cross is my refuge.' I'm amazed that any of us survived it. Well, I tore them up and put them in the bin, better than breaking glass. So there, that's why you're getting this letter, and I will now begin to use your letter-case. (Maybe I shouldn't have torn the cards; maybe we should keep those monuments.)

About the others, let me tell you my thoughts at the moment. Helena is busy, but has had more consecutive days off recently, so we've had some pleasant walks and talks. She's a terribly complete person; I suspect it's all the travelling does that. I think, perhaps, that even if there were things wrong in your life, you could always relegate them to a place of minor importance if you were going to Rome in the morning. Or New York. Perhaps I'm a masochist, but I want to hear from her always about the places. She has even begun to take some photographs for me. And although it does sometimes make me feel the blandness of my own life, at other times her descriptions (she's a great teller of tales) are essential sweetnesses in my weeks. And some day when I have my children reared, I won't be wondering where to go, my list will be ready. There I go again, wishing time away. I suppose I am sometimes envious of her and Kevin's relationship, one of the only ones I've ever seen where each of them is naturally both man and woman. They're like family to one another – even in the way they bicker about small things! If I were to say to Desmond some of the things she says to Kevin, I'd never hear the end of it. Mind you, I'm not sure I could take the public raising of his eyes to the ceiling that Kevin does. Helena is tough, no doubt. And yet I bet they're having it off more often than the rest of us. She and I don't discuss things like that; I think that she thinks that I'm too naïve. Or maybe it's best not to know your neighbour's sexual habits anyway.

Bernard is great at the moment, just started his new part-time job. And I'm on speaking terms with your tenants, although I haven't yet figured out the differences between them. They have a great variety of music. I sometimes hear it drifting in – Bach, Beatles, Bowie, Ella Fitzgerald. They're too young for the Beatles but someone must have got hooked by an older brother or sister. I like them. The girl looks as if she thinks she's making a patchwork quilt when she dresses every morning. One of the fellows has a gorgeous smile; he'll cause trouble. He looks out under one eye when he's looking at you. I was thinking that he should go far, but maybe men won't like him for it and women won't get him much further than the couch. Desmond is fine, busy and concerned with quotas and teaching. I see too little of him but it's hard to complain, I know he's working hard. Nor would it do any good. And it is also humiliating to ask someone to talk to you, don't you think? It's like being a child: 'Mammy, Rosaleen won't talk to me.' So maybe I prefer to see little of him because at least he's not in my presence not talking to me. Do you get me? The children are great – I'll send some photos soon. I must go now because it's time to pick them up; in fact, if I don't hurry they'll be swinging their legs like the kid in the Flash ad. It's OK: you wouldn't, and shouldn't, know it.

Your dream was interesting. I have no idea what it could mean. Must hurry.

Love,
Connie

Dear Connie,

This is really a rushed note but I got your letter this morning and thought I would reply immediately, the reason being that I was worried about describing my dream and thought I might have overstepped the mark. So I was terribly relieved to get such a lovely letter from you. You make me think of women, and women plus children, in such a different way. Your thoughts contain within them not just the basis of your ideas but the critical analysis as well. I must go today and search for some books for you, particularly one – *Of Woman Born*. I was looking through it in a friend's apartment.

Sometimes it's hard to know what to write to you; we live such different lives now. We did at home too, but at least I knew what was going on around me, the news, the gossip, the good, the bad. Now I'm cut off, and when I do hear of the things that would normally preoccupy us, through the *Irish Voice* or an Irish newspaper, it is too late to write to you about them; they will have been superseded. On Saturday I'm going to buy some new clothes. I feel I need a changeover into my new life and changing one's clothes is always a good marker. Did you ever notice that when people break up they rout their wardrobes soon afterwards?

> Love,
> Fergal

Dear Fergal,

Who's the friend? I've read *Of Woman Born*. It was years ago! Desmond and I are on a few days' break in Clare, not the place of your dreams. It's beautiful and I'm shocked at how quickly I could forget just how wonderful this corner can be, how I can sink into here. Helena and Bernard pulled this surprise on me; between them they're minding my brood. I've been gone twenty-four hours and I've forgotten I ever had them. Life is sweet, the sea, the sun, could you believe? Glasses of Guinness whenever – and, oh, you know the rest.

> Lots of love,
> Connie

PS. Yesterday I watched a seal sunning itself; made me think of the necessity of being good to oneself, even animals do it.

POSTCARD
To Fergal from Desmond

Fergal,

Connie and I are having a short break in Clare; my father and Helena are minding the children; I really don't know how they will manage. Connie keeps me up to date on your progress. Life is fine with me, but it is pleasant to get away from college and college politics. I suspect you feel that in regard to the whole country. I wouldn't mind myself, sometimes. I think we will leave here tomorrow and go to Galway, perhaps; it seems very quiet with just myself and Connie. This postcard seems bigger than the normal.

> Yours,
> Desmond

To Connie and Desmond from Fergal

Dear Connie and Desmond,

How lovely to get your postcards. I had just come back myself from a trip to a few places. No one here goes to such and such a place, they take a trip there, and in a way I suppose it's an appropriate word, the place is so vast. Mine was just a small trip really: New York, St Paul-Minneapolis, Washington and back to New York. Mind you, I set out on it as if it was a huge undertaking, not realising how piffling most Americans can consider that distance. The size of the place definitely adds restlessness to the other forms of life; the airports are full of nomads moving out, in, up, down, back.

I write to tell you of my trip; a risk, I know, because the details of other people's travels can sometimes be irritating. Maybe I'm telling you because the young woman beside me on the plane between Pittsburgh and St Paul-Minneapolis was writing to her friend, back in some part of Yugoslavia, and the thought of her has stayed with me since. No matter what slaughter, or rather where the slaughter has moved to, people still travel and write letters. How amazing; you'd think we'd all be paralysed by grief. I was so struck by her thinking that her journey might be worth recounting to someone in a war zone that I've decided to tell you about mine. The woman was in the window seat and was an accommodating sort. She allowed me to look past her and even pointed out things that she could see before me, like the beginning of Lake Erie or other things that she happened to see on her occasional glance up from the page to the window. It was during one of her longer looks out the window that I sneaked a peep at her page. It was such an ordinary letter, making such passing reference to the butchery of her own place, that it intrigued me. She wrote of the moment and I wondered if she might mention me. Why? Well, why not? She was writing of her journey as it unfolded, so why wouldn't she mention me? Well, she didn't, not that I could see anyway.

My own journey began in a rather hazardous way. I went to Newark, which is a crazy-looking airport, planes seem to be taking off above and below each other. As we're sitting waiting to leave, we get the announcement that due to thunderstorms we have to wait longer. For three hours we sat there, sweltering, while the captain explained stacking and queuing and God knows what else to us. And people took it out on the stewards. 'But my connection!' What a job! Actually watching the planes queuing like a vast snake was interesting therapy for a bad flyer like me; they looked so normal cosied all together, not at all the threats I usually imagine when I have to think about them. Of course, by the time we got to Pittsburgh the outgoing flights were stopped, so we had to stay in a hotel. We don't just live America through films – try saying Pittsburgh without adding Pennsylvania. In the hotel bar I listened to a couple squabbling. Apparently he wouldn't talk to her. What's new? I treated myself to a margarita and it made me feel as if I was in Pittsburgh Pennsylvania. (A client rang me up at work one day saying he was calling from Albuquerque and I said, 'Ha ha, you only imagine it, no one actually rings from Albuquerque' – sorry, that's another story.) Next morning it was raining and the place smelled of tyres. I'm sure it didn't, but that's what I remember.

My flight was interesting. Over Milwaukee I saw the first parched fields I've seen in a long time. (Yes, that's the place where the fellow murdered dozens, I think, of young men and ate some of them. But who wants to let one lunatic mar a view from a plane?) Further out, the newly ploughed fields over the earth looked like recently swept rooms or hurricanes in flight. Some fields had swathes cut out of them like question marks. I stayed for a few days with our old friend Pádraig; you, of course, remember him. Well, he's still a mad eejit who keeps the music up too loud. He's married to, I fear, a rather obnoxious woman whose sense of inferiority manifests itself in an overbearing bossy manner. Not comfortable. They argued continuously and I was sometimes rigid with a sense of boredom and annoyance at their bad manners. But then I remembered how he liked to show off, and perhaps that's what his marriage is. Alone with me he behaved in that very emigrant way, wanting me to meet people that he knew in New York, people that we used to know when we were in our early twenties, people I had no interest in whatsoever. But emigrants do that, they want relatives at home to be fascinated by other relations' progress in Florida, Kentucky, wherever. They're shocked if the Irish people haven't a fidge of interest, because that means that they then, too, could be forgotten. I escaped to go by car to Pine Lake to visit a man with whom I briefly worked last year.

I hired a car and the first thing I had to do was buy coffee to put in the coffee-holder, and crisps, of course. I drove the automatic at the stately speed of under fifty-five miles per hour with the air-conditioning on, and I went over the Mississippi and I became an American. I was in the film. I was the film. The summer-house, a stately, solid wooden affair with plenty of silver in the drawers handed down by money; the G and T's, the warmth, the wine, the lake, the boat, the new friends, the calmness of people here; it nearly made me weep. I thought I was on a voyage on a ship. On my way back, when I was less awestruck, I noticed how right the film was. You can see this place; it is harder to feel it. My last duty back in Minneapolis was to shop in the Mall of America, the largest in the United States. After half an hour it's just a shopping centre, but people do fly in there to shop, and joggers lap its insides on winter mornings. I wanted to stay in Minneapolis and it's some time since I felt that about any place. (I always felt that in Mayo, never Clare.) Maybe we do have past lives lived in specific places. For instance, I never wanted to stay in Boston, nor in Sligo.

I'm afraid my flight to Washington was a disaster. The earth was too visible, or too far away, or we were too high up, or too low down, or maybe it was the margaritas from the night before. The wheels came down when we were still too far up and the plane seemed to lurch downwards. I hate being such a sporadically incapable air traveller. And I really never know when it's going to hit. In my hotel in Washington, with more margaritas, I saw my first fireflies. How often the writers mention them; I must have read the name hundreds of times, yet they did not describe them. The lawn looked as if clear-flashing Christmas lights had been strewn across it. Or so I thought on first glance, until the lights began to fly. Fascinating little beasts. Watching them made me feel about how we're all made up, machines really, with bits that light up. Those bits are our hearts, I presume. Yes, that's what fireflies are really; the Pompidou Centre model of the human brain.

In the morning I 'did' the Washington that we know from Mícheál O'Hehir's radio description of Kennedy's funeral, and also the one from every daily news. Our tour guide was a Kennedy lookalike, Irish-America throws them up; it's the looks refined by good living. What would have become a peering, lined, sad face of postcards breathes out with wealth into a Kennedy. He had once worked in the White House basement and had some great stories (Johnson pissing out over the balcony on to journalists and that sort of thing). He gossiped warmly about the ones he knew and it frightened me somewhat to be so near and to hear the human weaknesses of the men who wield such enormous power. What struck me most about Arlington cemetery were the rows of white crosses, the acres of dead men. I hadn't intended to feel what I felt at Kennedy's grave but it's hard, regardless of doubts, not to sense a murder of hope. And then Bobby's simple white cross, one faded, ordinary carnation lying there, it could all have been too much. And as for the Vietnamese memorial, think as I did about the slaughter of the Vietnamese, I still had feeling left over for some of those men. I felt some forgiveness – their actions seemed more pitiable than malicious for a few minutes. The alphabetical order of the names of the dead comes as a shock – you can find your son's, your husband's, more quickly and put your hand over it, taking all your memories into your fingertips from the stone. People do. Then the Lincoln memorial: well, I never knew he made such enlightened speeches; my American history is still too sketchy. After that we sauntered by the White House. Reagan has succeeded in closing it off, in making a fortress of it, and who will reverse that? We had lunch in the Dubliner (where else?), a crazy name for a pub that needs coolers. The Senate houses, Capitol Hill, I'd had enough in this day to make me think.

I fear I must admit that I did not take the shuttle back; I got the train instead, through Baltimore, Delaware, Philadelphia. I arrived at Penn and made my way home, as one tends to do on a Sunday. But New York is like nowhere else on a Sunday and for that I'm grateful. When I got your cards I thought to write immediately. I hope you both had a lovely time in Clare, and Galway if you went there. And I'll be in touch again soon. Regards to Bernard and Helena.

> Your fond friend,
> Fergal

Dear Helena,

I went out to see my cousin who was on a stopover at JFK yesterday evening and I remembered that I hadn't been in touch with you for a while. I know you may like the Italian flights, but I do miss your stopover here, and I'm glad to know that you'll be back in a few months. I got two postcards from Connie and Desmond on their short break; I was delighted to know that they got off together – nothing like a free weekend in the west to make people appreciate each other. Of course it can work the other way too; the weekend that I went away with my wife, only two weeks after the honey-moon, put paid to a whole intended life. One could almost laugh.

> Yours,
>   Fergal

To Fergal from Helena
Rome

Dear Fergal,

I don't know about being back in New York. I quite enjoy having someone to write to between the shower and supper; it structures my evening off. Obviously I can't write home as I'm usually back the next day. Connie gave me your letter to read, lovely journey, I thought; I was in St Paul-Minneapolis only once.

I had to fly over here unexpectedly this evening in order to work the journey back tomorrow because one of our staff got sick. It's odd flying when I'm not working; I watch people differently. Actually, I just watch people; whereas when I'm working I either pass people or stare at them. The first I looked at today were a couple and child who went up the escalator before me, the man moved directly in front of me, the woman three steps ahead holding the child by the hip as it tried to wriggle out of her grasp. She had a lovely profile, a nonchalant way of holding her body. I honestly don't think he noticed. I think he was dreading the Costa del Wherever with a child in tow. I found myself staring at them, wondering, and thought I was becoming like men, the way they stare at women's legs and hips as they walk past. But then I realised that no, the kind of men who stare that way only see legs and hips, or breasts and whatever; they don't imagine the life of the person.

On the plane I met an old school friend; well, 'friend' might be stretching it a little. You would probably know her name – Mona Lowe, now works in RTÉ. But she had a life before that one, a sort of international PR person, I think, a life that consisted of lots of bed-hopping; one, in fact, that couldn't have had much else in it if I am any judge of time. But then maybe these things can be done much faster than I think. She told me the most extraordinary stories of life on the road, or, to be more exact, life on the tiles. She said that when she was living like this she genuinely believed that the more she 'sinned' the less harm it would do her, because she could forget more of the transgression. Her debut with strange men had started when she stayed overnight with a work colleague on her way to somewhere – I can't quite remember, there was a complicated reason for something or other. Gerard, let's call him Gerard, I've forgotten his real name, in this case he wasn't famous, said that he wasn't a very good host, when she arrived. She wrongly thought that he meant the opposite. His wife was away for a month, she was a fashion buyer, and the kitchen bore the marks of an incompetent man, the pots and the things that could be seen were filthy and he had no embarrassment about it. He had ignored her all evening, but then after they shared a beer, things began to change. When they got to the bed she was uneasy, but he was totally in control. He wanted her to put on the condom. He thought that, considering he had to wear it, this was the least she could do. She hadn't a clue how to do it, somehow presuming that it was the least men could do, put on their own condoms. It wasn't that she objected to doing her share. For instance, she didn't believe that only the men should change the tyre when you got a flat. Anyway, she got on with it, the whole thing being both as good and as bad as she had known it

70

would be. His kisses were good enough. As long as she kept her eyes closed she could make something of him. His fetish for feeling her nipples through her clothes was rather thrilling and the rest was satisfactory. But, she said, they could take no breaks because they would have had to start all over again; nothing lingered once they realised who they were. In some strange way, despite the earlier confidence, he was too timid for her and she was too shy to push him. Afterwards was awful, she said. She put her clothes on quickly; he lingered on the bed displaying a body that she had little interest in, and certainly didn't want to see now that she was satisfied. He suggested that she must be out of practice, her coming had been so loud. Nasty little jibe. He moaned about her having her clothes on so soon and said that he'd like a rub. Apparently she made a note never to get herself into that situation again, one she obviously lost. He then began to talk about his wife. He said she was a 'good' person. I was wondering how a fashion buyer can be a 'good' person. I'm not saying they're bad, but how, particularly, would they be good? What would they do to make them good? How would anyone know that they were good? And then I thought, Perhaps he was sending some message to Mona. She honestly did tell me all these things; I was praying that she would keep her voice down.

I can't remember half of the stories but they all had little losses in them. She had sex with a man in a hotel room and when he went to sleep she moved herself over to the other bed. In the morning he left before her, saying a brief grumpy good-bye. Before she booked out, for some odd reason, she checked the bed that had been partially made, the one he had slept in, and, lo and behold, he had wet it. Sheets, duvet, mattress, soaked. What infuriated her was that he had slunk out without saying, or taking responsibility, so that the hotel staff would think it was she who had done it. She stripped the bed clothes and did her best to dry the mattress, hungover and fuming all the time. Later in the day they bumped into each other and he behaved as if nothing had happened. I think she enjoyed the power of knowing that he was having to live the rest of his life wondering if she had checked the bed. Her revenge, she said, was in telling me – not just the story, but his name. Apparently the sex

71

was lousy too! An all-round piddling affair, she said.

And there were losses of property too. She said that if you left anything behind in these illicit night manoeuvrings you never got it back. Once a man admitted throwing her blouse out of his car into the ditch. Her good blouse that her grandmother had bought her for Christmas! She said that nothing could have been worth losing the blouse. But she eventually got scared, she told me. She would be away somewhere and wake reluctantly, her sins waiting for her. 'Oh Jesus,' she thought one morning, unbearably, 'did I come on to the taxi driver last night, did I kiss the taxi driver?' She tried to go back to sleep. Maybe it would go away. Surely no one could kiss the taxi driver; even if he was the last man you were likely to see that night? But closing her eyes didn't shut down her fright; she could still see the picture, gradually defrosting. She wondered if she kept putting questions to herself, 'Did I kiss the taxi driver last night?', as if she really didn't know, would that protect her from having to say, 'I kissed the taxi driver last night.' Did the fact that she woke up asking the question mean that she had done the question? So she opened her eyes reluctantly, thinking that it was better to face it now. Apparently, that signalled a change in her lifestyle. I should think so; rather dangerous behaviour, I thought to myself.

I was overwhelmed by her life. I couldn't figure out why someone would put themselves at such risk, and then I thought that maybe she was right, maybe she thought at some stage, now is the time I should be enjoying myself, before, before whatever. But then what does enjoying oneself mean? Is it getting tipsy? Is it that five minutes before getting tipsy, or is it managing to conquer sexually, or is it not a spring day? I'm afraid I wouldn't be cut out for that sort of caper! I certainly had nothing to match in the conversation and was not tempted to try.

After her deluge of recounting she asked me, suddenly, if I had any photographs of Kevin or Ciarán with me. I can tell you I'd forgotten about them during the previous minutes. Photographs! Now there's an odd thing. It used to shock people that I did not carry their photographs. Now I do. But it still shocks people that I do not add and subtract my five or whatever hours to think of what they're doing. I believe Ciarán is in good hands, so why worry?

People expect me to worry about what will happen to him when he grows up. Firstly, he might be unlucky and nothing might happen to him; secondly, life is happening to him, and finally what might not happen to me if I didn't keep moving? It offends me that mothers are expected to put their lives into their children's as if children were trustee banks. And we're supposed to worry all the time, to catch our breaths at the awfulness of things that might happen. I worry only when I've been sitting in one place too long. On my week off I changed the furniture in the house, for the sake of changing the outlook, not for the sake of having it to say that I've done it. I love my husband but I don't spend my time missing him, well, sometimes, maybe at half ten or eleven at night, when there's no one else around, but mostly I don't; what's there to miss? He's somewhere, isn't he? But I do carry photographs now, a few of Ciarán, some of him and me, and more of Kevin. I don't think I need them. I used to laugh at people who carried them, but one morning I woke up in New York and I couldn't remember what they looked like and I began to worry, what if I completely forgot? You may ask how could a wife, or more particularly a mother, forget? You're right, but it scared me. You see, flying can do peculiar things. Sometimes when I've been working a lot, I fly all night in my sleep, and I wake up suddenly as if afraid that I will find out that I'm not in the bed. I touch Kevin at moments like that, often guiltily, because it's surely not a compliment to use someone as an aerial. You see, when you're in the air a lot you lose the perspective of people as people: everyone is simply a passenger, the way some nurses see everyone as patients. It's not a bad way to see people really, as passengers, it often gives them more importance than they have in real life. When those nights of uncertainty happen to me I cannot go back to sleep. And if they happen away from home and I haven't got Kevin beside me, I think about him and Ciarán all night. Strange really, how people whom one never knew up until one day become so much part of your life.

Anyway, I showed Mona the photographs and we got on to a different tack, which was a relief in a way. Although when I thought about it afterwards, I had to admire her nerve. Did I tell you? God, no, I didn't. Connie is coming with me next time I have a few days off here. I'm really looking forward to that. I want so much to be on holiday with her, to lounge about uninterrupted in her essential company. Must rush, the others are ready for dinner.

Lots of love,
Helena

Fergal,

Well, here I am. The lights go down in the piazza; Helena and I have just eaten. I had pasta and saltimbucca alla romana. How come we can't cook like this? How come we never think of it? The mopeds twitter past and the furs are being put on. It's still nippy in the evenings. It's simply gorgeous being here with her, pampering all the special things in our friendship. Postcards are supposed to make people feel better but I'm going to make them feel terrible at home when I tell them that the sun has been shining all day. You, of course, always feel OK. Still, I hope. I'll write in a few days, tomorrow perhaps.

Love,
Connie

Dear Fergal,

This is all rather sudden arriving here! I know that Helena thought I
was coming, and believed me when I said that I would, but *I* didn't.
A very strange thing happened to me. I went to a work 'do' with
Desmond and had nothing to say to anyone. I went to the swimming pool the next day. I remember noticing that there were a lot
of freckled people in the pool; I've always liked freckles. And suddenly I was crying. I had to keep swimming with my head under
water so that people wouldn't notice. I was still crying in the
shower and just made it home before collapsing into unstoppable
tears. I decided that crying in the swimming pool is some sort of
sign and made my mind up. Perhaps it was the break in Clare that
did it. I couldn't any longer wait for my satisfaction to arrive in
small doses.

In the passport office I listened to a woman plus baby, obviously
visiting her old job and her old working friends. The women still
working there were clearly bored with her; she was out of their
look now, and I wondered if she had always been this boring. The
woman with the baby may have been wondering if the others had
always been caught up in such trivial nonsense as hair, clothes, and
who was playing where next week. 'What's a passport?' a child
asked and his mother did her best to answer. I switched off, suddenly despising children, the way one shockingly can sometimes,
and I was terribly glad that I was on my way. I don't know what
Desmond thinks; I know that I had to come. And I hope that it will
settle me for a while.

We are staying in a hotel which Helena knew about. My room
has wooden shutters (but of course) that open out on to a walled
private square. I'm dazzled by the tiles when I waken. The place is
so beautiful it makes me shiver. At night I can hear the swans over
the Tiber sounding like distant people making love. I feel so good I
want to flirt all the time, even with myself. It's a long time since I
felt this good. I look in the mirror and I honestly don't recognise
myself; the blue in my eyes matches the blue in my shirt. Last week

if I'd been asked what colour my eyes were I would have had to say, 'Can't remember, certainly more a matt finish than a gloss.'

I was shocked by the sights I saw today, the years, the history. What do any of us know? St Peter's! St Peter's would make me want to be a proper Catholic. Well, maybe that's taking it a little far, but my God, did they have taste! It's funny, in Rome you can see the sense of stained-glass windows and resurrection scenes in D'Olier Street or in Doolin. I was thinking fondly today of the Mass in Latin which I just vaguely remember. I found myself remembering my saints and my hymns and my prayers. And then I remembered the guilt. Well, it doesn't strike me that the Romans suffer from too much of that.

I eat in the evening and I dream. The food, the wine, the glamour, the noises, the smells. The glamorous here are so glamorous, the rich, so rich. We're off out now for more of the same and tomorrow it will still be here.

Connie

PS. I never did post this. I think we went a little astray on some of the drink that night. When I woke, I was taken aback by the sounds in my head, but eventually I did get my brain in working order. And then Helena had to go. I found Rome a little difficult to be in alone; I was getting slightly less fascinated by the flirting, and I think you need someone, you know, to ooh and aah with, and to understand why you're suddenly tired. As a city Rome can be titillating in a sometimes unsatisfying way, so I decided to come to Verona and here I am. It was a spur-of-the-moment thing; I've always liked the ads for here. They had some late fog as I came in on the train; now I know why the wine tastes so good. The fog, like some spirit-ridden mist, is dropped down through the branches to the bottom of the vine trees.

I had dinner last night in a sweet little place, even if they had some difficulty with the *uno* person and the *uno* dinner. But they put me safely in the back corner where I wouldn't ruin business. On my way it was chilly, and the city was quite deserted – the fog, I supposed – but there were packs of lads roaming around the streets and hanging around the telephone boxes. I had all sorts of lock-up-your-daughter plots worked out as an answer to that, when I remembered the national service. They were, in fact, hanging about with nothing to do, away from home, and they were ringing their mammies. In the restaurant one man had difficulty accepting me sitting there on my own reading a book; he looked at me a lot, then shifted in his seat uncomfortably. The woman with him was so glamorous, it looked as if she and I belonged to a different species. I suppose he thinks women only have to look like his companion and only have to sit and be treated well. Aah! It's not that way for all of us and some of us might not want it to be so. The more plebeian couple beside them appeared riveted by each other. I think he was asking her why she filed her nails rather than cut them. She shuddered as if he'd suggested cutting her fingers off. I could see that the shudder had him hooked. The waiter left them discreetly alone; in Italy they know that we deserve all the moments of happiness that we can get.

I feared that I might begin to have things too much like home thoughts, so I had a brandy and retired to sleep; well, to finish this letter really and now to sleep. Tomorrow I'm off to Venice, with a stop to see the frescoes in Padua. Aren't I brave? Certainly braver than I thought I could be. Actually, I only wrote that so that I could see it written down. Tomorrow I'm off to Venice!

To Fergal from Bernard

Dear Fergal,

I do not believe that I owe you a letter so this feels like getting into the black, but I do owe you a thank-you for the wonderful recipe. My bagels are the talk of the street; I'm thinking of gradually introducing them to the job. The first attempt was a little doughy but I'm getting better. I'm getting better at cooking generally and eating is not quite the chore it was last year. Having come to cooking late, I use recipe books a lot, so perhaps that explains why I'm as good as I am.

The job is going well. We sell all types of glass, large orders for building firms, tiny panes to tiny boys who are getting it fixed before the neighbours come home. We usually sell glass a little cheaper to them; it seems too harsh to take all their piggy-bank money. There's one pair who come in here, a twin boy and girl, and it's always a long narrow yellow strip they want. They're compact against the outside world, a very secretive pair; perhaps they're storing the glass somewhere. There's another young fellow who comes in to buy broken bits. He wants to make his own glass-house; I want to point out the difficulties, but then who am I? It will be the best glasshouse he'll ever stand in. We also do mirrors, laminated glass, leaded lights, perspex, that sort of thing. All very flat glass, but it feels good to the hand. The only problem is that the front shop manager has a terrible accent. Actually, no, it's not his accent; it's the actual pitch of his voice which goes through your head like a hacksaw.

I walk to work, across by Slattery's, onto Leinster Road the back way, down by Harold's Cross into Clanbrassil Street, so I'm exorcising my pain as well as walking. I like Dublin, I think, or at least it surprises me that I dislike it as little as I do. And I have met one of your tenants, Stephen is his name. Properly this time, I mean. A few weeks ago I was at Heuston station waiting for the train to Waterford; I had decided to visit for a day, and it had become a task rather than the nerve-wracking experience I thought it might be. Or perhaps I tried to make it into a task so I could bear it. The young fellow nodded at me, knowing me from the street, I suppose, and I was glad to engage him in small talk. He said that he was going to visit a friend of his in Portlaoise jail, what he called a political prisoner. I must have laughed, because he then said that the man hadn't always been a friend of his. I thought that kind of him, because those of us who detest the way the last twenty or so years have gone are not always so tolerant. We drown our opposites with self-righteousness instantly, and leave no room for discussion. He said that he visits three prisoners who have few visitors; he said he was an anarchist. I said that I thought that anarchists would be opposed to nationalism, and there ensued a lively spar, at the end of which, I had to say, that there was more Christianity in the anarchist than in the Christian. He took me up on that as well, pointing out that Christians have a mistaken belief that they are the only people with good hearts. My train came and that was that. The level of aggravation and interest that he had arisen in me helped me through the day, the old streets, the grave-yard.

The following week, when I was walking home from work, I went into an old glass shop, much more my sort of place, I'd thought, as I had walked past it every morning. But I decided it was a bit rich of me to be thinking of better choices of workplace at my age. And there he was working behind the counter. 'So we do have something in common,' I said. I asked him around for tea last night and they all came. What a lively bunch. One anar-chist, one socialist, one feminist, or crossovers of all three, all engaged in subterranean banter and seriousness. They told stories enthusiastically, as one will at that age, if you haven't been con-vinced to tread carefully. They talked of friends of theirs who had done shocking and outrageous things, but somehow their descrip-tions made them seem all right to me. I don't know why. Perhaps I admired their dedication to causes, even wrong ones. Perhaps I really did see astonishing selflessness for the first time in my life. Oh, I'd read about it, but one doesn't even think that three young, badly dressed tenants on your street could be so unegotis-tical. Because I do know it to be true that those who start to affect change never get thanked. Change is always wrongly believed to have come one day with the sunrise. The long and the short of the evening was that I agreed to write to this man, this prisoner, who apparently has few friends. I only just managed not to say 'I'm sure'. The man's name is Senan Lillis and he didn't actually kill anyone in the 'war', as they insisted on calling it; he only robbed a bank, or had something to do with a bank robbery. This morning, having had my night's sleep away from such idealism, I wanted not to write to this Senan, but I feel that I've committed myself in some way – not to him, but to those young tenants of yours. I suppose a letter can't do any harm. And maybe, since I've always believed that chance is a serious part of life, it is the best thing. So for now I leave and will write to you again soon.

> Regards,
> Bernard

PS. And thanks again for the recipe.

Dear Helena,

Thank you for your most interesting letter from Rome. Yes, I do remember Mona what's her name, vaguely. And I'm glad Connie got to Italy and all that, but really I'm writing because of Bernard. I had a most peculiar letter from him about starting to write to some fellow in Portlaoise prison. Really, I hope he's all right. I hope no one is trying to take advantage of him. Could you check and see what you think? Just when he'd got a job too; what an odd thing to happen. Write me and let me know. I really will reply to your fascinating letter.

> Fergal

To Fergal from Helena
Dublin

Dear Fergal,

Sorry for not replying sooner to your postcard but I had a visitor. My head has been cleared and rinsed out by the departure of Sinéad. I really couldn't believe how difficult it would be to have someone like her in my hair. For a small person, boy, could she seep out of the pores of every corner in the house, spreading tension as fast as incense. She had an otherworldliness, being a serious macrobiotic cook, that should have been OK with me, because I can be fascinated by those preoccupations, and am often envious of the peace that care of the physical body can bring. But her relaxation was a desperate one. It spread out from her like damp. I, as you know, had always been close to her and shunned the idea that others had of her, the idea that there was no depth in her, only a shallow, complete self-absorption. The only aggravation I had ever had was the way she checked her appearance continuously, looking at her blouse, settling her hair, glancing in mirrors. Now I'm afraid I join the others and, alas, surpass their distaste of her, probably because I had been so loyal for so long.

I realise that Sinéad fed off my interest in her. I now see that she has an oppressive air of always having the right answer, and I was a great sucker for all she said about recipes to sort the inner soul. She is wired up to a state of possessiveness of her position, even in the simplest of conversations. I used to think that it was a jealousy of people, of acquaintances, an inability to mix with more than one person at a time, and in a sense that is what is wrong with her, but only because she fears that any extra person might be the one to usurp her position. In group situations she hated people speaking to me, and yet it wasn't as if she wanted to talk to me then; it was simply that she wanted me fully as her personal blotting paper. Once, during her month-long stay, she went away for a weekend and I breathed so freely on waking up that Saturday, that I knew I could only bear a little more. I opened the fridge door, forgetting that I hadn't bought sausages and bacon for weeks, and I noticed the invasion of all these tinfoil-covered dishes. I had loved them in the first week, seeing them as beacons in a well-organised life; now they represented an aggressive take-over of me. They smelled obnoxious. In short, she almost ruined me and nearly destroyed my social life. My dear husband isn't in such good humour either but we'll get over all this; we're good at collectively forgetting nasty things. But I don't think I'm good at losing friends. Now to the question in your letter.

Bernard seems OK to me, I wouldn't worry too much about him writing to Portlaoise. As you know I'm apolitical myself when it comes to these matters. Kevin says that apoliticism is another word for conservatism. He says that that is not an insult, just a fact. But here's something rather weird; Connie is writing to this fellow too! Now there's one for the books. When he writes back, will Desmond open the letters? Can't see him being too happy about that.

Anyway, as I say, don't worry. I'd like to lie in bed for three days to recover my equilibrium after Sinéad, but I think I'm on Rome again tomorrow. Hear from you soon.

Helena

Just a short note, Connie. I must say I find this new-found interest in prisoners' conditions a little irritating. I would never have seen either you or Bernard as Amnesty types. Forgive me – my annoyance probably comes from feeling so left out. Of course I'm interested in history, always have been. With regards to the northern question, I have kept myself informed of every new twist in our tale. In discussions I have always prevaricated wisely because I don't want to take sides; it is too difficult a matter. I am therefore terribly surprised that you and Bernard, whom I wasn't aware of being in any way interested, should take sides so quickly. I've tried to put this as kindly as possible, but really, I am concerned.

Fergal

Dear Fergal,

I was surprised to get your card this morning. Firstly, I felt it petty of you not to refer to my Italian holiday, and my letter describing it. Secondly, you sounded as if it's all right for you to take political decisions, or wrong decisions, because you've read your quota of history books, but not me. Isn't that a little patronising? And any-way, a letter is hardly taking sides. Also, Fergal, how can you pre-sume to know what my opinions are or have been? I have not always lived in the same street or, indeed, the same city or country as you. I hope this does not sound too harsh.

Connie

Dear Helena,

Now it appears I've put my foot in it with Connie. It's always been the same; the bloody North breaks up friendships all over the place. Connie says she's not taking sides, but really! Writing to a Provo is hardly sitting on the fence. Quite frankly I feel like throwing those tenants out, but I'm afraid of upsetting Bernard and Connie. Also, it's quite a difficult thing to do by letter. What do you think, Helena? Not just about the tenants but about Connie and Bernard? Don't tell me that you think that it's all going to be OK.

Fergal

5

Bernard Cunningham's wife had died and a month later he heard a rumour that the new management were going to 'synthesise' Waterford Glass, his Waterford Glass. A man, filthy with richness, had done a survey and, apparently, wealthy buyers did not know that Waterford was Waterford, Ireland. So some of the glass could be made less expensively in other places where labour was cheap and you could work men down to their bones. Which was the worst thing, he wondered, the disaster that had happened first or the one thing that he had left being also taken away. During his life with Moira, glass and Desmond, their child, had been their days. World news, yes, elections, flu, seasons, weddings, relations (in small doses), all those, yes, but mostly glass and Desmond. Not just any glass, Waterford cut crystal. He was a known expert; he knew the journey of each piece and felt himself to be in the presence of something more than inanimate objects. When finished cutting he would put his hand around the piece; he handled glass the way many a person dreams of handling another's body.

He then went home (never via the pub), closed the door behind him, and in his house he lived the next good part of his life. Moira and he had loved, married and loved. They had one child, Desmond, who was bright, a little reserved maybe, because of being an only child, but doing fine, and achieving at school. Why they had no more children was not talked about; it certainly was not for lack of loving. Bernard and Moira would never have known that Desmond felt cold, outside their love, that he was afraid of their sufficiency, that he grew up hating any love that shut him away. He determined to make his life in some institution, some work that didn't finish at five, some lifetime pursuit that would, because of its own validity, leave only small room for the personal burying in someone else's life that most people crave as a religious form.

Moira died too young. Bernard had not known that forever with her was going to be so short; he knew that the forever without her would be longer. People came with sympathy and remedies for his life; he knew that there would be none. Silence was his sentence, a half-life. People said, 'Ah, Bernard, she was a wonderful woman', 'God knows, she was always in the same good humour.' People didn't know what they were talking about. Desmond's neighbours came. They gathered together outside the church, not sure what to say or do and wishing they could get to the nearest pub soon (that one a few miles back looked OK). Would you look at that umbrella in front of us? An ad for Wormdrench, not the sort of brolly to take to a funeral.

So Desmond's neighbours were there; what had that to do with him and Moira? Nothing. It was for Desmond they had come, to pay acceptance to the fact that he was from Waterford, not Dublin, that he had not always been married with three children, that he had been a child. What did it matter who was there?

Desmond himself was touched by the neighbours' presence, but then figured that Waterford was not really that far for them to come. Bernard ruminated on all sorts of stupid things in order to make himself believe, just for flashes of moments, that this was not happening. What did it matter who came to the funeral? The funeral was now over, Moira committed to the earth remarkably fast.

In the months that followed, Bernard thought all his waking hours not just of Moira's life, but of life itself. As he had seen it leave Moira, it seemed such an inconsequential thing. And what happened in life, the tragedies, the luck, were such random things.

Some people were born with tragic faces so that they would look right when life got around to hurling its store at them. Bernard nearly drove himself mad. He wondered if it wouldn't be easier if he'd loved Moira less. But whatever way people love is how much they love, so he supposed there was no more and no less in any of it.

When Bernard had come back to Waterford to a job he'd always wanted since he'd watched the men coming home from work, he'd thought that that would be all his luck. But six weeks later he met Moira. They loved as musicians will, who smile at each other even when they don't know the whole tune, but recognise a familiar part. Things rarely happen as a result of intention. Most often events fall over us, usually like snowflakes rather than hailstones, softly, insistently. And then a life and lives are made from that event. Bernard knew his politics and his work but he had never known that a person could have those same certainties about themselves. Moira had. She had invented herself. She didn't look at other people to see who to be. Some people want to know others only so they know how to behave in front of them. Then those people whom they admire put a strain on them because they have to be pleased. Not Moira. Her life thus far had been spent rearing herself, a completely self-alienated timespan that was not a selfish thing – it was simply her reality. When she met Bernard she included him in it and he couldn't get over the attention. They married quickly, being certain and being right.

They set up a life that had little need for anything but themselves, seeing the interference of others' lives as a just bearable, hopefully short, intrusion. Neither of them became mere functions for the other; unusually, both, not just one of them, stayed in love. If a person becomes surrounded by people who can't dance they soon forget the rhythm. Bernard and Moira set themselves to exclude distractions from their waltz. Perhaps poor Desmond was one of those distractions? They would never have meant to harm him. And now Moira was gone. This question of being. I am, therefore I am. And she was. Has this God been waiting all along? Some people's lives are so bad they want to keep living until history changes around to their turn, he and Moira wanted to keep living because they had such plenty. God had become so grudging, so much like the rest of them, he held little interest for Bernard now. If forever had only not been so short, if only there were time to make even the tiniest of shadows into nothing. Bernard nearly could not bear it.

Desmond, a good son to whom he couldn't talk, asked him to come to live in Dublin beside them. He liked his daughter-in-law, Connie, and he thought he remembered that he liked their neighbours. He could talk to his tiny grandchildren. And now this rumour that Waterford glass need not be made in Waterford. Buyers are not concerned about the place of origin, only the product and design, they had been told. We will offer voluntary redundancies. Bernhard saw little else for it, leave and forget, or try.

He knew somehow that he should wait a little longer, should stay put, and should shed some years in the exact spot that they had accumulated. He knew that it would be better for him in the end, but that presumed a desire to postpone his end and in that eighth week it seemed a pointless wish. He tampered a little with exteriors and with new paint, he switched the table and chairs; he blindly gave away most of her clothes and jewellery; he wept almost uncontrollably, his eyes and face and nose were raw. His need of her voice and touch and lips was extreme. Connie came and locked the house and brought him with her. He didn't even say goodbye to the neighbours.

He found his new house to be satisfactory in all ways except one, and that one would never be. So in a controlled fashion he set about constructing his days. He had been reared in a way that had had a political edge to it, and he returned somewhat to that, cloaking himself in a stream of things rather than in his own heart. It helped, and anything that helped was worth a try. He moved and moved his furniture again until he was satisfied. He cleaned and moved his glass collection. He reluctantly started a garden; dabbling in growth seemed to be particularly cruel. And when the first spring came he resented the coming to life of the shoots, he resented people's cheerfulness. And yet the effort began to pay in an easing of the pain. He would always need Moira but he could also try to need other friends and people.

And so he established a tentative relationship with Desmond and

Connie's neighbour Fergal, and also with Kevin and I. It was tentative because he did not wish to intrude too much. Although he certainly didn't seem to be intruding on Desmond. There really seemed to be nothing that either of them could say which might bridge the gap between them. The uneasy failure of it sent both of them into respective independency of each other, and that was no bad thing, they told themselves, not each other. Once a month they went for a drink but after the third time Desmond always brought a work companion or some other acquaintance with him. And Bernard felt it easier too.

A new life opened for Bernard, a kind of second bachelorhood. Mistakes are made in that state because it cannot be learned overnight. Those who have always lived on their own have particular knowledge not easily come by. Bernard was sometimes too familiar; then when he would realise his mistake he would not be forthcoming enough. But with all his errors he finally found a level, particularly with Connie and with Fergal.

He missed Fergal and meant to write more often. The job was a godsend, although the glass was all flat. And now a new, wonderful thought was slowly insinuating itself past his doubts. He would make glass, crystal, ornaments, drinking cups, himself. He would turn his garage into a factory. He would learn to colour glass. For God's sake, he would go to Venice, maybe. It was while these thoughts were germinating that he decided he had better visit Waterford, old friends, and a grave. Nothing as yet had let him place Moira in that grave and a visit might be a necessary move back into reality.

It would be best not to tell Connie that he was going to Waterford because she would fret, or she would come with him and make him remember by remarking on things. This way he could cope, dealing only with the moments that could be borne, closing down the rest. Memory is a very brutal thing.

It was indeed a great distraction meeting the young fellow from Fergal's house. It was indeed good to meet him again. It was undoubtedly a good idea to invite him for tea and it was nice that they all came. They brought with them differences as large as making glass. They told stories well, they had an innocence. They did not slip in political points that can give a person uneasy guilt feelings; they were too unshy about their beliefs for that. He liked them. How unlike Desmond the two young men were. And when they asked him if he would write to their friend, well, he wasn't really their friend, it seemed a harmless thing to do. 'You'd have time, Mr Cunningham,' Stephen said. 'And it would mean a lot to Senan.' Bernard had a particular view about the North – the Provos were wrong. And that was that. Very occasionally he allowed himself to try to understand why they were there, how they had come about, and the effort annoyed him tremendously. So Senan was wrong. But even God, not always to be relied upon for consideration and mercy, had advised the visiting of prisoners. And maybe he could influence this man? And maybe he would learn something himself from mixing with the enemy? And it certainly made a change.

In the meantime, there was the matter of the garage and glass. Bernard went shopping. The garage had not been used for years and was reluctant to exchange its musty smell for anything cleaner. Bernard had to try a few times before he could make himself destroy the damp, rotting shelves; he feared the past that he might be enraging, he heard the murmur of ghosts. The work attracted neighbours to the door, to peer, to check, to be glad for change. And they brought stories which pulled Bernard in closer. They were careful with questions because they knew that he was Des's recently widowed father. A man might be very sensitive at a time like that. He felt their care and it built up scabs on his raw flesh. The garage took on the look of a well-designed room in which to be busy. The smell of varnish and new paint wafted out to the street, so other people began to paint their windows and doors. By that time Bernard had stocked up on tools. He'd got a blower, he found the endless other requirements. Connie helped him, pottering for odds and ends with the baby tied to her front. Funny how they did that these days, nice for the baby, I suppose, but you'd think after the pregnancy that the mother would have had enough of her balance being ruined. And then he concentrated. As he worked he felt someone in the room with him, distracting and helping in turn. The colours didn't suit, he added and watched.

He fused, he drew deep breaths, he stared, he mixed. He let the cold water flow over his hands until it hurt, but he didn't notice. Here and this would do.

6

Dear Senan,

Your friend may have, will have, mentioned to you that I was
going to drop a line, as he said that you don't have much
correspondence. I should say at the outset that I'm not used to writing to people I don't know. And certainly not to prisoners. But then
there's no harm in trying something new. I didn't mean the remark
about prisoners to be derogatory; it looks so when I read it back, but
really, this is so new to me, I will have to keep tearing it up and
starting again if I correct everything that might be sensitive. I think
perhaps it will be easier when you write to me and tell me what
your interests are and what you read. I read quite a lot myself, more
so since my wife died. At least this last few months. When she died I
couldn't be bothered reading, facts seemed so alien, and fiction so
pointless. I preferred the radio, then, voices had a little context.
But now I'm back reading, so perhaps we can share books. I don't
know what the situation would be about me sending you books.

I'm just beginning to make my own glass, after spending most of
my working life in Waterford. It's a gesture, like swimming ten
yards from the shipwreck instead of gulping water, even though
twelve yards in the pool has always been your personal best.

I've recently moved to Dublin and find it surprisingly OK. I miss walks around the lake that used to be near us in Waterford – it is still in the same place, of course; it is only me who has moved. But I walk now up Palmerston Road, round the park and then take my choice of paths home. I don't know if you are familiar with Dublin. Making glass came as a surprise thought to me; it is astonishing how little we know of our own potential, and it has never struck me in all the years I worked that I should try this. Do you have useful ways of spending your days?

Often when I walk in the park there are cancer patients from St Luke's walking around too, sometimes with a relative. I can always tell that's who they are: a particular atmosphere clings to them, a particular way of gulping air, as if it could be stored up. Then I am glad that Moira died so fast and so unknowingly, and then I think of how I've reduced them to patients, stolen their lives away from them. Treated them as if everything they had learned and loved, the music, the joy, had disappeared because of ill-health. Other walks are much more cheerful.

I hope you are well, and look forward to hearing from you soon. Let me know if you have requests for particular books and I might be able to help.

Yours sincerely,
Bernard Cunningham

the year 2000. 'So what?' you may say; it's only time. But
millenniums surely mean something. I dread it, actually. I
ographical picture of the turn of the last century, a picture
by the historical shifts about to take place. I have an uncle
born on Easter Sunday 1916, and another on my father's
was born the day after the executions ended, and an aunt
born on the day that the War of Independence started –
the only reason that I know that Dan Breen fired the first
Soloheadbeg. And another the day after the Treaty was
Those first decades of this century seem to have been busy,
killing. Maybe it is always so, but we expect things to be
at the beginning of a century, cleaner, somehow, and so
ce in a clearer way the goings-on. I dread it, because every-
know exactly where they were. I prefer uncertainties about
ings; uncertainty is less limiting. Will the papers review the
usand years, the 'highlights'? Don't laugh, I bet they will.
't think that I'm a very political person. I went to one of the
strike demonstrations, but didn't everyone? I was there the
he riot and I was so shocked at what I saw, I kept my mouth
errific, wasn't I? I remember when they started to die, people
ask completely uninvolved people, 'Are you going up to the
?' It was as familiar as 'Are you going to the Féile?' I did go to
blic meeting; actually, I didn't go, I just stopped at the plat-
s I was passing. But I did not think like the speakers and went
quickly. I fear, sometimes, that philosophy itself has been
because it was captured by one sex. And politics, all politics,
umed to have a predestined route. No one on that platform
ed that sometimes things just happen. What is this division
en men and women? Is the downward, inward path that
less powerful? Who is not telling us what? If a person hides
imp, someone else has to limp for them. So you can see that
ng was not really the place for me. I did go to one other kind
eting, a tenants' association thing, but I spent the time longing
atch between my shoulder blades. I didn't go a second time.
lespite this lamentable distance from the political processes, I
ve that there should be philosophy departments attached to
nity hospitals. I think women philosophise in a different

Dear Bernard,

Thank you ever so much for your letter and I look forward to our
correspondence. I can imagine exactly how you feel about starting
to write to a prisoner – me to be precise. We often distance our
terms here in an effort to remove ourselves from ourselves.

I should begin by saying that our letters will be read and that
occasionally parts of them will be censored; this has got to do with
the fact that there are limits put on our communication. It is all right
for me to explain it to you once. We are not supposed to discuss
political activities as such, although I slip here often because I now
think that everything is political, so when I slide over into the pro-
scribed, I do so without noticing. We can discuss broad general
issues, and things related to our welfare, health, well-being etc.
Personally, I think it best to forget about the rules, write freely and
then let them censor whatever they want. Gives them something to
do. You will notice that there is a given crossness between them and
us. I fear, also, that ignoring the rules may have been a general prin-
ciple with me some years ago, but I've learned a lot in here.

Yes, I would be delighted if you could loan me the odd book;
your choice would be wonderful. I like the idea of someone else's
suggestions because it is sometimes difficult to get new ideas or
move forward here. It's fine if one of us has a good visitor. There
was a man here from Waterford for a year and he had a great visitor,
a book reviewer. I don't think he ever let her talk about anything
else, judging by the workshops he would give us after every visit.
(She was an enthusiastic visitor, genuine. Sometimes, you may find
this hard to believe, we get prisoner groupies here, and those visits
can be pretty sick experiences, as you can imagine.) I should tell you
not to send hardbacks, as the covers will be taken off them. For
obvious reasons, you might say, but nevertheless it galls me. I can
send them back out via Stephen. I hope you won't mind some
delay, because books get passed around a lot in here, but I promise
you they will eventually be returned.

I'm studying at the moment, doing an Open University course on history and appreciation of art. In a sense I am getting much more out of it in here than I would outside, because I have to visualise what's written about, paint it myself practically. So any catalogues you can find would be useful. I was never interested in art before I came here. I found little validity in trying to understand something we don't understand, well, I don't understand, so the first course I tried depressed me thoroughly. I could see myself and my arrogances and, therefore, my mistakes too clearly. Doing my time is bad enough, I don't need my nose rubbed in it. But now I thoroughly enjoy my course. Do artists ever know the escape routes they give us?

How interesting, making your own glass. I'm useless with my hands. In my first week, which seems like years ago, which is years ago, I made a bodhrán for my sister-in-law. She told me that it sounded like a Lambeg in her eardrum, but that I had plenty of time to perfect the art. She was the only one I could ever joke with about my life and times, or what it would be better to call my predicament. But, unfortunately, she went to live in Australia when I had been here a while. In some ways I think the fact of me and my actions drove my brother and her, no, not her, my brother, away. There he didn't have to explain. I also once tried a few days in the leather workshop, equally unsuccessfully. I think I saw it more as the family man's place, fathers making presents for children out of wood and husbands making purses for their wives. You speak of your wife with love; it's hard for me to know what to say to you but I feel I should say something. In here we learn two opposites, that everything must be said openly, and yet that everything can be unsaid and is no less real for that. So if you talk of her I will try to imagine what she was like. So few people talk of their loved ones; is it fear, I wonder, or are they not loved ones at all. My relationships with women have been varied, and now that I am so wise, I suppose it will be too late for me when I get out. I didn't live in Dublin for long. It was a rather unsettled time for me. The only consolation was pints at night. Fear and indecision were ever present for me. But my good friend, who ended up in here too, loved the place and never

stopped talking about it. He's out now not get visits from previous inmates.

Time for dinner. I look forward to h

Regards,
Senan Lillis

Dear Senan,

Well, here goes; I'll try. Your friend Step pen-pal; I don't know. He's not actually tenant in my friend's house, but of course this.

I have three children and spend my day in which to think; that is when I have ti have time to think. I suspect our lives are also sure that there are startling similarities. think they might be; I don't know what th ers are. But children do get older and easi voice that comes from having too many my husband hates it; it's the insistent voice children get. I suppose I'll be able to grow have to hide a lot of things; last week o threw all the children's toys into the garde in the morning, a little early in the day to be and heard the performance I called in to her She begged me not to tell anyone – telling know she didn't mean anything serious by anyone. I like my children, I like their pers looks, there's a thing or two that I'd chang them. That's a real bonus – not everyone like

And so I write to you from the kitchen. same time, in the last decades of the one thousa

be alive
turns of
have a g
disturbe
who w
side wh
who w
that wa
shot at
signed.
a lot o
differe
we not
one w
these t
last th
I do
hunge
day o
shut –
would
funer
one p
form
away
tainte
is pre
belie
betw
much
their
mee
of m
to so
But
belie
mat

way, but there's no training for it; it's too crooked, too jumpy.

I will conclude this letter because really I may have been writing a lot of rubbish that does not interest you at all. It's like setting up a game; the first player can only do so much until finding out what the other is up to.

Writing this has been easier than I thought – a little like writing to my friend Fergal, although he would be shocked at that. He strongly disapproves of me writing to you.

Hope this is all right,
Connie Cunningham

To Connie from Senan

Dear Connie,

Thank you for your much appreciated letter. When Stephen told me that both you and Bernard (your father-in-law, I believe) might write, I was pleased, as you can imagine. It's like meeting new people. But he didn't tell me that you were going to be so lively, and maybe even a little provocative. But, of course, none of us really knows the other (well, I expect that you know your father-in-law). Stephen has been visiting me for over two years, but you never really know visitors whom you hadn't met before. The conditions naturally exert a certain strain. I'm very fond of him and he has been a loyal visitor. That can mean a lot.

You make your neighbourhood and your children sound most interesting – your neighbour throws the head and you cover up, your children are good-looking. What more could I need to know? Yes, I think I may understand similarities between our positions, certain lacks in our freedom of movements and the need for self-dependence. After that we probably diverge. Your ruminations on the eclipsing of one century by another remind me only that I will be out by then. By the way, we never say that time is 'only' anything in here!

I should explain that there are rules about what we can write to each other, but your letter did get through unscathed. I think you are very political by thinking that you are not. What ages are your children? I expect you don't get much time to read. I remember my nieces and nephews, before they went away. They took up a tremendous amount of space and sound. My sister-in-law brought them in here a few times, although I was never sure if that was a good idea. I can understand why fathers should see their children, or rather, why children should be able to see their fathers, but I'm not sure if jail is a good subconscious thought and perhaps it should be avoided if possible. One of my nephews always picked a flower and stuck it in the wire grid between us, but because of the space between that grid and the next one I could never reach it. Those visits were, in a way, some of my very worst moments. My sister-in-law sends me photographs of them now, and those pictures mark my time more clearly than lines on my own face or the grey hairs that appear overnight. I think that the wives and children of the men in here have an even harder life than us. We get used to it; our lives are regulated and we have constant company.

I see by your address that you live very near Bernard. Would it be impertinent of me to ask you for a photograph? I look forward to your next letter and thank you again for taking the time to write.

> Yours sincerely,
> Senan Lillis

CENSORED
POSTCARD
To Stephen from Senan

Dear Stephen,

I meant to write sooner to thank you for your visit and for the letters from your friends. The old man has a matter of factness about him, about his life, that is refreshing. Connie dropped me a few pictures yesterday and they did not surprise me. What's her husband's name? I got the books you left in. How was your weekend in the west? Would there be any possibility that you could get me any book that could give me an idea of the Irish artists of the sixties. A catalogue, maybe, from some gallery, if there is such a thing, no rush. Looking forward to seeing you again.

Senan

To Senan from Stephen

Dear Senan,

Well, this book is the best I could do. I may see something else when I get a chance to look around. Pity the lovely hardback will have to go. We thought Gina was pregnant last week, so we hung about a lot, doing nothing, waiting. We hoped she wasn't, but pretended that we hoped she was, just in case. She wasn't! Much relief, particularly for Gina. I am glad Bernard and Connie wrote. They make an interesting pair; I think she gets on better with him than with her husband, and he better with her than with his son. (Desmond is her husband's name.) Then there's Helena, an air-hostess who flits in and out, and of course I hear of Fergal all the time, our absent landlord, who seems like an OK sort.

Last night we all got depressed. I think we had too much cheap wine, and this new health kick of Gina and Liam's makes us too unfit for the like of that. We went round and round in one of those circular political morasses and couldn't get out. Gina came to the conclusion that we were missing out on many of the good and innocent things in life because we're always thinking causes rather than us. By bedtime we had become a house of 'ex's' (not that one can become an ex-anarchist, no more than one can ever shed Catholicism). I think she's right. I notice that all my age group are distancing themselves from campaigns and getting jobs in newspapers and in RTÉ. But they'll be sorry. I can hear you saying, 'No, they won't.' I can hear myself saying it too.

Stephen

To Fergal from Connie

Dear Fergal,

It's a long time since we communicated, and frankly I would be upset if I thought that we couldn't work this out. I want to write you an ordinary letter, but I feel that I must first address your fears, or whatever they are, and although I'm trying not to re-express my horror at your reaction, I would be dishonest if I didn't say that it still rankles. If I were to discuss this sort of thing with Desmond I would expect certain reactions and so I did not bring it up. But of course Bernard told him on their monthly drinks together – livened up the proceedings, no doubt. But I don't expect those reactions from you; you are after all a travelled and a free person who, surely, should have an open mind.

It actually astonishes me how closed you are being, and I remember how an acquaintance of mine in London used to complain about the selfish, unhelpful attitudes of people from the twenty-six counties, the Free State, or whatever he called it. I never passed much remarks on him, but now I can hear his voice clearly. Are you suggesting that I believe in violence? Because if you are, you couldn't be further from the truth. (I, after all, have had children.) But there is one thing about me, and maybe this difference has been accentuated over the last few years unnoticed by both of us – I'm a realist. By that I mean I'm stuck in reality, firmly stuck in reality, and I believe that what is happening in the North is happening not for no reason. That's as much sympathy as I have – it's not happening for no reason.

Of course I think about the brutalising of everyone, the wrongness of it, the narrowness, but I also know that these notions have been given to me, and I believe that my view is simplistic and ill-informed. This I know because I know, and don't snort that instinct can be dangerous. I am also not unaware of history, as your tone suggested, and have indeed, surprisingly, read at least three newspapers a week, even after having children. OK, I am not bereft without a news fix within five minutes of waking – I have other things to think of – but I do keep pretty up to date with what's what. I also watch news and views programmes. I find myself being defensive again. But you see, I don't have to justify myself to myself; I'm simply writing to a man in prison. Yes, it's a leap to take. Good Lord, I have to do *some* jumping. Of course I wouldn't approve of what he's done, but I presume I wouldn't actually approve of anything any prisoner has done – the fact that I might be able to stretch my imagination to understand why he has done it does not make me a supporter. Maybe law and order seems more distant to me, perhaps even suspect, and maybe that shocks you, but there you are – I am not a carbon copy of something you think. I like your tenants too. I really do envy the courage to choose that sort of freedom. I suppose they won't always have it, but they will always have something from it, even if it is merely a contradictory streak. I know, I had a year living with people like them. In London. Irish people. Whacky, serious, very, very political (every-thing was political), down to the shoes you wore, and the lies you told – but they were great fun. A knowledgeable house because everyone threw their bits in, so it was easy to become informed. I suspect that is what your house is now – your walls will be more mature when you come back; if you come back, of course.

So now, excuses made, I should just add that my correspondence with this prisoner (Senan is his name) is not going to become a central part of my life. Writing to him is peculiar, really, because once I got over the initial thought of it, I can write as if he were simply a stranger whom I was slowly getting to know. Getting let-ters back is always such a shock because of the censored mark on the top and because sometimes lines are crossed out. We write of ordin-ary things, although I sometimes am embarrassed by how attractive my ordinary things might seem. Who would ever have thought that my life could appear glamorous and free and deeply varied?

He has an interest in art because of some course he's doing, so maybe you'd pick up a book or two when you have time – you would obviously be more in the line of browsing than I am. But don't if you can't imagine that they're just for me, if you feel compromised by it. God, I do feel estranged from you, I feel as if I'm cajoling a teenager to be on my side.

Other matters. The children are all fine and life proceeds as normal. I've recovered from Italy but do feel a little still that it was a more important visit than it might have been for someone else, or would have been for me some years ago. I felt like a reluctant virgin as I walked around galleries – I stress reluctant, because virginity is not a bad thing unless the virgin wants rid of it. And I certainly had an unsettling desire to know more than I do. I remember once asking someone how a person could start listening to classical music, as if that world of listening was disbarred to me and I needed an atlas. The man I asked – London again – seemed to be taken aback, but then gave me a list of records. I'm afraid I haven't progressed from there and still listen to only those three.

The child will start pre-school next month and then that's me off from another starting block. Maybe I'll be able to come home and have an hour's stolen sleep. I'm so tired these days, always longing for my bed. Desmond is well, rushing around as usual and being late home. At last you would have something in common with him; he flinches when I get a letter from Senan. I think he's afraid that the postman will know. I wonder if the prisoner was a woman would it be easier for him. There, I'm searching for a compliment, because I doubt if he sees me any more as a 'viable' sexual being. Next weekend I and the children visit my parents – Desmond's not coming. I think he hates it, and I don't blame him because it takes me some time to settle in too, and it's easier for me because after all one does have loyalties that are forever. That's what loyalty means.

Love, and hope to hear from you very soon,
Connie

Dear Helena,

I have just got a letter from Connie. I'm amazed at how blasé she is about corresponding with a Provo. She even tried to implicate me by asking me to get books for him. I will in my arse browse around New York looking for books for a Provo. She was complaining that his letters were censored. Has she gone off her head altogether? What does she expect? Of course they're censored – the authorities need to know what these people are thinking. She writes as if it were normal behaviour to be communicating with paramilitaries. I don't know, I wish I was there. Of course, if I hadn't left this would never have happened. Enough of that. When are you coming back on the New York route?

Life is good, work is going well. I love the sounds and smells here more every week. I still notice them, though not continuously now. Dating, as quaintness would have it, can be difficult. It's hard to get the signals right. Not just here, I suppose, but things do tend to be more extreme in this city than anywhere else. Men used to do all the asking, which was awful for them, always trying to work up the courage. And it couldn't have been too satisfying for the women, waiting and taking no part in their destiny. So now they ask too, sometimes, and sometimes don't. So it's awful for every-body, every way now. The men try to ask and wait to be asked. The women do the same. And boy, if you get the message wrong, are you in trouble! You stand near people attempting to act on instinct, but mild flirting for one person can be another's bedding invitation. There is this woman who has been in my, our, company a lot these past few months. She grew on me; I missed her if she wasn't there and I felt it when she talked to other people. If there were more than one car she always offered to come in mine; she sat beside me if we were having meals out; she smiled a lot at me. Well, you're right, I did. I touched her as you would touch a fence to see if it was electric. It was her, I fear, who got the shock. Apparently she found me so amazingly unattractive that she felt completely safe with me. Boy, did that run the flag down my pole! Now I can't enjoy her company at all. She says it's all right and not to let so small a thing as crossed messages come between us. Well that's OK for her. I'm the one who pored over messages that weren't ever being sent at all. I give up. I even feel guilty, and I've never been one for that. You know when Carmel, my wife, walked out the door, I knew that I should feel guilty about not feeling any remorse, but I didn't. I've always known when I should feel guilty but have never quite mastered the actuality of it for more than a few minutes. Ah well, I'll get over it. One always does; there's no such thing as permanent heartbreak. Well, I don't think there is but I've just remembered some of those poets. Maybe poets are different.

Last week I met a man who knew Abby Hoffman. Interesting, isn't it, to be in the way of meeting people who knew Abby Hoffman? On the one hand, you meet some of my co-workers, enough said, and the next minute you're standing close enough to touch all that is best and wise and caring and funny. Well, not that Abby was quite all that, but he was some of it. I just had an argument at work about US foreign policy: I said that in Ireland most people thought that – I was cut short and the man I was speaking to asked, 'What business is it of theirs what America does in Iraq?' I love it; he really does think that it's no one's business but America's. A 'what's it to you?' view of world politics. And then I met the man who knew Abby Hoffman. So there goes my life, a bit of this and that, eating away at it. I do hope you're over again soon and look forward to it very much.

Regards,
Fergal

To Fergal from Connie

Dear Fergal,

Today has been a lovely day, remarkably warm. Last night we went to a fireworks display that was put on in the Phoenix Park. It was utterly magnificent – such basic principles can give such joy. The children loved it, of course, and so did I. Some smaller kids were frightened because of the noise. The thunder of it reminded me of what it must have been like during the air wars. I imagined the great and beautiful flashes were raining down bodies instead of sparkles, but I scolded myself back from gloom; it is also important to forget. I once read of how a river had disappeared, or so the people with the map thought, until they found that it had changed course because it had become dammed up with the bodies of the slaughtered. The victims had been tied together, the person at the beginning of the line was shot, all the others were dragged down with the first falling. So they fell in straight connected lines and changed the course of the river. Charming thoughts for a fireworks display! The best part was the lighting-up in spurts; some spluttered to a quiet demise gracefully, but you could never be sure, because others exploded into massive waterfalls of colour, raising a stunned gasp from the crowd. And, of course, others looked so like majestic sperm searching for an explosion, so obvious it was a delightful shared picture among the adults. The display lasted over half an hour, terrifying the birds and bees, no doubt. An occasional lone crow would fly across the sky bewildered, and then fly back again, like a vulture disturbing a beautiful painting. And yet there was something vaguely dissatisfying, because nothing is left to the imagination in fireworks; you could not figure out if it would get much better, or if that's the best it could be. But it was this dissatisfaction that made it enjoyable, because then the whole sky would be crackling and roaring and shooting into colour saying, 'See! you unbeliever, watch me!' If you closed your eyes, you still saw with the inner eye. Not like you would a painting, that is, minutely, but rather with an overall eye. And then there would be another orchestrated rumble and you would open your eyes to the snow-flakes of light falling over you. A person never forgets who was with them at fireworks, and you feel, at least I did, a soulful sentimentality for missing people. So I hope you are well and that you will write soon. Bernard sends his regards; he's too busy to write at the moment, excited about his glass endeavours.

Love,
Connie

Dear Connie,

Brief note: we went to a play last night that had no words in it! Truly. More than forty actors just walking and half-doing things and then moving over for someone else. Handke, an Austrian fellow, I think, wrote it. It was very beautiful for a while, but was aggravatingly too long – pity. It would make you look at people on the street in a different light. Such a peculiar thing, really, all these people not looking at each other, and being busy about the same things. We then had a drink in the hotel and overheard a heated argument about the north of Ireland. I was thinking of your Senan as I listened to it because, although you know how I stay out of these things, I couldn't help bristling at some of the outlandish generalisations that were being made, and I was thinking different life, different city, different sex, who knows what any of us would do? Humiliation can turn into a terrible force. And if there's ever an end to it I can imagine who'll get to rewrite the story. And who knows what goes on any place? If we took the lids off people's houses, heaven alone knows what would be going on in our streets, never mind further afield.

I know you're concerned about Fergal, but really, you shouldn't write too often if he doesn't reply. I think you shouldn't take responsibility for his hurts; you have done nothing wrong. You should value yourself more, and not throw yourself at his feet, as the wise women used to say. If you're at their feet there is always this temptation for them to walk on you. Perhaps he's jealous? My, what a nest you've stirred up! I'll be chaotically busy for the next month, because a lot of people seem to be sick. Remember me talking about Lucy? Well, she finally had to get her veins done. Yesterday I went shopping with her for a suspender belt. She tried not getting it and hoping that the elastic stockings would stay up themselves underneath ordinary tights, but they kept slipping down, making ridges like little pillows below the tights. She was funny about the suspenders; she didn't want to get them on her own. She said that when she put the belt on it was as bad as she thought it would be. The gap between the frilly bit and the stock-ing tops was twenty years wide, the visible shape was as she had hoped it wouldn't be. She couldn't reach the first back fastener without putting her spine out. The last back one couldn't be done at all due to the vast geographical strain that was now pulling on the first three. So she'll be off for a few weeks. The same day as she had the veins done, Rita joined the Recovery from Alcohol course – Drink School, she calls it. Next door the junkies are trying too, they call it High School. So she'll also be off for a few weeks. I don't yet know what my shifts will be.

> Love,
> Helena

To Senan from Connie

Dear Senan,

I came across this catalogue of Lucien Freud's work and I thought I'd send it to you. I remember I got it on my honeymoon, so perhaps you'd keep it for me. I fell in love with his paintings, the subtlety of his own presence in so many of them, discarded rags, a chair, discarded paint, all that. Of course I wouldn't have noticed that if Desmond hadn't pointed it out to me, but once he did I could see him everywhere. I remember some of the ones that are not men-tioned in this catalogue, one of his mother after she had died. When you stood far away from it you could imagine that the skin was silk. And the one that's there of the sleeping couple; I love the way her tiny leg is thrown over his, dropped like a light bone on the bulk of his leg. Hope you like it, anyway, and do keep it for me. No rush in sending it back, I'll wait until you're out.

I found the catalogue among a stack of old magazines. I was thinking of all those articles read. At the time you think they are interesting and important, but you've forgotten them within two days, completely. Like, does it really matter what kind of childhood your man who starred in what's-the-film had? Of course it does, while you're reading it, because it makes you feel good about how your own children have such a better life (they only tell you if the childhood has been awful). But ten minutes later you've probably forgotten the star's name. And which film was it?

Children's lives can be made too important as well. Mothers cannot guard against all evil. Children have to have normal worries; how awful it is to put their fingers into their mouths after they've had them in their ears; would the mother ever speed up in this car; I'm getting bored; how far is it to home now? We can forget too easily that we have to live as well. I notice how similar we are when the leaves fall or there's a snowstorm. We walk the children to school in the snow, children ourselves again. We stamp our feet loudly at the hall doors, pleased with the certainty of cold weather. No, mothers aren't very different from their children sometimes. When my children went into Junior Infants (Junior Infants; I ask you, what was wrong with Low Babies?) all I could think of was that I remembered clearly my own first day in Low Babies. After I dropped them off one day that first week I went to get the chequebook to do the shopping, but couldn't find it anywhere. I spent hours searching and searching and finally cancelled the card. The next day some other mother rang me to say that my chequebook was in her daughter's room. Apparently one of mine was having a conversation with this girl, and felt sorry for her because she had no chequebook, so brought her mine to school. Lovely gesture, but it doesn't mean that I didn't get mad. But antidotes always come up.

That's all for now. Just thought I'd send this catalogue and also my good wishes.

Regards,
Connie

Dear Connie,

So, enclosed all the instructions for applying for a visit. I very much hope you can manage it, although I know how much of a drag it can be. I've asked one of the screws to photocopy the catalogue for me, that way I'll post it back tomorrow. I'd hate to have a honeymoon memento hanging around here; one never knows what could happen it. Spontaneous combustion can sometimes occur. I'm also writing to Bernard; he too says that he'd like a visit, so perhaps the two of you will come together. I keep looking at the couple – they look so comfortable, even on my wall! It must be great to be able to see and feel as clearly as painters, good painters, do. Then again, sometimes it must be unbearable.

> Regards,
> Senan

Dear Senan,

I really am terribly sorry that I didn't make the visit. I had everything organised; I went to the guards and got my photograph and form signed. I had my pass and went as far as the gates. I think, perhaps, it was Stephen talking on the way down; I got too nervous. I hope we will continue to write to each other.

> Connie

To Connie from Senan

Dear Connie,

Thank you for your note. I was very disappointed that you didn't turn up and, I must admit, not just a little angry because someone else might have come to see me. Visits are not very easily organised, you know. I don't think you've been honest with yourself; I think you just couldn't make the leap to being a person who had visited a jail – not an unusual problem, I must admit. I think you see me as a prisoner, not as a person, and indeed that is what I am for the moment. Of course, after I get out I'll be an ex-prisoner, to some people, but to myself, both now and in the future, I am and always will be

Senan Lillis

PS. There is another thing that will surprise you – this war will not go on forever. And when it stops, I, and the like of me, will have to be forgiven. And I will have to forgive those who took the lives of my friends, and those who took all those years away from me, and those who still will not forgive me. And the thing that annoys me is that the rewriters will be crawling all over the place within a week of the treaty, and we will have to let them waffle to their hearts' content, piling lie upon lie. Oh, the joys of having made martyrs of ourselves!

To Senan from Connie

Dear Senan,

Yes, I'm sorry. Let me try to explain. You are right when you say that I see you as a prisoner and not as a person, but maybe that is not something that anybody can avoid. Although I should know how annoying that can sometimes be – once a mother, etc. – you, however, will be able to leave the classification behind you. What a lousy excuse. Look – I just couldn't. I felt that it somehow would put me in a too distinct category, that of people who have visited people in jail. I couldn't do it. I intended to but I lost my nerve. So I'm making no excuses. Also, if I'm to be truthful, the idea was causing a lot of serious angst in the house with my husband and although you may think that a minor problem, lives have to be lived out here too. As for forgiveness when the time comes, I'm sure we'll manage. But you have to accept that there's a colossal gap between you and others. Of course I know that prisoners are only the ones who get caught, and that the top echelons are built on columns of law-breakers, but that doesn't change the reality of your situation. Look – I don't wish to preach. It sounds as if I'm trying to get myself out of the corner and I'm not. I am sorry that I messed up your visit – truly sorry – I'm also sorry that I've offended you because of a step I could not take, but that's the way it is. As you said yourself, regretfully guilt got a lot of people involved. I just passed up on that emotion this time. So until I hear from you again, goodbye and good luck.

Connie

To Fergal from Helena
Dublin

Dear Fergal,

Just had a wonderful two days in London with Kevin; we walked the feet off each other. We had to go to see Lucien Freud's exhibition because Connie's always talking about him. Well, not always, but she mentions him every now and again. Then we went to see Francis Bacon's portraits. The only one I liked was the self-portrait done in 1969. Maybe I also liked the self-portrait done in 1972, but like me, he was a little downcast that year, I think. Then off to the Turner shortlist: straight lines, concrete rooms, snaps, as we used to call them, and drills of rice. Rather liked the rice. And then we had the real treat – Howard Hodgkin at the d'Offay. There were colours to make you cry and titles to make you laugh. Desmond had given us the list of what to see. That night we went to see *Vita and Virginia* in the Ambassador. A wonderful, wonderful play, based on the letters from one to the other. It was terrific, because the two of them moved, inches away from each other, as if the other wasn't there. It was exquisite and intimate and gorgeously precious, as well as sad, of course. We had brandy afterwards, only way to go. Great few days.

But this, of course, is not why I'm writing. I'm writing because of Connie. Firstly, I think she really is getting depressed. I think her life has closed in around her and she looks awful. I tried to get her to go to a psychotherapist – just for a visit or two, not a serious long-term thing, just a visit or two, but I think she felt insulted. Selfishly, this terrified me because it set me thinking what I would do if our friendship was put in danger. I told her that I had gone once, which is true – three visits, two and a half actually, the first one finished very quickly. I didn't go because it was a fad or because I had more money than sense – all kippers and lace, fur coat and no knickers, so to speak. I went because I really did feel awful and was seriously ratty. I didn't like the way I was behaving. Behaving! I was a monster. To Kevin – a man, whom you know, doesn't deserve that. The whole thing, my whole behaviour, had begun to feel seriously wrong, so I did it. It wasn't much help; especially when the therapist laughed and said things like 'that's an interesting way of looking at it'. He was supposed to be giving me the new ways of looking at it! But it did help in some peculiar way. I discovered when it was that I'd begun to feel bad; a simple thing really, the woman in the keep-fit class had died beside me in the morning, keeled over, heart attack, dead in a minute. And I lost Ciarán that afternoon. I was late collecting him and he'd gone to a friend's house. But describing to the guards his clothes and eye-colour and the type of shoes he had set up some terrible echo in my brain. Well, it had been a bad day. I told Connie all of this but she wasn't convinced.

However, my feeling is that there are a few things wrong.

Desmond really does get more and more self-centred. Writing to the prisoner has shaken Connie up a lot, especially seeing he seems to have been very disappointed by her not showing up on a visit. Yes, she did apply to visit him, went through the whole works, the police, and all that, surprised me too. But mostly I think it is you not writing that is the problem. You know that you have a special friendship, and I think it would be a terrible waste to let it go. You know that yourself, and it's ridiculous to let it happen over something as trivial as writing to a prisoner. Oh, I know, you say that's not trivial but really, Fergal, it is. It takes all kinds to fill an aeroplane, so come down from your high horse. I know you will think that I'm interfering, but I care too much for both of you to let this continue – so do me a favour, don't think about it, just sit down now and write. Will be back in New York soon.

Regards,
Helena

7

Fergal Carraher was, like the rest of us, a sum total of what had and hadn't happened to him. And like people to whom a lot does and doesn't happen when they are children, he had developed an extra layer of skin. He was the door and the door-keeper of his own self. He knew that it was best if children's days were full but unremarkable. He had thought this out when he was twenty and become afraid when he remembered the terrible unpredictability of his own childhood. The awakening could have left havoc, and did for a short while, until he pulled himself together, and found ways to excuse, and ways to stop rummaging dangerously in the past. He had been the youngest, much youngest, of a family, all of whom had gone by the time he was seven. Up until then the noise they had made was comforting, and prevented him from noticing. But when the last sibling left, to flit between the others in England or Munich, an unbearable sadness came over the house. His parents and himself seemed to have been stopped, rabbits frozen in a spotlight glare. He began to notice and to hear from this rigid stance, and saw that his mother and father never spoke civilly to each other unless they were outside the house. It seemed that his mother conspired to meet his father at the gate in the evenings and to ask primly and loudly in front of the neighbours, 'How are you, PJ?' He'd answer 'Great', and look as if he wanted to kick her in the shins. Or so the look seemed to say. Fergal saw it and knew.

His father spent a lot of time writing letters to his family, particularly the daughters. This was in the evening. Silence, more silence, piling up in his child's heart to cause untold damage and to give a quiver to his voice for the rest of his life; a tone that checked out if it was OK to talk. And then his mother would put him to bed, and although she was a woman who, if given a chance, might have told a daughter to leave a night-light on with a young child, she forgot with him and put the light off. The switch was too high for him to reach then.

As he lay in his bed the darkness would gather speed with a foreboding confidence, winning, winning, becoming full-bodied. He could hear the man outside the shop, 'You'll never find now until you see a stretch in the days.' Oh, he wished and wished. The silence downstairs would break, perhaps it was only thunder.

'How come you never . . .'

'You always . . .'

'None of this would have happened if you hadn't started . . .'

'None of this would have happened if you hadn't talked to that nosey parker in the shop . . .'

Fergal would close his eyes and pretend the sun was shining. Then he would put the three of them in separate circles on a sandy beach, separate so they couldn't get at each other. But they could, and crescendos of fury would work its way up the wall. Then the noise could get no louder, so Fergal would think, this is the worst it will be, not that bad now that it's here, the same as always, no worse, and he would sleep with that sound floating in a cloud above his heavy eyes.

One morning when his mother was at the shop, Fergal watched his father getting ready for work, in great haste. He looked at him sideways because he could see light around him. His father seemed to flash like lightning, and he said, 'Goodbye, son' when he reached the door. He put his hand out to touch Fergal's head but changed his mind. When his mother came back she noticed nothing and got Fergal ready for school. That day he and the girl from the same class got prizes in a race but the girl was given *Kidnapped* and he was given the girl's book. And when he came home from school his mother was pale and then there was only him and her. He wondered if he had told his mother about the light around his father when she had come back from the shop, if she could have done anything about it, caught him before he got to the bus, maybe.

Very soon afterwards someone came and took the furniture. Fergal came in from school and there was the empty sound that happened when his mother cleared the kitchen to wash the floor. But there was no bucket and no papers on a wet floor. Neither was there a couch nor armchairs. Everything was going fast.

His mother and Fergal moved house. For a while they lived in a condemned house. It belonged to the owner of the factory, so no one would say anything to him about the disgrace of that house. Not because he had direct political influence that could be used against them, but because he was a busy man and so, surely, wouldn't have time to even notice, and they or their relations worked for him. In time, as the house got even worse, someone might say, 'God help the Carrahers, it's a disgrace', but the longer they lived there the more likely someone else was to answer, 'They wouldn't want any better.' Fergal's mother must have known this so they moved again to a row of houses where the women stood with their babies in their arms at the doors, not like other places where women moved inside when people passed. Here the girls got pregnant and the sons got girls pregnant and it was noisy. Out the road the old men were older-looking and resented how diluted their sons and daughters had become by going to cities, but not here. It was busy and Fergal's days began to even out.

Fergal's mother put her life and aspirations firmly behind her son. There was never any question but that he would succeed at school and that he would have to have a uniform for the school he would be going to next, and that he would have to get a bus to that school. They talked little of his siblings who were gone, and never of his father. He completed his Leaving Certificate and while they waited for the results they busied themselves with the tiny garden and the library books that were changed every week. He built a rockery and did odd jobs for farmers and builders. The results came, he would go to university.

One Saturday Molly Carraher got flu, but she had always believed herself to be a wiry woman and did not visit or send for the doctor. Before Fergal went to bed she spoke to him in a fever. She told him that she would have preferred not to have to speak to him of certain things, but seeing that she had to, she should tell him about his father. His father's father, Fergal's grandfather, had thumped Fergal's grandmother in the stomach when the baby was inside her. She said, matter of factly, that up until that incident he had apparently been a decent man. The child was born with a damaged shoulder ('You remember your father's gammy shoulder?'). The guilt got to his grandfather and he had to leave or wilt. He went to London to work and always sent money home. Granny Carraher had told his father when he grew up that she had the London address and perhaps he'd like to see him sometime. Perhaps if he'd straightened himself out he might be all right, but if he hadn't, and was still battering women, she'd prefer if he didn't. Fergal's father had declined. But it left him with a history of running. So London, and later Munich and other places where his children lived came onto his map. 'Things got bad, money was tight, and he ran away.' She told Fergal that his father had left an undeveloped film in a drawer and that she used to look at it fearfully for a month or so. But eventually she got the nerve to bring it to the chemist (in the next town, of course, where she was not known). In truth she was relieved to see that the photos showed her and Fergal, and men with sons at football matches, and not some woman. 'He was a terrible man, your father, you'd never know where he was.' She had thought that nervously to herself as she had waited for the chemist to hand back the pictures. Now she said it aloud, forgivingly. 'There are new machines in Dublin, Mrs Clarke was telling me, where you can see the photos coming off the belt. When Mrs Clarke told me that, I thought I would not have liked to have had to watch your father's film coming off that machine. Imagine standing at the counter getting a prescription and seeing photographs of your husband or your wife with someone else.' His mother then said, 'My parents never forgave me for your father leaving.' She added: 'Why would I worry about dying without my parents' forgiveness? After all, my husband died without mine, and I would certainly die without his.'

The talk of dying frightened Fergal and he asked his mother to stop. He looked at her and saw that there was no light left in her face; her eyes had been cut off at the back and were connected to nothing. He ran next door and they got the doctor. But Fergal's mother was not going to speak again and had forgiven as much as she could.

But Fergal could not forgive her, yet. And even worse, there were then the brothers and sisters. Two of them couldn't come to the funeral; two did, one brother, one sister. They stayed in the hotel with their spouses. They spent the days there going over futile superseded anecdotes from their mother's past which bore no resemblance to Fergal's and her life. It was a different woman they knew. They also spent a lot of time excusing the other two who couldn't come; as emigrants themselves they knew how hard it was to get away at such short notice, the fares were very dear when you had to buy them immediately. How terribly inconsiderate of Mrs Carraher not to give them a bit of notice! They walked around the town smartly, happy to renew old acquaintances on this shortest of stays, happy to wonder unreasonably about the untravelled lives of their school friends. Their father was mentioned only once by the brother from Munich, who then covered it up as if Fergal would not want to know about him. Fergal had been hoping to pick up information with the corners of his ears as he walked among the guests at the wake. Of course they weren't guests, but he could not think of them as mourners either; he felt himself to be the one single mourner. But nothing more was said that might give Fergal clues as to what the man had done, thought, or how he had lived.

They left for the airport together in a hired car. Fergal knew that they couldn't wait to go. He didn't excuse them one bit, not even on the grounds that they had left so long ago and were then embarrassed by the outcome of events. He refused to believe that there could be any excuse for anything about them, even their clothes. They, for their part, left happy with how they'd got along with him; after all, it wasn't easy, they had been gone from home, as was their right at their ages, but it wasn't their fault that they had been followed by their father. The past, their childhoods, had collapsed when the last one banged the door on the way out. (Well, there was still Fergal. Well, yes, Fergal.) Even those who had not intended to stay away did so, because they had no intentions of walking back to misery. And Fergal was fine, going to university; just as well he had something to do now, couldn't have been easy living there alone with her. Maybe some of them should have come home (back, you mean, not home), even occasionally. Too late now. The brother and the sister thought collectively, but said nothing, as their respective spouses discussed the roads, the trees, houses they passed, people on the side of the road. Funny, he didn't look like any of the rest of them really. He'd be fine now, he'd have a new life, and they had given him all their addresses. It was too late to give him their father's, the sister had always had it, and would have given it if it had been asked for, but would never have offered it. You never know what their mother might have said about him. They would have been horrified to discover that she had said nothing, nothing at all, all those years, until an hour before her death, and even then reluctantly.

Fergal started to pay bills and close house. The brother had sneakily paid the undertaker; the sister had paid the publican. Why couldn't they have said, 'We'll pay that'? Then he could have argued a little but let them pay it. Instead he had embarrassed himself by offering to pay two bills that were already cleared. The undertaker and the publican would both know that even the brief façade of family had been a farce. And if *they* knew, then everyone would know. But why should he care? He was going. But he did care; he wanted to leave an intact history behind him, an ordered memory of himself and his mother. If only he had her to talk to. She would have known what to do, and how to do it, and how to cover the last tracks of doubt. He collected his savings and hers from the post offfice: added together they were a more paltry sum than he had expected. And so the gravestone was out of the question. He got a large stone from the quarry and chiselled it into some kind of monument. He knew this was not the done thing, and that people would know that the money must have run out; he hoped that a rumour would be started by one of them, one to the effect that he

119

had artistic leanings. One never knew one's luck. And a rumour like that would spread because, if given a way out, these townspeople could be generous. He was reluctant to put pebble stones on top of the grave but he would not be here to tend flowers or pull weeds. Perhaps the pebble stones would go well with his own chiselled stone.

Then there was the house. To be returned to the county council. Who would live in it next? He nearly wrote to his brothers and sisters to see if any of them would like any of the furniture. But then they had not known it, and the two that had been here for the funeral had not remarked upon anything. He could not take it with him to a flat. He would keep some little things and they could be his private fund of his past; he would tell no one. He didn't know why it should be secret, why he should be secretive, but he was certain that that should be his behavioural mode from now on. As far as possible. He tidied the garden on the day before he left and even moved a few flowers to what he had discovered last summer was a brighter corner. The garden was hard. He cried then, squeezing 'Mother, Mother' and 'God, God, oh God' through his blubbering mouth. Sooner than he should have, he stopped himself and said, 'Right! right!' The night before he left, neighbours called in but were uncertain how to behave, or what to say; the circumstances were unusual. They came in the morning too and were easier because there were things to do like bags, very few of them, to be carried, and a bus to be got. They shook hands, or embraced him, or kissed him, and waved energetically.

Fergal booked himself into a sort of hostel and, remarkably, set about constructing a new life. In the confused first weeks of a college life, he told different stories to different people when asked questions. He ended up having coffee and beer with several different people, some of whom he remembered and some not. Often they would ask where each other was from, numbers of brothers and sisters, what fathers did, all those markings. Fergal answered as he felt at that moment and could not always remember to whom he had told what. There may still be people who think that his father and mother run a bed and breakfast in County Carlow, but he doesn't know who they are. In those first few weeks everyone seemed confused, so he ducked in and out of the general chaos and succeeded in finding a level. He attributed all panic and sudden breathlessness to college nervousness; hadn't everyone else got it? At the end of one lecture, history, maybe, he hadn't been listening, he met Ollie from Leitrim who hadn't yet got his living arrangements sorted out, so they went for cups of cold splashed coffee and arranged to share a flat.

Ollie, Oliver McGrath, lived by scam. His brain was constantly speeding, in motion, deciding new ways and new means. Some of these were necessary for living purposes; others were merely enjoyable pranks that prevented his mind from becoming lazy or ordinary. Ollie had an irrational fear of becoming ordinary. In the first week of their flat-sharing he had researched possible insurance scams; he had assembled all the paraphernalia to join the Automobile Association. It offered cover for breakdown. He had no car. 'But we could get a free night in a hotel when our car has broken down and we're waiting for it to be fixed. A flashy hotel.' There was no point in mentioning that Fergal had no car either. He had also put an old pair of shoes among the new ones in British Home Stores; he said that that was his political action. He had stolen a supermarket trolley, it was parked in the hallway. Ollie also did endless competitions; the table was littered with coupons.

Because the edges of Fergal's normality had melted in the last month, he did not worry about Oliver, as others might have done. Instead, he became the minder, buying milk and bread and making sure there was always a tin of beans and a few eggs in the cupboard. One evening he even bought rice to make rice pudding. Ollie didn't ask him why he never went home at the weekend. A few months passed satisfactorily. Ollie went on holiday to Wales not, he explained, to have a holiday, but to partake of the pleasures of a new scam that had come to his mind regarding traveller's cheques. Unfortunately for Ollie it wasn't a very new scam at all, and he was picked up within fifteen minutes of cashing his first cheque. He was brought to a holding room where the questioning started, not about traveller's cheques, but about every unsolved bombing that had occurred in England for the last ten years. Eventually, a sergeant decided that he was too young and too disconnected to be a plausible defendant, so he was allowed to leave. There was a message from his father at the exiting desk; the police had telephoned him. Ollie hadn't, nor had he asked to, make any other calls; the ignorance of his rights had indeed been one up in his favour. The message from Ollie's father was that he would pick him up at the boat on his return. From there they went to the flat and packed his belongings, Ollie's father staring at Fergal as if he were the God-father, and who could blame him? It is hard to believe that a child of one's own could break the law in such a blatant way unless they had been influenced by some evil force. The father then brought Ollie home to the family supermarket in Ballinamore where he could keep an eye on him, leaving Fergal to find himself a new flat-mate. There was that Connie who wanted to move out of her digs and definitely wanted to share in a mixed house. And so Connie moved into Ollie's room, replacing scams with calm.

For the next three years they lived in the same flat, shaping each other's lives unnoticed by themselves. They moved often, enjoying the possibilities of changing address with such little fuss. They learned to talk to each other remarkably quickly for two strangers, in the way that rarely happens. Fergal talked to Connie about his past life, about the loneliness; he acknowledged bewilderment. She was the first person who had ever heard his feelings detailed and the first person he ever went shopping with. They went browsing for books and fitted on clothes on Saturdays. Connie had forgotten that he was a man, almost before she had noticed. He told her his terrible dreams, and they were many. She was the only person who witnessed his breakdown; she saw him putting himself together again as if he were a game of Lego. Her own dreams were easy and she always woke ready for breakfast. Connie didn't tell as much about her past; she said that there was nothing to tell. And Fergal didn't push her. Maybe there was nothing much to tell, or maybe she was hiding something, and if that was so it was all right by him. But she talked incessantly not of their pasts but of their presents and knitted a language in which they found whatever comfort they needed. Indeed, Fergal was lucky, because who knows what might have happened to him just then if he hadn't met her? He knew this but doubted if Connie did, because she didn't need him as much as he needed her. Their closeness was never directly remarked upon to them, but it was noticed. Their other friends knew the limits of intrusion, knew that they were not allowed in past a certain level. This closed door was essential, so that both Connie and Fergal could build their own defences, become sophisticated, restructure the effects that their histories had had upon them. And they passed their exams.

Fergal travelled a little then; most of his friends did. But he was surprised to find that he did need familiar things and wished a lot to be home. Funny, he didn't like Ireland the year that Connie was away; his thermometer was missing. However, she was only in London, so he visited her one weekend, but it turned out to be such a disaster he pretended it had never happened. She was shifty, secretive, and uneasy. Terrible, really. But once she came back to Ireland, she became well again.

Fergal himself got a good job and filled his time with being in his mid-twenties, with having money and good places to spend it. He socialised often with Connie; indeed he was with her the night she met her husband. Unfortunately, his relationship with Desmond did not develop beyond discomfort but with great luck, again, that didn't appear to affect Connie and himself. Their friendship continued to last.

Fergal met a woman, Carmel, when he was on a brief, working-away break in London. On the bus home one evening he was mesmerised by the make-up lines behind the ears of the passenger in front of him. It was so messy looking it gave the game away, but the woman didn't seem to mind. She got off at the same stop as Fergal and as luck (I don't say which kind) would have it, she tripped as he walked off in the opposite direction and fell, the contents of her bag spreading out over the footpath. Fergal turned around, helped her to her feet and, because she recognised his accent, was happy to let him help her pick up the bits and pieces that made up her personal baggage.

There were several toilet bags all bursting with lipsticks, mascaras, colours. As he ran after falling bottles she laughed at what he might think.

'Oh, you see these, I'm an actress, you know.'

'Ah, I see; that explains . . .' Fergal faltered.

'Explains what?'

All this, all this, he thought, and said in time. Mentioning a rim of make-up behind her ears would have seemed over-personal. And so began a fast romance, tinged with the usual words and coincidences of feelings so beloved of those caught in speedy freefalls. Carmel was jumpy, already disappointed, looking always, in public, as if Fergal had just said the wrong thing; in private she puckered up her face like a jazz player. She jumbled her sentences together and patronised a certain amount of air between herself and Fergal. She spoke to him as if holding a telephone mouthpiece at a little distance. But they noticed none of this. Because of the speed, Fergal was a little taken aback and told a lie or two; he hadn't the time to figure out how much truth to tell, how far Carmel's sympathy might stretch. But they noticed none of this either. Each time he met her he used the first words to wet his tongue. Touch me, oh God, touch me, he would think. Afterwards his legs would tremble so much he could barely walk and he had better not look at her or it would start all over again. They married with unnecessary haste and took the bafflement of living together well for a few weeks. Perhaps they were like others of that time who married because they needed to go to bed with each other regularly and couldn't be bothered putting up the small fights necessary to achieve that. But you cannot move into a kitchen with someone who doesn't want to bump into you. They told friends of their news and arranged to meet them on their return to Ireland; that would help. They were going to travel to the west for a weekend together, and then they would live in Dublin.

Something happened in the west. Fergal had a bad dream. And so did Carmel. Carmel's consisted of her passing what appeared to be a prune, then being crowded by women who told her this was a miscarriage. She peeled off the layers to find inside a perfectly formed skull which spoke to her. She woke petrified but said nothing. Fergal talked and screamed in his sleep so it was harder for him to avoid explaining his nightmare. And then other lies were uncovered. Carmel was startled. Something else must also have happened, but only Fergal, Carmel, and probably Connie, know about it. Carmel 'left the marriage' the next day, as if a piece of paper which had declared what both of them had said under the influence of lust was an actual place, or thing, that could be related to spatially, and left. Fergal felt something, but not guilt, which he knew he should have felt. It suited him that Carmel was an actor.

In the next few weeks back in Dublin he wandered a lot, walking across the bridges that go back and forth over the Liffey. He thought about how he had wanted to live his life and how, by virtue of one mistake, that that would not now be possible. Actions could not be erased. Wasn't he himself a sufferer from people trying to do that? But the mistake was not so bad; it could have had a gory ending but didn't. He went to libraries a lot; for some reason they offered a specific comfort. He watched women taking escapist literature, or dreams, from the shelves. But he knew by looking at them that they had their longings under control. Longing didn't mean that they believed it would happen. He lost a lot of weight and even his feet grew thin. He had been put out again, like a young swan, out until he would find a mate. But he wasn't ready. Like the swan who comforted himself with the company of hares and birds and young foxes who came to wait with him, he would comfort himself with Connie, more work, and a house, perhaps. A house of his own in which to put order on things.

Because small bits of luck were often with Fergal (although overall one couldn't say he'd had a charmed life), Connie, and now her family, moved close to him and the regularity of past confidences was resumed. But he wasn't that lucky, so redundancy was no surprise. Depressing unemployment was a heartless, cruel stroke on him and Connie was right – he would leave for a year; apparently he would be able to get work in New York.

8

Dear Connie,

Hello from New York. Yes, I should have written to you before now; yes, I'm not good at apologising, and yes, you're right, of course. I cannot expect you to be a carbon copy of me. I shall now relegate your prison communication to its rightful place; God knows, I'm good at forgetting things. I do not have any excuse to offer except that, perhaps, your friendship is the longest consistent thing I've had in my life, other than my mother, and I panic at the thought of anything that might jeopardise it; anything that might signal its loss. Panic unreasonably, but you know that. Let me tell you about loss.

Before I left Dublin, before I was made redundant, I should say, the typist in our office – but of course you'll remember – Hannah, scatty Hannah, came to work one day red-eyed, like seriously red-eyed, it wasn't the sort of thing you could ignore. I knew that if I asked her what was wrong that she would cry again, so for her sake, I left it until lunch time. We went to the coffee shop around the corner, where she blubbered her way through soup, and I felt weak with the pain of watching her. No, her husband had not died or run away; instead she had left her daughter to the airport that morning.

I asked where the daughter had gone, and what she would be doing, but Hannah swiped her hand at the air, as if those things were totally unimportant. She said that at moments it was like a death, flashes of memory that she couldn't get rid of. The main thing was that she hadn't been prepared for the overwhelming feeling of grief. All her aunts and uncles were out of Ireland; she had been reared on emigrant letters. All her brothers were away too, not great communicators, but bank holidays were punctuated with phone calls. Rather pointless, she had always thought them. She had felt, before this particular day, that yes, she would miss her daughter. She had been edgy for a few weeks prior to the departure date, but she had busied herself with preparations, endless lists of things to be done. Now that she was gone she couldn't believe just how devastated she was. She also hated the 'now you know' voice of her mother that was ringing in her ears, although she hadn't spoken to her yet, and couldn't. And in her circular descriptions I recognised my own missings; they were like kicks in the stomach. I remember not sleeping, months of waking up in the middle of the night, and you'll remember the bad dreams. We got through lunch time and she said that she felt better, fit to face the afternoon typing stupid, meaningless letters coming over her earphones, in voices that, today, she hated, smug unhurt tones. Of course I told her that she couldn't be sure about them; maybe they had suffered the same pain. Well, she said, she wasn't likely to find out, because she had no intentions of putting a notice up on her desk, and with that remark we managed to get back to normal office demeanour.

All that afternoon I thought of the intense silence that we have wrapped around this problem, and it is a problem. I saw clearly how the bad songs on Radio Éireann could be sending people all around the country into paroxysms of loss. It's funny how in books, too, we're left at the moment of grief but never brought forward into the following days, weeks, months. It's the same in films. There is a death, a departure, and the chapter changes or the camera moves. We don't want to know how the people who are left behind feel; we're afraid that we'll be touched by their agony. We are kind, but really don't wish to delve, because even if we did it would be no help. Then again, perhaps we shouldn't because if all of us felt the same intense pain at the same time we would be no practical help to each other. We'd all be a joined-up sniffling mess. That's loss. And I've been thinking of it today when I became stupefied by the fear of losing your friendship or, indeed, destroying it myself. By the way, Hannah got all right in time and joined the ranks of people who flinch slightly or pause dreamily for a mere second when asked how their emigrants are doing. So forgive me. And I hope we can recover our lost ground.

I've been thinking, too, about Desmond; odd day I'm having. I can just see him and Bernard doing their best to communicate but at least they have pints in front of them once a month. I may seriously try to find my oldest brother soon; as far as I know he hasn't kicked the bucket yet. Oddly enough, it's getting in touch with the others for his address that puts me off most. I don't seem to be able to forgive their collective behaviour at the time of my mother's death, the two that stayed away and the others flithering around the place as if it was a normal Christmas get-together. What a mess. I now also think that I should have kept some of the furniture; there were odd things, knick-knacks, pictures, crockery, even pots and pans and some bits of rubbish (well, not rubbish), farm implements that my mother had kept from my grandparents' house. The longer I spend here the more I remember of my last years at home with her, and I occasionally regret that I had not been more together when leaving the house. I could have organised some way of keeping a few things. No, maybe I was right because those things would remind me always. Hannah didn't open the door of her daughter's room for weeks; she said that I must think her mad, but no, I didn't; I wouldn't even take the road to our town, not even yet.

My job is going well, the apartment is grand, flowers and plants beginning to be mastered, the love life makes me sigh when I think about it, which I try not to. I've joined a gym (takes some of the heat off) and am now in a sort of regular pattern – funny how quickly routine catches up. And I'm beginning not to notice the wonderful things. I go to the Eagle once a week and there we hook into the music, hoping that someone really good will be over from Ireland. Not that 'our own' aren't good enough, but the real thing still has serious magic. Thursday nights are terrible gambles: if I don't go then I'll miss the session of a life; no matter what I ever talk about again, someone will say, 'Ah, but you missed so-and-so, didn't you, Fergal', and someone else will say, 'That's right, you weren't here that night, Fergal. Where were you, by the way?' So I go, no matter what else is on. As well as listening to the music, we exchange clips of news that people have gleaned from newspapers and phone calls, the latest film or play to do with Ireland; there are usually ferocious arguments about these. Some people love anything that shows a green field and the Liffey; others, like myself, spend most of the time cringing at the dripping saccharine that we've just seen. Of course when the arguments get too uncosy we immediately switch to New York – handy that. By the time we leave we're a peculiar mixture, all rattled by faraway places, home, yet delighted to be escaping to apartments that have nothing to do with such a place. Yes, Thursday can be bad for the blood pressure.

So you had fireworks in Dublin – how unIrish! And you are the proof of that. I think, Connie dear, when you're watching fireworks you're not supposed to be analysing them. I think you're supposed to treat them like a roller coaster, and all you should be thinking about is yourself and how you're enjoying yourself. Maybe you weren't cut out for such enjoyment. Talking about enjoyment, do you know what I've gone and done – taken up cigarettes again. I know this could be seen as the greatest contrariness imaginable, seeing that people give them up before they come here so they can slip into the new health machine, but there you go. I awoke one morning and longed for a fag with such desperateness that I took it to be a sign. They help too, you know; the smoke breaks are the commas and semicolons of the day. The first one is always an exclamation mark. Yes, it's a pity, but so are many worse things.

Now, Connie, I must go. I apologise again. I've already forgotten that you lost your head and started writing to a criminal. Oops. I know I'm forgiven, and I know this, not because I'm a cocky blackguard, but because you always do forgive me. Hope to hear from you soon, very soon.

Lots of love,
Fergal

Dear Fergal,

Well, it has been a long time since I put pen to paper. I seem to
intend to write and feel positively happy about sitting down to
communicate, but once I do, I think, no, I can't be bothered, and I
leave it. But this time I'm going to persevere. It's the glass, I suppose, which has turned my head. I now have my system worked
out. The garage is organised perfectly, maybe too perfectly. I seem
to get as much enjoyment out of the rearranging of it to suit my
needs as I do from the actual glass. Here's a picture. As you can see
it looks the real thing. The right-hand side, by the door, is where I
blow. The heat is such that I usually blow with the door open – as
you probably know, this is a delicate part of the process and all conditions must be right. Blowing is the dizzying part. I must not blow
too hard, nor too easy, and must turn the rod at just the right speed.
Except for the turning, I presume it's like playing a wind instru-
ment. Mind you, if you get a note wrong you can still continue
the tune. I'm now concentrating on practice; although I know the
steps from Waterford, it's different when I'm making it myself. It's
more enjoyable but I also have to take on myself the responsibility
of failure. A child watches her mother when the dinner is ready,
waving the red cloth to the men in the potato field, she knows that
that's the best part. She grows up, marries, and gets to wave her
own cloth, but then it's not so exciting, the different men's tastes
could make her dinner a disaster. What do they get at home? Maybe
potatoes better done? Well, I'm not that unlucky, because no one
has to see my disasters if I don't want to show them. I've started
making lamps, a space for the bulb then layers of the flat glass getting smaller and moving in different directions. I know you can't
visualise that, but it's there; I should have one perfect enough for
your house soon. Yes, I will send a photograph of that too. Maybe
I'll take up photography as well. All these possibilities come to me,
ways of filling my time, good ways, not merely means of stopping
myself staring at the wall. Of course I'm aware that if I take up night
classes the teacher will be younger and think I'm an old man, maybe
find me surprisingly interesting, as if all old people were from the

one part of a sagging cake. Funny how the younger one is, the more one is supposed to have experienced interesting things. Funny when youngsters look at a street they see it full of people except when they come to the old, whom they see merely as the old.

This morning I had another letter from our friend in prison. I say 'friend' in the broadest possible sense. Not to repeat gossip, or to make you nervous about how your friends see you, but I should like to bring up this issue with you. You see, age lessens a person's fear to tackle thorny subjects. I understand perfectly how, when you're away from here, the imagined spectacle of Connie and myself writing to an inmate of Portlaoise presents a different picture than the actual reality. In fact, the man didn't do too much. Now I know that seems as if I'm making an excuse for him, but let me tell you it was a relief to me. You see, with my own views of the futility of the Provo position I would, before now, have felt that 'not too much' was too much. However, for some reason, a shyness in the face of Stephen's dedication, perhaps, I didn't ask what he was in for in the beginning, so I was relieved to find out that he had merely hired out a car for someone. Now the relief was followed by the realisation that the car was used in a bank robbery to secure funds for the organisation and that Senan could not have been a complete innocent; he surely didn't think that they were going away for a long weekend break. However, I've been struck by the bravery exhibited of taking one's medicine for such a trivial thing – he got an inordinately long sentence in the Special Criminal Court. Stephen says it was vindictive because the actual robbers were never caught. Of course they will be caught for something else eventually. I also began to think that one could be drawn into actions of this sort because of people one knows – fate and politics and geography are not unconnected. We in the South do not know what loyalty, what driven heavy history, propelled people. Although Monaghan is, of course, technically in the South, it acts in a schizophrenic manner and a large number of northerners were driven there in the sixties. All this is by way of not simply trying to see some sort of justification for Senan's actions, but of understanding for myself how the collision of facts creates diverse actions. Be this as it may, I still do not support the Provos. However, the experience has brought to my attention a rather pathetic response on our part: the 'I'm less of a supporter than you' syndrome. That kind of pettiness seems pointless and unproductive to me and with that in mind I did visit Senan.

But I won't be doing it again. Not because I don't want to, but because I couldn't bear it. From the moment I applied for the visit I regretted it. The guards treated me as if I was a dangerous criminal, but that was nothing to the visit itself. Some of the officers were obviously kind to relations, some looked down through their nostrils in a way that could only be described as provocative and almost brutal. Being patted on the inside and outside leg, having to take my shoes off during the search, left me disconcerted. I nearly turned back but didn't want to waste the man's visit, so I proceeded. I remember very little of what we talked about; I was overwhelmed by the waste of lives, completely overwhelmed. I was nervous and ill at ease; the poor prisoner had to do all the work, and do you know, I would not recognise him if I saw him again. I thought that the time would never be up and I fear Senan may also have longed for that. So it's back to letter-writing; I think that I really am too old for that sort of upset.

I was glad of glass the next day, a bright shining morning when the sounds of life are clear, and after breakfast I got straight down to making. The great thing about being a human being, as opposed to what, I don't know, books, films, maybe, is that we can absorb conflicting ideas easily. We are allowed to be more expansive than one idea, and we can also forget; our thoughts are not hammered irreparably into us. Well, they are, but the mind can flit past, corroding bits if it wishes to. Don't we forget, every single day, all the awful things and, indeed, we forget the simple acts of accident that bring us into a world where we get indigestion as opposed to stomachs bloated from hunger? That's me being self-righteous − surely we cannot wallow in guilt because of good luck. This comes to mind only because Helena had a sort of party in her house, friends of hers from the street. I fear that there was a great irresistible variety of drink, duty-free collected over a long time, I presume. You'd think at my age that the memory of hangovers would be stronger than the instant desire for alcoholic-induced bliss, aaw no!

So, Fergal, I think I need to have an hour's sleep, which might help to calm my liver, so I'll sign off hoping that you're well, and also hoping that I'll hear from you soon.

Yours,
Bernard

Hello Kevin,

What an odd thing to do, write to you, even if it is a fax and seems more like a phone call. I suppose I should do it more often but I always feel that we have talked all we need while I'm there and that my absence while working gives us both time to remake ourselves into ourselves, after the experience of making ourselves into each other. I wonder how we would cope if I stopped going away? But I'm faxing because the answering-machine appears not to be working, and I forgot and need to tell you about Ciarán's school sports 'thing'. We have to say by tomorrow morning whether we want him to go on the tour, and if so, whether we want to fund-raise or pay the whole whack, a considerable amount as far as I remember. Neither of us would have time to fund-raise, so I suppose we'll have to go for the second option. Mind you, fund-raising might be a good idea, because I think perhaps, even though we might hate it, one of us should get to know a few of the other parents, and that might be the way to do it. I now leave this in your delicate, capable hands and you can decide. You'll find the forms etc. in the drawer to the right of the television. Lots of love, see you tomorrow night.

Helena

133

Dear Fergal,

Got your letter and it was great to hear from you. Loss! Don't mention it. Fear! Who said one time, 'Listen, my fears would give your fears the shits'? Isn't loss a great word? It conjures up thoughts of all the wide-open pits that there are, primed, waiting for us fools to fall into them. But then again, we wouldn't experience loss if we never had a good thing in our lives. Of course that's the cliché that you could get murdered for, the love of your life has just walked out, you're a pathetic mess given to seriously worrying breakdowns in all sorts of public places, actually you never park your car, you leave the engine running, and your best friend says, 'Better to have loved and lost than never to have loved at all.' But I'd like to help you find your brother. If you'd really hate to get in touch with the rest of them, I'll do it. Remember, it's not just that I'm curious, but I did travel down many of those dark nights and wouldn't mind fitting a piece of the jigsaw, if we could find it. Although of course I also think that you'd need to be careful, or at least be well-prepared. Heaven alone knows what you'd find. Exciting though? Couldn't it be? I'm all for giving it a try, so let me know first.

Today, I wondered, maybe men don't feel the same things as women when it comes to their children. Jesus, how wonderfully original of me. No, forget the originality; how bloody pathetic and arse-licking the 'maybe' seems. In any case, I actually feel the growth of each child; I can almost hear it. The words they say, the clashes they have, are edifices being constructed around me. What happens when they go, I can only imagine. But all friendships, yours and mine as well, create their own needinesses. Where does this leave us with loss? Maybe the more of it we've had the more we can cope with, because we never expect anything to turn out like the sweet songs. No, I'm wrong there; don't children with too much loss chop up frogs and burn horses and all that?

Last week I went to the school sports, a day I detest beyond belief, because of the heartbreak of losing. My first time, Ciarán was racing in the egg-and-spoon race with his friend, but every time either of them passed the other they waited to let the friend catch up. I thought it was such a wonderful slap in the face for competition. The fathers were horrified (except for the father of Ciarán's little friend, how lucky for him). And of course if Kevin had been there he would have laughed. I actually heard one of the other men saying, as he walked away with his friend to another race in order to harass both their sons, 'Well if the father reacts like that, what do you expect?' These are four-and-a-half-year-olds, some of whom break down into the most heartbreaking wails when they lose. It's the first seriously confusing cruelty that most of them have come across. Of course I watch adult sport, nothing more relaxing than watching a few fellows having the dream of their lives come true by putting a ball between two posts. And of course they didn't get there by keeping pace in the egg-and-spoon race and all that, I know; but still I hate school sports. Funny, then, that I like betting so much. But caution keeps me from doing it too often. Yet there's nothing quite like the sound of horses' hooves, four of them carrying your money in their stride. But sport is for men, I think. I was once in love with one of our local stars, who was also supposedly the secretary of the club. For two years I addressed all his postcards about meetings for him; he'd give them to me when we met on the road. Funny how it was the only time I met him – before the monthly meeting. I would address them and then hide them under the waistband of my underclothes for the next few days until he accidentally met me again. I wonder how many others preceded and succeeded me, and if the other players ever smelt flesh from their meeting notices. You could hardly call that being in the thick of the sporting world! But boy, did I think I was an important cog in the whole razzmatazz of the machine. Dear me. Then on Sundays I would watch him, trying to scan my eyes over the other players so no one would notice that they were riveted to his knobbly body. I thought him the most gorgeous of human beings. In truth, he was an ugly-looking little squirt. The blindness of love is startling and wonderful, partly because it is often so terribly far off the mark. Later I refereed the first camogie match in the next village; I was never asked to do it again. As far as I remember I stopped running after a while, having realised that the players knew the rules better than I did and could get on with the game without my efforts. The truest metaphor ever for my life, perhaps? And yet, if sport is for men, how come the terraces are packed with women? Who, secretly, are the men playing for? Surely not always for the blokes speaking out of the corners of their mouths. Desmond and I watch the soccer matches on TV together, about the only thing that has been consistently done with regular goodwill in the last few years. Naturally, he doesn't credit me with too much knowing, but I take bets to myself on the scores and am surprisingly right very often. But who ever thinks that a woman's passion about a team is in the same league as a man's? Now who? Enough of this.

Helena had a party last week. God, it's so long since I was at a party and it was terrific. Some people were so wound up in the beginning, like circus performers before a show, but a few drinks loosened them, as if they'd finished their night to a good audience. People do live such interesting lives! Or was that the drink, of which, I must say, there was rivers. Some of them were a little over-confident, but that's just in contrast to me. I enjoyed myself thoroughly, didn't get too drunk, and managed to mention the children to no one. No one at all. Success. The next morning I was rather worried about some of the things I might have said, but consoled myself that at least I hadn't done what one fellow standing beside me had. He was under the weather, carried away on some flirting that he was dipping in and out of, and then he bit a hole in the woman's jumper. It was one of those playful, jokey things that took the lurch into disaster – apparently it was a very good jumper! Desmond was in his element, as he can be on those occasions. He can make himself the interesting centre with such little ease, I realise how difficult home must be for him. Oh! I wish you'd been there. I do miss you ferociously at times. I wonder where does all that communication we used to have go. Does it wither away without being watered or does it build up angrily inside me? And if so, what will the explosion be like? But mostly I manage to think of you benignly. You are not forgotten although, really, it isn't possible to remember all the time. People who go away want to be thought about, naturally, but they do not realise what they're asking. If those left behind were really to remember them, they would have to think about them all the time, meditate upon them each day, not do anything else to fill in the time that was once theirs. Now how much would that cost and who?

I've just been to the library; they've changed the books around and people do get so ratty about things like that. Librarians don't understand that people consider the place part of their front rooms – they know where the books are, how dare anyone move them. One woman nearly ate the face off the young fellow about the new regime of charging even if the books were only a day overdue. 'But we don't do that here,' she protested. 'They only do that in the ILAC, and other ones that are computerised.' Really she had meant to say, 'What made you people think you had the right to change our bookshelves? Doesn't anyone understand constancy any more?' Then an old woman asked for help with the large-print books, which they had also moved, rather silly of them. 'Now what would you like, romance or thriller?' 'History, please,' she said, and I never heard such weight in the word. They're putting up a fight, certainly. I got the mountains of books for my offspring and the one for myself. I'll have to watch myself; my reading has become sporadic and forgettable. One of these days I'll waken up and I'll know nothing but maintenance of people. What are you working at now, Connie? Maintenance. Now when was it that I was in Italy? And the days are dark again, too. Moan, moan, moan, but you understand.

Your tenants are all fine; they asked me in the other evening for a glass of wine. With the children. I couldn't refuse the offer. The wine was shocking but they were friendly. I was afraid the kids might wreck the place so I didn't stay long. You'll be delighted that one of them asked, that is, one of the children, 'Where's Fergal?' When I said, 'In New York', they all looked at me for a second and collectively banished you in a flash. You see, no one is any use to children unless they are there, there and there. Except, of course, the people in bedtime stories.

Maybe I'll have a party. Desmond would probably love that, and then I could also meet some of his friends. I would have to start by praying that no one got an earache in the middle of it – forget the food or drink, minor problems those. Yes, I think I'll have a party. I'll write and let you know how it goes. So until then

Your fond friend,
Connie

To Bernard from Fergal

Dear Bernard,

Lovely to get your letter. My, have you done a job on that garage! Forget the photography; what about interior design? Enclosed a few wonderful catalogues on lamps. How the eye becomes overfed and thus unappreciative. After getting your letter I started looking at the lamps in my apartment, and the office, in the coffee bars, restaurants, bars, and noticed that there's a world of lamps and lamp-making that I had never noticed nor knew existed. The catalogue is from an exhibition that I happened to see when walking around last Saturday. I spoke to the man about lamps and about not noticing them. He said that the better ones are not supposed to be noticed. I couldn't reconcile that with the effort that appears to have gone into this show, but who was I to argue?

My reading is still greatly encouraged by the library system. I go in to marvel at the number of books and come out laden with tomes by people I've heard of forever but never actually seen in print. This week it's George Sand and Anthony Trollope. Lovely combination! Would you believe, I've never read either of them before? All I know about them was that George was a woman like George Eliot and that John Major likes Anthony Trollope. Where I got that last bit of information I have no idea, some side-inch in some Sunday news magazine on some Sunday night. In Ireland I always read the Sunday papers at night. Here I read them, or should I say it, during the day. This obviously means that I have nothing else to do on a Sunday. I suppose you've read Trollope? What an interesting story about the priest – terribly un-anti-Irish for its time, or did *Punch* only get into its stride after the Famine? If that is so, then the story could have been guilt. I notice in the introduction a passing reference to the crop failure which caused the Famine. My blood rises as uncontrollably within me as if I was in the middle of a personal brawl. So perhaps I should understand the North better? History, history, bloody history. The best history is the one furthest away, the one you can see yourself in without it being a part of you, like 'The making of Europe, conquest, colonisation and cultural change'. Great stuff, all the buildings, all the distant wars, all the glass a person could need. But George Sand, now that's a different matter. And Trollope's other story – the obvious is not the obvious. Of course you could take it as a part of a pat, flat love story if you wished but there's something else there; a picture has been painted that distorts the cosy view. Well, if John Major likes him perhaps he will be the next new Gladstone. Maybe he doesn't like him at all. I could have imagined that I read that. I wonder what Trollope was doing in Ireland.

So my reading is going well, the place in which escape is accomplished is well established, the foundations are sound. You see, I normally think of buildings, solid things. You are probably more adventurous, you think glass; or maybe you are more romantic, so you think delicate. If 'Love is the seventh wave' – sorry it's a song – you'd stand watching it, you'd wait for it to come in so you might marvel. I'd stand there waiting for it to crash. Speaking of songs, I'm going to learn one; it's called 'Do me justice'. I heard it the very night I had been thinking about *Punch* cartoons, so it was a sign. Then I'll have a party piece. Or should I say I'll have a party piece for some parties? One has to be careful not to be classified. Now all I have to do is find out how to sing my way up and down a scale.

Last month I went for a day's outing away from New York. The quietness disconcerted me and I worried that I have, indeed, become addicted to noise. Not that my apartment is too noisy; it just sounds of trains rumbling away in its walls. I cannot imagine the building without that noise. Then there is the noise of dogs barking from afar – some nearer than others, but all a distance away, making them sound like barking dogs with scarves over their mouths. And there is also the noise of cars honking and parking and people fighting and doors banging, but nothing serious like some places here, where you'd think you were sleeping in the middle of a traffic island. Mind you, I remember a flat in North Frederick Street I shared with Connie. That was indeed the noisiest experience I've ever had. It was wonderful sharing flats with Connie; it was my first experience of the comfort of what a normal sibling relationship would be like. Of course, I could be wrong here, because maybe that's not what normal sibling relationships are like. How would I know? You see, we cannot compare things if we've only one experience of them. But I thought that that may have been what it was like. That flat in particular was interesting – there were desks for studying at – and it was certainly a new experience for both of us. One of the desks was so beautiful Connie said it would make you want to be a writer. I said no, that although an easel – a beautiful easel – if there is such a thing, could conjure up desires to be a painter, a desk could not be associated only, indeed even mostly, with writers, because so many other things happened at them. God, wasn't I a snotty little prick! Know-all. But of course I wasn't; I was a quivering mess of insecurity. I used to feel my stomach moving around inside me. Connie was great, like a big sister, organised; she organised me and I found that a great comfort. On her occasional visits home she came back with home-made bread, jam, fresh eggs, flowers. All the things I hadn't got, she shared. Without ever noticing that she was doing so. Funny how I remember that flat, everything about it, the cooker, the carpet, the spring in the floor, the noises. Although mind you, I think I can remember most places I lived in vividly, but I chose not to dwell on them because a past life is really past and not always gratefully savoured because of its very pastness. But that place in particular comes into my head often; I think that I even remember conversations I had there. The flat belonged to a beautician and her dentist husband who lived downstairs, seriously flashy people by our standards. Apparently the beautician had visited Connie's school in her final year, telling the girls how to present themselves to the world. Connie never did inform the landlady of this. There were very strict rules in the house, and I'm afraid we broke some of them, so we got thrown out. I suppose I shouldn't be telling you all of these things about your daughter-in-law. But she was different then. I don't know what I mean by that so let it go.

Lunch is nearly over so I'll post this immediately, otherwise it will stay lying on this desk until it has shrivelled with the power of the central heating.

Regards to all.

Your friend,
Fergal

LETTERCARD
To Fergal from Bernard

Hello Fergal,

Thank you for your interesting letter received today. Glass proceeds in fits and starts. You must make time to find out about George Sand – now there was a woman! A truly wonderful woman. She wrote the politics and the passions; how timid we still are here in comparison. My aunt gave me a biography of her when I was about thirteen; there are several of them so you'll find one easily. My aunt, as well as my mother, was in the suffrage movement and helped organise the 1937 meeting of women in the Mansion House, protesting the articles which they felt were damaging in the new constitution. Of course I wasn't told this, neither about the meeting (who was?) nor about my aunt's part in it. I found it out in her letters after she had died. So I associate my aunt, a feisty (I think that's the new word), serious, but amused by George Sand, woman, and I wonder about the kind of a life my aunt really did live. Trollope – you know, of course, that his mother was a writer and supported her husband and seven children with her writings – was sent to Ireland as a deputy postal surveyor, and I have to agree with you that in some stories he does show remarkable individuality when it comes to his perceptions of Ireland. However, I'm not sure that some question marks don't hang over his novels. As for *Punch*, I'm enclosing a book with this card on the history of the cartoons and you will be able to judge for yourself when he first began to throw his particular slant on Ireland. No, thank you indeed for writing about Connie in a natural way. I sometimes worry about her these days; she seems so less perky than the person I first met and doubtless even more so than the person you knew. Perhaps it will pass when the last of the children goes to school. Will write again soon.

Bernard

POSTCARD
To Bernard from Fergal

Dear Bernard,

How prompt. Well, thank you for your letter received this morning and thank you for your information. Now I need to read something else. Fast replies, now that's communication! Of course there is no reason why we cannot live without it but it cheers up a day no end. I also will write soon.

Fergal

To Fergal from Helena

The Shelbourne

Dear Fergal,

Short note to let you know that I'll be back on the New York route in a few weeks. I'm having a cup of coffee, waiting for my friend Julie. Yes, that's the one you rather fancied, I think. I had just woken up from an afternoon nap; you know, that terrible climb up from devastating depression after a daytime sleep – all to do with the blood sugar. I could explain it but I won't; it's knowledge you don't need unless, like me, you had to get some explanation to avoid topping yourself. But it only takes ten minutes to be sane again. However, what a ten minutes! So I thought here would be a good place to meet; always cheers me up. The reason I had to have a sleep was because the people who live at the back of us were hammering until the middle of the night. It infuriates me when they do that, but they're originally from the country and when they're working they obviously forget that they have neighbours. Touching really, if you didn't have an early start. And the mornings that I can sleep in, they're usually arguing. They finish off their rows over breakfast, if they didn't reach the climatic conclusion the night before! Connie is having a party on Saturday, which will be great because I have Sunday and Monday off. A colossal scandal is about to break about a paedophile priest. I like that one – if he were an ordinary man he'd be a child-abuser; it's like the way the poor are shoplifters and the rich are kleptomaniacs – can't help themselves, poor things. Of course, maybe it won't break. Anyway, see you very soon. I am now looking forward to New York again; I need a change from Rome and London.

> Love,
> Helena

PS. Connie has started going to night classes, art and philosophy! I think Desmond is gobsmacked. I don't know how long they'll last – the classes, I mean; because I can't see Desmond forking out the baby-sitting money, and I certainly can't see him coming home at a regular hour two nights a week. Good for Connie, anyway; she needs something, and she's such a star for everyone else, it's time she got a little selfish. Saints can be hard to take. Not that Connie tries to be good, she just is.

Dear Fergal,

I've just cleaned the post-party mess, the children are all at school, the plastic bags have been knotted to await the bin man and I feel bereft. The party was great; well, Desmond didn't come home until it was well started and he arrived drunk with two women from the office. If there'd only been one I might have suspected him of something, but I got over it, because he then sobered up admirably and entertained us all night with great stories from work. I think Bernard was a little surprised.

You know the way a party should just be a party, not the first, not the last. Conversation will be forgotten, surely, people will be mislaid, all that. But somehow, this one was different. I wore the black dress with the white pockets. I wore it because I put it on earlier and it fitted me, much to my surprise. After having three children the dress shouldn't fit me, so I was pleased, ridiculously. I don't get much time to think about my body so surprises or compliments are truly welcomed.

The children went to sleep like angels, smiling as they did, perfect, in other words. After they went asleep I started cooking snacks and preparing nibbles. The cooking food gave off vapours like expectations at Christmas time. When I had the table ready I lined the drink up, trying not to make it look like a bar waiting for customers. I was beginning to get nervous, you see, panicked that my friends were shoddy and then remembering that I'd invited new people from my classes. I forgot to tell you about those – some other time. Then I worried that the new people wouldn't get on with Desmond's friends. But after the shower and putting on my dress I began not to care. The fire was just right; we've got a new gas contraption because it looks as if coal will soon be banned completely. At this stage I was getting annoyed with Desmond; I knew he had to go to a staff meeting, some emergency, but still I felt that he could have emergenised out of there as well. Helena and Kevin arrived first, content as usual, giving me confidence. We started on the red wine and I would have been quite happy then, even if no one else had come. Then Bernard, of course; he gets more dapper every time I see him; he was dressed up and he's loosened extraordinarily, his face doesn't look so grief-stricken any more. We talked about you, wondering how you were getting on and if you'd ever come back. I suppose Helena will be able to tell us more when she sees you. It's funny how you can get drawn into a moment of missing people, the excited feeling that they will walk in the door and be with you, a conspiracy of pretence, and then a sharp missing beyond belief pulls you back into the room so that you have to busy yourself with other thoughts. Your tenants came too, looking the same as always, solidly certain, unharassed by any limits on their expectations, and bearing lots of not home-made wine.

After that the party filled up in one's and two's and the noise moved into comfortable rhythms. One of your tenants seamlessly organised the music to fit in with the accelerating moods. I'd nearly forgotten about Desmond by the time he arrived and the wine had made me less annoyed. So we had a great night. It's lovely to have people around you who titillate curiosity; all a rather silly business, really, because what can we possibly know about what goes on in other people's heads? Still, there's something innocently satisfying about a party. We talked and danced until dawn, I think, and I felt invigorated. Not too much, I hope; I'm afraid the components of my existence could only handle a slight shift.

Yesterday was mellow and I blessed the children, they'll never know how deeply, for being placid and dreamy. Helena and Kevin came over again and we finished some wine and conversation. Now this morning, now that I'm finished tidying, and have cleaned the evidence, I feel sad in some way, lonely, really, which is a terrible thing to admit. But I'll be OK, it's probably just a hangover.

And how are you? I'm enclosing some recent paper clippings and also all last week's job ads. They'll give you an idea of what's around. I don't read them all the time so I'm not sure if that was a good week, but I suppose we can presume that it was fairly representative.

So my dear, until I hear from you, goodbye and fond wishes.

Love,
Connie

Dear Fergal,

Monday afternoon, lolling about; just to let you know that I'll be at
the hotel by nine on Thursday next – not this Thursday. Would
love to see you. I'm going over to Connie now in a minute; she
had a party last Saturday night and honestly, Desmond is a right
bastard. Kevin and I arrived to find that she had done all the
preparations herself; well at least Desmond had been gone to some
meeting since one so I presume he didn't prepare anything before he
left. There she was all dressed up on her own. But she was in good
form, very dreamy, as you know she can get. Then when Desmond
did come in with two women from work (meeting my eye!) he
was loudmouthed and overbearing. Anxious and nervous, I
thought, and wondered why. It was a day's work moving him
around the house so that no one person had to get stuck with his
stories. I think Bernard was horrified. I suspect that he thinks his
son is not a great husband. Will fill you in on all the news soon.

Helena

Dear Helena,

Don't worry; your friend has just explained that you couldn't make
it. Your phone call obviously didn't catch me on my meanderings
between work and here. I got both a letter from Connie and your
postcard this week. What the hell is going on with her? She even
told me what she was wearing at the party. Not that there's anything wrong with that; it's just the exactness of her descriptions left
me worried. It's like as if she explained the outside of things

meticulously, in order to avoid what was inside. Why did I feel that the bottom or the sides or the circular motions that keep a life together are collapsing on her? She didn't say anything but I just felt it. Perhaps I'm worrying needlessly. Do give me a ring at work before you leave tomorrow. As for Desmond, perhaps it's time someone spoke to him. Now who could do that? I certainly wouldn't relish the thought. Maybe he's pushing Connie to some limit to find where the cracks are. Talk to you tomorrow and if you get back from your philanderings and feel up to it, I'll be at the Eagle tonight from ten until one-ish.

Fergal

CENSORED
To Stephen, Bernard and Connie
from Senan

Dear Stephen, Bernard and Connie,

This note may surprise you but believe me it can do nothing to cause reeling like what I've got. Apparently I'm getting out early, early. I have no idea why; good behaviour is the reason given. It's rather a shock, welcome, of course, but I have to rush my emotions together and we definitely train ourselves here to take things slowly, so that we retain some control over our own reactions. It's either that or tablets. So I'm having a preparatory weekend with my family in seven days and then I'm being loosed soon after that. I do not know what I'm going to do but I will at least call on you all once, perhaps in the next month.

Yours,
Senan

9

The date was 18 March. Senan Lillis came out of the first door of Portlaoise prison and the screw closed and locked it behind him. He didn't even step outside to have a look at Senan's fast-disappearing back. Another screw led him down the path to the next door, unlocked it, then another led him down to the gate, unlocked it, and let him out and locked it again. 'Good luck,' he muttered.

Senan had been told that he was to get out on Wednesday but because that was a bank holiday, they had kept him in until today. They could have let him out on the Tuesday but one officer had a particular grudge against him, and he would not, could not, bring himself to give him an extra day of his life back. Senan didn't mind; he had been here for all those years so he might as well spend St Patrick's Night with his mates. What would he be doing outside, anyway? It's unlikely that he would be going to a concert in the Point, he didn't think he could bear a packed pub, and he wasn't going home to Monaghan yet; he wanted one week for himself.

His mother and father had never approved. In the last two years the visits had become more bearable; three years gone, they would have a drink on their way home after the meal in Tracey's. They were less sprung, more settled in their parental duty, but that did not mean that they approved. They did not know whether this should be shown to Senan when he came home. If it was, would it stop him from getting involved again? Or if it was, would they lose him totally and leave him free to rent another car, maybe worse this time, and if it wasn't shown, would that leave him free? They tossed around in bed at night burdened with this question. No one could tell them that the man was hovering in the regions of thirty now.

They need not have worried, because Senan Lillis had no intention of lifting a finger again for bloody Ireland; he never really had the intention of doing it in the first place – or had he? Who knows? He doesn't, and if he doesn't, no one else does either, no matter what they say about individual responsibility.

Senan had not, in fact, come fully fledged nor blindly to the Provos. Theirs was what would now be called loosely a republican house, although that was not a term that they would ever have dreamt of using. They were not marked out, no more than the Fine Gaelers were; they simply farmed their land, milked their cows, went to Mass, drank and danced, and breathed air in and out like everyone else. They always bought the *Irish Press* and not the *Independent*. Senan's grandfather would have remembered the War of Independence, but talked vaguely of it, as if vagueness could make it not have happened. One of his grandmothers had reason to remember it clearly but she never spoke of it at all in case the words would bring horror into her life. As for the Civil War, they really were convinced that their wishing could make it go away. They voted Fianna Fáil and talked, on the rare occasions that politics were mentioned, as if that was the only party. Consequently, Senan was interested only in Fine Gael, as if that contrariness could offer him escape from the normal claustrophobia of childhood.

The late sixties and early seventies brought the Civil Rights Movement and People's Democracy over their wavelengths and into their kitchen. Senan's father listened intently but said nothing. Senan's mother and grandmother gave out tiny bursts of fear and his grandmother would say, 'Any day now someone will get killed.' Already a few Catholics had been killed, but that was put down to one small group of individuals and if only it wouldn't happen now, then that could be forgotten. One morning the newsreader said that a young Catholic from Armagh had been beaten to death and everyone stiffened at the table, fearing to say a word in case a good thought would tempt fate or a bad one would bring comeuppance. There were refugees then, although they weren't quite called that, but what were they if they had left behind them burned-out houses and their lives, or if they had driven down the road speeded by fear? The language of their new place was the same, but it was hard for teenagers to take Saturday nights in Monaghan seriously; the rules of the game were different enough to make them uneasy.

Their neighbour, the only real republican in the guards' sights, soon began to call more often and to goad Senan's parents into argument. Senan began to see sense in this man's position; history seemed able to right itself. The neighbour also began to have unexplained visitors, and once brought two young men, named ridiculously Seán and Séamus, to the house. They scared Senan and now he shifted to a truly anti-republican frame of mind. He even refused to write to this neighbour when he was sent to jail for six months, supposedly for being in the IRA, a fact that had not one scrap of evidence to support it.

Even Senan's parents thought he should write to the prisoner, in the fashion of good neighbours. But he wouldn't, and soon afterwards escaped from his choking childhood, got to Dublin and started work in a mediocre job in a printing shop.

As life began to happen to him he allowed all sorts of people and places to swing him this way and that. He began to contemplate the news, to buy three newspapers every day, to argue, to get angry. He was drawn to one pub where the northerners drank. He heard people ask men, 'Where are you from?' — 'Derry, Armagh, Fermanagh.' 'And do you go home often?' 'As often as possible', and you knew then, when they said that, that they were not on the run. After work on Thursdays and Fridays Senan went to this pub and listened to what was not being said as well as to the convinced arguments that went on around the outer circles. The women were more interesting here too; they'd thrown off reserve and saw thought as a vital part of attraction, as vital as looks or clothes and certainly more important than cars. People were honest here. There were surges of unselfishness among them. Sometimes he would be told stories that left marks on him as surely as if he'd been beaten himself. Internment had happened to some of these people as if it were in the natural course of growing up, and it had left a wash of huge anger in them. Soon he too was being harassed by the Special Branch, because of where he was drinking, arrested occasionally, abused and scared. But he knew that he was not allowed to be frightened, fear was defeat; the only answer to an unwarranted arrest was to do something that would warrant the next one.

Yet Senan was not completely convinced. Without knowing why, he felt that he should leave the country, should put some distance between himself and happening history. He toyed with the idea of further study, of indiscriminate travel. The dithering gave him a nervous, malleable feeling and he agreed one night to rent a car for one of the fellows, Martin, who drank in the bar. Martin said that he couldn't do it himself because he had a conviction for drunk driving on his licence, and asked if he, Senan, would do it for him tomorrow, using his own licence and getting open-drive insurance. Nothing to worry about. It was just for the weekend and he'd have the car back with him on Sunday night. So he did, and Senan left it back by nine o'clock on Monday morning, as arranged. But then the Special Branch called at work looking for him, asking about a rented car, and Senan got properly nervous. He packed his clothes that evening, having printed himself a few new IDs at work, which he then scuffed and scarred to make them look used. Brushing the paper with a nail brush thoroughly scared him. Scared is not stiff; it's hot and fluid and noisy in your ears. How had he got here, what was he doing on this train to Dún Laoghaire? Surely you couldn't just land up shit creek minus a paddle if you had never even got on the boat. If only he could get to Euston and over to that small hotel where he and his mother had stayed when they went to London for her younger sister's wedding. If only he could get this one night, no, the next two days, over, he would be fine.

Senan, now called Tim Gallagher, found the hotel. The landlady was courteous and helpful. He would be staying for one night, he was down for an interview, from his job in Edinburgh, he said. How quickly he was lying now, untruths jumbling carelessly from his mouth. He would have to keep moving. In the breakfast room the next morning he felt his mother, and remembered nothing of how she had aggravated him ever, remembered nothing but good and strong and reliable things.

Tim got a job – labouring, of course; it was safer. He got a room in a shared house, an ex-squat of some dubious legality. At night he could feel his nerves itch. He tried to think simply of things, not to listen to too much news, and to dismiss political discussion. He rang his parents from a public phone box on the street, saying that he had got an unexpected offer to come to London, and felt that it would be good for him. He sensed that they didn't believe him. He told them that he'd had to take the decision in a hurry because if he hadn't come immediately, the printing job, with much more training than at home, would have been gone. A printer: suit you better to be something a little less volatile, something that could keep you at home. Still, a while away will do you no harm. He would have a permanent flat soon; at the moment he was travelling to different branches of the firm and had no definite address, he'd be in touch by phone though. This was no good – how could he keep this up?

As the months went by, Tim developed a hump on his back. Sometimes he got psoriasis; at night he watched the veins in his arms jumping inside like frogs; his arms had got thin. He dreaded weekends. Streets that were, in reality, open seemed hidden, frightening places. As he walked around he felt that no one, no neighbour, no brother, neither of his parents, would recognise him if they saw him on one of these streets, and although unrecognisability should have felt good to him, it didn't. He was being erased. He would not stay in London; his being there under an assumed name made him appear guilty of a far worse crime than he had been party to. Truly, he hadn't the strength to be political. His desire to be innocent led him to sometimes believe that he was.

And so one day he decided to go home. Or thought he did. He packed only a small bag and went to Heathrow airport, thinking that he would sit there for a while, lay out all the possibilities and see what the options looked like when removed from the actual street where he lived, the actual job, the actual city. In an airport, where freedom is the biggest word, he would come to some conclusion. He went to the Aer Lingus desk and asked when the next flight went to Dublin; this was so that he could put that into the equation. He was told forty-five minutes, 'Smoking or non-smoking, sir?' and he said, 'Smoking.'

When he was on the plane he marvelled at the fact that he had taken no decision. Of course there was no one to meet Senan at the airport, except the guards. And this time the Bridewell was for real. The car ate up the miles down the airport dual-carriageway, up Dorset Street, up Capel Street, and made straight for the station. He would have loved it in another situation. Indeed, he had flashes of homecoming comfort, despite the circumstances. He was plead-ing guilty to hiring out a car under false pretences. For someone who actually admitted that he had an unclean driving licence. Yes. All that he had done. But he did not know what the car was used for. Of course the guards did not believe that. And he would not tell the name of the man who asked him. In truth he had forgotten, he didn't know him that well; he was embarrassed himself at this admission. Embarrassment for him was not what the guards felt. Each time he was left alone he bunched up his body, his arms hold-ing himself as if they belonged to someone else, some dream-like comforter who would be able to suck him inside her body, and he would have disappeared next time they came back. Gone into thin air, gone to where the lost sentences on computers go – there would only be his date of birth on the machine in the Bridewell, not only the accusations, but the prisoner too, would be gone. He was cold. And sore. And insulted. He would never have believed that men could say such terrible things about other people, about men, about women. About mothers. That was the vilest, a cesspool of words that surely could never have been thought, pointless degradations, because they showed only the worthlessness of the sayer. He would never think about them again; he would now think about the prac-ticalities of telling. He would not, of course, try to imagine what his parents would feel, that would be unbearable. A solicitor came. He tutted at Senan when told that he had admitted everything.

'But not about the robbery?'

'What robbery?' Senan asked.

And the solicitor believed him, because anyone who would

admit to hiring out a car for someone he didn't know, who drank in *that* pub, and didn't expect to be charged with something bigger, was definitely innocent. Surely the guards would see that too. He didn't even know the man's name. Now Senan asked him to tell his parents – no, tell his brother – who could tell the parents in person rather than over the phone. The solicitor hated this bit. No, he didn't want anything – well, a clean shirt and his suit from the wardrobe at home. His mother would take it out as if for a funeral, almost his own. His father would watch her from the corner of his eye, silent, blaming, because at least blame was active. As the Special Branch came in with the charges, Senan remembered the name of the man: Martin, Martin something, but why tell on him? It was not going to be of any use to him now. Maybe he should check with the solicitor, ah hell, too late, see what happens, at least the questioning is over, now there is only a court case and whatever follows.

Senan was brought to the 'Special' to be accused. He mused on the word while they read the unspeakable. A special court because no case was heard before a jury? Or could you say that the crimes themselves were special? He would have pleaded guilty to hiring out a car under false pretences, but he wasn't charged with that; instead he stood accused of conspiring to rob an Allied Irish Bank on May the whatever in the town of Monaghan. Convenient enough, he thought, he would know Monaghan well. He didn't even know if the Allied Irish Bank in Monaghan had ever been robbed. He was remanded in custody and brought to Portlaoise prison, handcuffed the whole fifty-three miles. As he left Green Street Court, the Special Criminal Court, cameras flashed like fire-flies and his photograph was in the morning papers with details of his arrest. Air-hostesses checked their timetables and, yes, one of them remembered him clearly. He wasn't nervous or anything like that, smoked the normal amount, one glass of wine (God, the last glass for a while), very good-looking, eyes you wouldn't forget, and in our job you see so many eyes, but not that many remain unforgettable. Deep blue, like the Hungarian blue you see every-where in Hungary (she knew that because on her breaks she always flew with Aer Lingus to Amsterdam and KLM to Budapest, or sometimes Aer Lingus to Zurich and the local flight to Budapest). She loved Budapest. That's what his eyes were like. As people read the newspaper and looked at his photograph, they thought of him largely in clichés, given notions, words that concealed meaning, if they had any, jumping quickly to other things and back again. But the air-hostess thought a little deeper, because it's odd to know that you've served someone on their way to such a different life. I suppose that's often the case when you think about it; even people flying home after forty or fifty years to die, but still prison seemed the most different. By the time the papers were being sold, Senan would have his first night over.

This is a bad stretch of road, he thought, a long, straight, dark mile that seemed to come from English moors or *The Hound of the Baskervilles*. The van bumped over it. A prison officer spoke to him; he knew they were called screws but couldn't bring himself quite there yet. He didn't answer him, not because he wanted to be rude, but because he didn't have anything to say. He would have time to be polite later. Manners were an odd thing; they were taught the same way as words and became part of you, like bloodstreams. He put his nose against the window like a child; he could have licked the glass. Everything was happening in slow motion, even desire. Why should he think now of walking through wet grass, of music loved? He would be able to have a tape-recorder, surely; he would have to stop thinking of things he loved that would now be impossible. A cat ran across the road, everything was so slow, took so long, he hoped the driver would brake in time, why did everything take almost forever, when before now time had always gone too fast? The town had a long beginning. When they came to the gates he thought it would take a distinct, memorable length of time to get in, but that's not what came to his mind when he woke. He couldn't remember very much; oh yes, the strip search, and what came to mind he quickly put aside. He, who had even hated communal showers after football. Which led him to the sound of kicking balls, and to the smell of seasons on a field. By the time the papers were being sold, Senan too was thinking of himself in jumps.

Although Senan was not, nor never had been, a Provo, they welcomed him onto their landing. He didn't know if this was the right move to make, but had no one to advise him, so decided to accept the offer, because there were more of them, so presumably time would be less claustrophobic. He thought that it would take him a long time to figure out who was who, and what they were in for, but unfortunately even that tiny possibility of using time was denied him. He discovered a remarkable capacity to remember names, charges, and years got. How would he have known that this would be the case? The only place that he had ever met so many men before was on the building site and there he had been depressing memory generally. The men were good to him, showing him the ropes, stepping into conversations like oil, when needed, stepping back out when he needed to be alone to contemplate the horror of his position. Maybe some of the men were not as friendly as others, but maybe that was because they saw too many coming in who would be gone out again before them. Maybe they could not afford warmth.

The drive to Dublin on the morning of the trial presented him with a series of dilemmas. Should he watch and feel everything because would this be his last trip up the road for a long time, or would he be coming back down this road in the darkening hours this evening, or would he perhaps never be on this road again, because certainly, if he got off, he would never drive to Portlaoise? Should he hope or should he despair and so perhaps get a surprise? The other men with him in the van were less bothered because they were attending for trials that had already got foregone conclusions or they were travelling to be given their sentences. They were not submerged in as much hope and fear as Senan was. He stayed down below while the others singly took their places in their seats upstairs, waved to wives, girlfriends, children, heard the judge, remained calm. And then it was his turn.

Both his mother and father were there; he thought that a bad idea because the pain could have been halved, although maybe sharing it would help them. Maybe that cliché was true. His brother was there, trying not to look ashamed. That was all. Others had friends but no unexpected body came in to witness him sitting in the accused's seat. No one for him to wave to. Better that way; it might have looked too casual, too uncontrite. He was quite astonished at how bad he sounded out of the mouths of others, surprised and almost amused at what he was supposed to have done, and finally shocked by the silence into which his own words of explanation and regret fell. No face registered belief in him. He dared not look at his family. He heard the sentences of his defence tumbling out, but could understand that they were not adding up to a convincing argument. This was not helped by the fact that counsel had had to be changed at the last minute because neither he nor his family could raise the exorbitant fee being asked, and senior counsel needed the money up front on the day. That's the way we do it. His solicitor explained that if he got off he might not pay. So the money was needed while he was a captive customer. His brother said that the fees were themselves criminal. How could anyone pay them unless someone else robbed a bank on their behalf and they too would have to pay the same fee, which in turn . . . ? He left the sentence unfinished. That was as understanding as he would get. Senan was found guilty of conspiracy to rob the bank and given five years. He was bundled into the van like a criminal. Someone pushed his neck down; all he could see was darkness, then he recognised his shoes.

In the beginning, visits proved to be difficult, worse than hospital occasions. Surely one could not be blamed for being sick? He dreaded the eyes of his parents, the attempts at lightening the conversation, the news from home, as if it had been catalogued, written down and learned off. 'So-and-so is back from London. Now imagine him coming back, and they always said it was the people from the New Houses who couldn't stay away.' Since when had returning home become a slur on one's character? Silence, but that had just been a sudden burst. There was to be no follow-up. The first five minutes were charged with sobs barely suppressed, ten minutes took care of the list, there was a short reprieve of naturalness, then conversation became a dry-mouthed effort, faltering over the slope of the last quarter-hour. Goodbyes were sensed before they came and many deep breaths were taken. The cell was sometimes a relief. But practice and repetition crafted these occasions into a semblance of well-meaning. By the time Stephen, a young witty anarchist, came to see him, Senan had the basics well learned.

In ordinary circumstances, Senan did not spend his time

questioning life (his or anyone else's) but he was not now in any ordinary place. It could be said that up until then he had been, in fact, too unquestioning, but then so are most of us – it is only the unhappy who pick at this and that thought, until their minds are open wounds. Or is it that the thoughtful must become unhappy? Life so far had given Senan the ordinary high points and aggravations. His placid temperament had diminished any major upsets, like losses of girlfriends. Not losses actually, as in mislayings, more like women slipping away in exasperation. There had not been many girlfriends, considering how many there could have been, due to his looks. There had been few because he didn't always have the stamina to understand, and he had found out that he couldn't fool them; there was nothing to be gained by feigning understanding, when both people knew that if he had just listened he could have got the picture with little difficulty. That's what he had particularly liked about that pub; there was an acceptance of people as they were, no pressures to be this or that; the manipulations of human beings by forces outside their control were of more concern than a personal history. It was accepted, in the few half-intimate conversations had on the sides of important discussions, that people would all make mistakes, how could they not? People knew too when they were being fooled, they knew that the majority opinion expressed about the beleaguered state of a poor British army and their powerless minions was flawed and dishonest. They knew that the prisoners of this decade, now going into these decades, were not evil people and if one or two of them were, that was to be expected. War didn't always bring out the best in men. But now here he was wondering why the first unfettered enjoyment of his adult life had to end up in a cell. Were the others still drinking in their corners? Did they mention him often? But it would serve no purpose to be bitter. Those people, who were more certain than he of this cause, they hadn't hired out cars for virtual strangers, or if they had, they hadn't been caught. He was always surprised when joined by one or other of them as the years went on. They would fill in the picture, as they saw it, and it was never as he had imagined it. Really he had known little then. Had he spent all of that time fooling himself?

The days had their own rhythms and the certainty of these gradually healed the soreness inside him; well, if not healed, at least soothed. He got down to living these days with the hope that when they became his past he would be able to remember as little of them as possible. It was only in his dreams now that real trouble happened. The patterns were broken sometimes, causing emotional flurries; a new prisoner – so that is what he had been like – or a man going home (this brought out the best he had ever seen in people); trouble on the landing, death, death, the news of which the screws had handled badly; springtime. The secret was not to let flurries become ulcers. Studying might help. Open University. The first course, sociology, was too close to the bone. How could a man in prison be expected to study deviance and control as if they were types of science? The political content of the course was presented falteringly, afraid that its own logic would demolish the previous assertions. So he went back to the workshop. But surprisingly his craft work did not improve. He had presumed, because of his pre-vious job, that he had some manual skills. Maybe history and appreciation of art would offer a quicker leap over the wall. And it did. You see, these painters had stayed the course. They had not ever said, look, you know, I cannot do it, I simply cannot take another day; I'm folding up and going away where you will not be able to find me. There were a few men in here who could not be reached any more, but Senan would surely stay as closely to the land of the living as he could. No matter that he felt the hatred which people had for him personally, no matter that the sounds of men putting in years could sometimes be too much for him, no matter anything, he would leave here still sane. Him against them and springtime. How did he know of the hatred, how could he sense, how could it filter through to here, this place whose daylight was even fractured? By watching the news. He still watched the news (nearly all of them did), letting it take them to named places remembered, watching it as if some day it would throw up something that would change their lives.

History and time, time and history, sizing each other up. All things smelt and felt. His touch became distant.

And into this came something to see, the pictures painted, they must have been done for him in particular, in his particular circumstances. This would be the saving of his senses.

One night when Senan was in London he had gone to a party; he hadn't often gone out with any of the others in the house, but that night it had seemed the right thing to do. He took a bus down the Holloway Road with Brian, hating this city because of himself. At the party he met a woman who surprised him. She wore a short black skirt, yellow tights, and a faded gold blouse. She had earrings and necklaces and rings. Senan was not in the habit of noticing all these details, but it helped to camouflage what threatened to be an overwhelming desire. He moved from foot to foot as the night went on, afraid that he would break their time by saying something foolish. In the end nothing harmful was said, their hands fell together and they speedily went upstairs where they locked the door. Senan forgot to tell Brian to get the taxi home alone. He often now replayed that night because it helped him. He was sure she wouldn't mind; it was not that his intentions were bad, it was just that he had not much else, and surely it was, too, some sort of compliment. The way they kissed, the way their touch was almost raw, the slow way they managed to undress quickly. How they brought up together lust in one night. They had each come to this evening with mannered talk and mild flirtatiousness. But now look at them on that bed.

When they woke in the morning, they made love again and then the questions started. Because of the lightness of the night Senan couldn't be Tim Gallagher and hinted as much. She asked him straight out if he'd ever killed anybody. 'Good God! No,' Senan said and blushed. Women were like that – they could be matter of fact about a huge question; they simply wanted to know where they stood. Perhaps it was because the reality was far from them; they didn't see themselves ever having to take those decisions. Men, for all their swagger, would prefer not to know, and that was not only because they were respecting serious matters. When Senan got home after that night he decided not to get in touch with the woman again; not because he didn't want to, but because he felt that it was too dangerous. She too was sorry when he didn't telephone at the agreed time, but thought that maybe it was just as well.

Stephen was visiting for some time when he brought the idea up of getting his two neighbours to write. He described them well. Senan knew, even before he opened Connie's letter, that this was the woman from the London party. When he read the letter he could even hear her voice, but maybe he was wrong? Imagination gone haywire. So he asked for a photograph, and saw that he was right. It would have been like that woman to send a photograph without fear. So she was married and had children. It happened. He discussed his quandary with one friend but advice was not forthcoming. He felt that he should let her know, and yet that could prove awkward for her. If he referred in a letter to having met her in London, might not the Special Branch call on her house? He couldn't find the right formula to tell Stephen either. Many times the screws were not asleep as they pretended, but were listening instead with double ears. And maybe, also, she would not want a neighbour knowing of her past? His impulse to accept a visit from her caused him serious worries. Would the shock be too infuriating for her? Would she remember that she had sent him a photograph? Would it indeed bring her worse problems? Was he accepting the visit, not only to clarify his identity but because he wanted to see her again, married or not? Then she didn't come. The reply to her explanation was suitably truthful. But Senan was relieved. He would continue writing and would visit her one time when he got out. If she freaked and thought him dishonest, so be it, he would at least be out by then and surely any hatred that she would direct at him could be submerged in the well-being of freedom. In the meantime he enjoyed her letters even more than he should have.

The passenger who got on the 11.20 Cork to Dublin train at Portlaoise on 18 March felt out of place and frightened, and had a nauseous excitement in his bowels. His clothes were years out of date, but he could also have been a slightly out-of-fashion farmer. He was still good-looking even if his blue eyes were more faded than you would expect. He was afraid to have a drink, the cost of the tea had staggered him. People don't notice fields, houses, other passengers, the way he did. It was the best journey of his life.

161

He stayed in a hostel for a week. It was suitable, not too comfortable. The cars and buses and crowds scared him, but his feet managed to take him tentatively up and down the streets. His brother, now back in Ireland, met him and they had a drink. The taste was shocking, the effect had a dangerous sense of overload. Emotions could explode if he wasn't careful. His parents made a valiant effort to have a welcome-home party, as if he were a mere emigrant returning. His mother bought him new clothes and he was ashamed of having no money. On arrival back in Dublin he telephoned Connie. She seemed nervous but told him to call the next morning at ten o'clock.

There was no easy way for Senan to excuse himself. The shock of seeing him on her doorstep (Connie recognised him immediately) made her draw him in quickly, as if the neighbours would know the whole story by the expression on her face, even from hundreds of yards away. 'I'm sorry,' he said, and tried to explain why he could not have told her. She raged, but understood really. 'Maybe,' she said. She became uncomfortable when he explained why in London he had not contacted her again, why he had thought it best. She didn't tell him that her body had longed for him many times, in the six months that had followed, even if her mind had warned against him. She didn't say that she had told no one in her present life of meeting him. Why would she have anyway? It was only a one-night stand she said, or lied. 'No one's life is easy,' she continued. 'But some are less easy,' he said. 'Oh, now, I wouldn't be sure of that.' There were some terrible pauses. And then surprising ease. Wouldn't Fergal love this, Connie thought sarcastically. Their conversation lapped up to each others', then moved out to sea again.

It is doubtful that either of them expected even a possibility of what happened next. It is certain that neither of them intended it to happen. Connie more so, although there cannot be degrees of non-intent. It must have been their fingers that hit off each others' as they both reached for the teapot. It is not possible to explain how they could not draw back from that one touch, or at least it's not possible to explain why one or both of them didn't simply try to pretend that there had been no mutual overwhelming charge dug out of memory. Surely one of them could have pretended that they hadn't noticed? But they didn't. And in five seconds there was no awkwardness left in that kitchen, the distance between it and the bed was measured on the one hand in inches, on the other in miles. Now look at them on that bed.

It appears that they both visited Bernard, and that Connie acted almost as she would have done if this had merely been the prisoner, the ex-prisoner, to whom they had both been writing. Bernard certainly noticed nothing stranger than he would have expected.

10

Stephen,

Hope you've enjoyed your fortnight in the wilds. Sorry we can't wait but we're getting a lift as far as Cork city and then we'll hitch the rest, off to Gerry's party for the weekend. The rent is in the usual place and we've left our share of the ESB bill. The tap is still dripping so we've tightened it with the wrench – see under kitchen sink. The pie in the fridge should still be edible if you're back tonight, Friday. So much for the mundanities. But guess what, we think – only think, mind you – we think Connie is having it off with your friend Senan, from Portlaoise. Yes, he's out, early it seems. We've seen him coming to Connie's every single day this week! And she called around here about the tap and honestly, you wouldn't recognise her. It's as if she's uncontrollably come back from the dead. Her clothes have all changed too. Truly, we don't think we've imagined it; in fact, we're practically certain. So how's that for news! If it's true, I'm delighted. I don't know what she's doing with that bag of bones, anyway. Joan says I'm being flippant, because I don't realise what a disaster it could be, due to Connie's responsibilities! Stick in the mud. So keep your eyes and ears open and see you on Monday.

> Gina

To Fergal from Helena
Dublin

Dear Fergal,

I won't be back for a month, as I'm taking my holidays and then going on the Rome route for a fortnight. Enjoyed meeting you last week etc. Look, I'm not going to waffle away here, I've wondered and wondered how to tell you this but there doesn't seem to be an easy way to lead in, so here goes. Remember the prisoner that Bernard and Connie were writing to; well, he's out. He came to see Connie and it appears that they had 'met' once in London when she was there (well, presumably she was there or they couldn't have met). Sorry, sorry. Anyway, she says that she didn't know that it was him she was writing to because he had a different name then. He, apparently, had realised that it was her, but couldn't tell her because the letters were read and he thought it best to wait until he got out. To get straight to the point, they have been having an affair for the last few weeks. A fully fledged, off-the-rails affair. Quite frankly, Connie is not herself, or maybe she is and she has been somebody else since I've known her. It was going on for a while (I don't know how long). One night, an hour after I had come back, Connie came over, very flushed and agitated. Kevin and I were having a drink together, but she wouldn't stay and said she would call in the morning after she had left the children to school. She did, and told me the whole story. My mouth just fell open down to my shoes. Connie! Of all the people in the world. You never know, do you?

She's not making any excuses, says she knows it's wrong and all that, but that she can't help herself. She says that it's the best thing

165

that has ever happened her. I questioned that slightly when I managed to get my mouth working and succeeded in getting a word in, but she insisted 'the best thing ever'. Quite frankly, I'm gobsmacked. I don't know whether to be outraged, shocked, or glad for her. I know that sounds ridiculously simplistic of me, but honestly, she looks great. She's almost dancing around the place, radiating some kind of basicness that I've never seen before. She has bought new clothes, looks smashing, Her house looks great too, and I swear the children appear to be cheered up no end. I can't explain it but it's true.

Now of course no one else knows this – I think. Although how Desmond doesn't suspect something, I have no idea. Mind you, he never paid much attention to her this last few years, so maybe he's gone blind as far as she's concerned, from lack of practice at looking. I haven't told Kevin yet, although I will have to soon; I thought I'd wait to see if it blows over because there is no point in the whole street knowing if it's only a temporary flash of madness. Mind you, it will be a relief to tell Kevin. Firstly, because I hate keeping secrets from him, and secondly, because I can't seem to think of anything else and I wish I could talk to him about it. By the way, after she told me that morning, she brazenly left at one o'clock to meet him. I suppose that's how you do it. Senan is his name, but of course you know that. I didn't know whether I was horrified or struck rigid with admiration. I have to confess that I couldn't resist having a peep out the window at him – not a bad-looking bloke at all, has some air of something different about him – he would, I suppose. I can tell you my housework took a battering, imagining what was going on across the street!

Look, Fergal, I feel that this will be a shock to you. Maybe I'm wrong; maybe you'll think it unremarkable and everyday; maybe it's me who is shocked and I wish someone else to be more upset than me, whatever. I thought, anyway, that I should tell you. I asked Connie if she had been in touch with you and she gave me a kind of distracted look, but didn't say not to tell you. Now I suppose I've done the wrong thing.

Helena

To Helena from Fergal

Dear Helena,

I got your letter this morning before I left for work and am still reeling. I suppose that's how it could be described. I want to know, Helena, no offence, if you too have gone off your head. Glad for her! This is a disaster! I bet he thought it best to wait until he got out! Suited him fine, still had his letters coming from her, didn't he, thought she might stop writing if she knew that he was a cheat as well as everything else. If the matter weren't so serious, I might be able to find your, 'some air of something different about him' amusing. Certainly there's some air of something different about him – he's a jailbird, isn't he? The long and short of it, Helena, is that Connie is sleeping with a Provo; a fucking Provo is what she is sleeping with. I don't care how many faults Desmond has – she didn't have to sink that low. I'm writing to her this second. Please call me when you are next over.

Fergal

PS. Of course Connie acted distractedly when you mentioned me; she knows damn rightly that I'll be the one person to burst her little bubble. And look where this mess has landed you; you're keeping secrets from your husband and you're worrying about whether you should or shouldn't tell me.

PPS. I'll send Connie's letter care of you in case Desmond might find it. Now look what she has us all at! And when did she 'meet' him? She never told me anything about it.

Connie,

I've just had a letter from Helena in which she told me about your carrying on with this Senan fellow. I must say I'm shocked beyond belief; not only because you're being unfaithful, committing adultery to be exact, but because of the type of person you're doing it with. I'm also horrified to hear that you already knew him – so that's why you said something about the fact that I don't know everything about you because I haven't always lived in the same country as you. Indeed, if your actions, now that I'm out of the same country again, are anything to go by, I'm not surprised that you said that. Does this in fact mean that all our friendship since that time has been dishonest? I really don't know what else to say. Write to tell me that it was all a mistake.

Fergal

Dear Fergal,

Now really, I have to say this to you; I don't like your tone of voice. Of course I know that you're shocked but I now realise that my worrying about whether to tell you or not had nothing to do with what's going on, but more to do with how badly you handled all this communication of Connie's with Senan from the first instant. By the way, I told Kevin and he just shrugged his shoulders and said that Desmond had it coming to him. He said that if she was going to have an affair, then Senan, of course, was the perfect candidate, just being out of jail and all that. I'm not quite sure what he meant but I can guess. No, you've got it wrong; you cannot just tar his whole character because of a mistake, and I do not believe that he intended any harm by not referring to their previous meeting – Connie doesn't seem to mind.

Which brings me to the most important part of this rushed letter. You are the person who is closest to Connie – a fact that I don't mind admitting I have often envied – and I think it little behoves you to adopt the high-handed critical tone that you took with her. Of course she showed me the letter; she was extremely upset by it. You'll be relieved to know that I didn't show her the one you sent to me, although it was for her sake, I can tell you, that I didn't, not yours. Adultery, adultery my eye; since when did we all revert back into the dark ages? Give us a break, Fergal, join a monastery. Mind you, that wouldn't guarantee strict moral standards any more. I digress. Yes, of course I see a difference between writing letters to someone and sleeping with them, but then you treated the letter-writing as if it also was a fully fledged betrayal. Of what I'd like to know? And I did not think I'd have to say this again; if you value your friendship with Connie, you need to get down off your high horse, or at least behave as if you were dismounting. OK, I don't want to be too hard on you, and obviously you're upset, but please try to calm down and leave a little room for someone else on the high moral ground. It would also help to think a little more ration-ally. Connie is going to write to you; she said that she was going to try explaining to you, although quite frankly I wouldn't relish her job. No, I didn't say that to her. I am perhaps more loyal than you think. I will get in touch on my next flight over, and I sincerely hope, for your sake as well as mine, that your heels will have cooled a little by then.

Helena

How badly I've 'handled all this communication'! You've all gone mad, including Kevin. She's sleeping with a Provo; she's endangering her whole life. God knows if she was daft enough to marry Desmond there must be something going on between them. Now she's jeopardising all that by having an affair with someone who would pack up in three seconds flat and be out of there if it suited him, or if he got the call.

All right, I may have reacted a little strongly, but what, Helena, was I supposed to do? Thank you for not showing her the letter I sent you. I'm away off to put my heels in a basin of ice.

Fergal

To Fergal from Connie

Dear Fergal,

It seems I'm going to have to make a serious attempt to tell you something about myself, and you're not the only person who hasn't known these things; the past few weeks have taught me more about myself than I've ever known. You'll excuse me if I ramble a little but by tying it together for you, as always, I will clarify it for myself as I go along. I am telling you all these things because you are one of the most important people in my life; I cannot live with your disapproval.

Firstly, us. Since we shared a flat you have been like a brother to me and I know I've been in some ways a whole family to you, but we did go our separate ways and you didn't always notice everything. After I met Desmond, naturally our relationship changed, or rather I changed, and you have to admit so did you, particularly after Carmel. You forget so easily that you were married yourself. But I changed even more after children, and you didn't notice because, perhaps, you were afraid to know some of my desperations. I'm not blaming you because, to be honest, I camouflaged it well, even for myself. The worst thing was not just the way my whole life was now revolving around babies, and the loneliness of that (although, of course, I loved them and I'm not going to patronise either you or myself by saying how much), but it was also Desmond. He stopped seeing me as anything but a mother, and because he was the person I saw most of, and certainly so after you went to New York, I began to see myself, too, as only that. A mother is grand, but nothing other than is not enough. You know those shocking pictures that I saw one time, on some anthropological programme about some tribe along the Andes, or somewhere, and the girls were tidying outside the tents while the boys parked toy trucks behind them – no, you don't remember? Well I do, and I can still hear you saying, not condescendingly, I have to say, but honestly, that you thought that, well, that's the way it is. But if it is, then the girls are going to have to get something else because tidying the tent, inside and out, can make your head blow up.

After I had the twins I argued a lot with Desmond, about reasons for this and that and reasons why we couldn't see eye to eye. The arguments were really about something else but we didn't realise it. Pity that he wasn't able for even a little more of me then, because I could certainly have still done with more of him. But we let it go and retreated into our separate nerve-ends; our lives became totally alien to each other's. The baby, I have to say, put the tin hat on it. I've never understood what the tin hat means but I know what it stands for. I developed a space in the middle of my head in which I let unpleasant things swirl about. I could imagine this place, full to the brim. I thought that I would always have to walk straight-backed, head up, or it might tip over, and all the bad things would drip through my brain and poison me. While men were writing sentimental poetry about me feeding babies, I was wishing that those babies were teenagers. I was trying to pull my nipple out of their mouths, without them noticing. If I was asked, which was rare, what I was thinking about, I always said 'nothing'. How could this be love? Quinnsworth, dead body fluid, and a sarcastic edge to a man's voice every evening when he came home. But what could I do? I had three children, for God's sake. They seemed to have happened to me, as if I had been caught napping and was told that I now had to pay the price. What choice did I have? None. I did try to bring this up with you a few times, but you skirted my fears wonderfully with all the assurance of a professional dancer. Can't say I blame you. No, I would have to get on with it and to hell with me.

As for London. No, I didn't tell you about everybody I met, no more than you did me. So we had a party in our house and I ended up with a man! In bed. Not all that unusual, even though it does seem odd now to have actually had sex with men I can't remember; how cavalier we were with our privacy. How careless too! We knew that men murdered women and, presumably, some of them nearly murdered women, but we were completely trusting of total strangers. Actually, I didn't do it much, now that I think of it. I probably can remember them all. On this night it was a man called Tim Gallagher; I even remember his second name. I have to tell you now that this was no ordinary night. We had the time of our lives. I had never believed that there could be anyone like him or, indeed, anyone like the me that was with him. Let's face it – sex is like everything else, some people are better at it than others. Do you know that I still remembered that night through all these years. And morning was no disappointment. But somehow I didn't believe him about his name. It was intuition, probably fostered by the great closeness we had just played. I must have asked him a lot of questions, and he must have hinted at something to me, and I remember we argued about the North, but of course that was nothing new then. How many of us did that every day without even realising, certainly then anyway? I suppose we've been training our forgetfulness since, as funeral heaps on top of funeral. One way or the other, I think I knew that that was not his real name. Now I said that 'we' had the time of our lives, but of course I began to doubt that when he didn't get in touch. In fact, I was very upset (devastated may sound a little dramatic). I had, after all, not known even his name twenty-four hours previously, or whoever's name it was. But I certainly thought that I was devastated. I dreamed about him all the time, felt diminished by the fact that he didn't get in touch. I could do nothing about it because I didn't know where he lived. In a matter of months I was the walking wounded and I had forgotten what confidence meant. But I had enough left, unknown to myself, had sense enough to fear what might happen if I didn't do something. So I came home. And I did forget him, or at least I relegated him to a manageable experience. The only difficulty I had was that sometimes if I had a drink I would want to talk about it, but in time I trained even that response out of me.

And then, of course, I met Desmond and you know the rest. So I missed you when you went away, and maybe writing letters to Senan brought something new into my life. No, it's not maybe; it definitely did. I could think that I was interesting again. So Senan came out and called to see me. He had agonised over me not knowing who he was, and I now know that he didn't get in touch with me because he couldn't, that is in London. I really did not need to know this any more but it was a pleasant surprise to be told. So I slept with him, just sailed into bed with him as if it wasn't wrong and as if it would have no repercussions. It could belong to my past, just be a continuation of a me that was no more; I'd come back to being a wife and mother in a minute when I got out of bed.

But of course that's not what happened. Sleeping with him (we haven't, of course, been able to sleep yet, we're on our guard too much) has changed me forever. I know you could say that that is ridiculous. I should have more sense than to think that someone else makes my well-being, but as you can imagine, I have already dealt with all those arguments. It's not that I have any illusions about this lasting or about any possibilities that there could be for Senan and me; it's more that the act of being touched by him (notice I see it as an act not as a passive happening) has shot me out of my past life; I mean, my past few years. That's what it feels like; there is such a distance now between me and the me of a month ago that I do not recognise the memory of myself. In time I'm sure I will again. I will be able to see some continuous line in my life, but at the moment, no; I'm too mesmerised by this surprise that I thought would be denied me forever. This will always now be the point where things have changed.

After that first day, when I thought about what I'd done, I did not feel any of the fear that I know you think I should have felt. I have never experienced such bodily longing. I now know what music is; it's the sound for stretching our emotions as far as they can go. It's the sum total of all the sounds that a stretched body takes to it. I'm listening to long songs and wailing music and I'm hearing every delicious sensation that I could ever have wanted. I am playing records; I find the radio a nuisance. After I 'slept' with him I could remember everything; that was the strangest part. Not about years ago, but about yesterday and the day before and last month and last Christmas. And having remembered I can now see.

Yes, Fergal, this will all end in tears. But I will always be glad about it. Even the children seem clearer to me now, more special. There will be no more waiting for disasters not to happen.

> Your friend,
> Connie

POSTCARD
To Helena from Fergal

Dear Helena,

Could you please tell Connie that I got her letter, and that I'm not ready to write just yet, but that my heart goes out to her and that I'm sorry if I've been very hard on her.

> Fergal

Dear Fergal,

Got your postcard. Perhaps you should tell Connie yourself, but no matter, I'll do it if you still need time. Listen, why am I talking like this to you? You're acting like a spurned lover yourself.

The scene now is that we're sure Bernard also knows, and neither Kevin nor myself know whether we should broach the subject or not; we'd hate to see him suffering alone. It's too awful for Connie; they have always got on so well. The affair continues, it seems, although Connie doesn't talk about it as much now. Either she's embarrassed by how open she has been about intimate thoughts, or it's not going too well. I'll find out in due course, no doubt. As far as we can figure, Desmond is still oblivious. Connie certainly hasn't told him yet. All is sweetness and light in the house, cheerful and breezy. By the way, I've met Senan; he's actually very interesting as well. I mean as well as being handsome. It was weird meeting him. Terribly sexual, really. I know, and have seen, quite a lot of unusual things, being an air-hostess, this and that, but there was something naked about the two of them together. I wish them well, with each other or apart. But of course the drama hasn't started yet. Don't you think tragedy has an oily feel to it?

See you soon,
Helena

To Helena from Fergal

Dear Helena,

I really wish you hadn't met this fellow; I would hate to see you encouraging Connie in any way by creating a normality about it. Poor Bernard. Poor Desmond. I wouldn't like to be about to lose her.

Fergal

To Fergal from Desmond

Dear Fergal,

This is normally the last thing on earth that I would do and no doubt you will find this a strange and peculiar letter but there is a matter which I need to discuss, and frankly, my possible choices of people with whom to do that are limited. So I have no choice but to write. You see, I need to talk to someone who knows Connie; the reason will become evident. To get straight to the point, I suspect that she might be having an affair. As you may have noticed, Connie is a very stable woman, has always liked women more than men, a fact that has, I must admit, suited me. To be frank, I also think that those women are better because they know precisely what they want from men; they've fulfilled their emotional needs elsewhere. However, although this was how things progressed at the beginning of our marriage, I have found that since our first child, children as it turned out, was born, Connie's emotional needs have become derailed. To be honest, her continuous knowing about children and her concomitant desire to know about herself and me has often embarrassed me. Now I know that embarrassment is a peculiar emotion for a husband to admit feeling about his wife; it also signals loss of control, but I think, perhaps, it is not as rare as we may assume.

As time has gone on I have persevered with these moods. I have my moral code, I pay my way. But recently I have seen a strange change in my wife – she has become cheerful. I do not mean simply cheerful in a normal way; it is more a superior cheerfulness that I find quite upsetting. This led me to believe that she might be having an affair. I thought at first that perhaps it might have been this prisoner fellow. You know, I'm sure, how women sometimes find uncouth types attractive; they can't avoid noticing them, being so used to the smooth skins of their fathers and husbands. Yes, this prisoner is out, my father told me when we were having a drink last week, and when I expressed surprise he asked if Connie had not told me? That set me to thinking, but she had a reasonable excuse and, anyway, she wouldn't really be the type to fall for a person like that. And also she couldn't possibly organise it with the children. There would not be time or place for preliminaries, etc. However, the fear has still persisted. Unlike my wife, I have never believed honesty in all matters to be essential, but it would still be unbearable to think of her having an affair behind my back. This may seem like a peculiar request, but as you do correspond with her I'm sure it would be possible for you to find out whether my fears are well-founded or groundless. I do not wish to break any confidences that you and she, as old friends, might have, but I trust you understand the importance of this one issue. If you do not have time to write my telephone number at work is 4931146.

Hope to hear from you soon.

Yours sincerely,
Desmond

To Fergal from Helena
Dublin

Dear Fergal,

The shit has hit the fan! Desmond came home one lunch time, deliberately, I presume; he must have got suspicious finally. Connie is bearing up remarkably well. She seems almost relieved, and still looks wonderful. Senan is now off the map, of course. I'll be in New York on Thursday. See you at the hotel? Or else leave a message for me.

Helena

To Fergal from Bernard

Dear Fergal,

This is rather a hasty note, but as I believe Helena is going to be starting regular flights again to New York, I wondered if over the next few months you might look for a few books for me. I believe it will be easier for you to get what I need as the choice is limited here. I'd like a few books that address themselves solely to design. This does not have to be only glass, it could be other materials, but I'm sure I'd find the glass-based ones inspiring. Have you finished George Sand or are you now reading something different?

As you may know (I didn't wish to enquire whether you did or didn't from anybody else), there has been a minor upset here. Some people would, of course, see it as major, and I'm sure I should be one of those, but things don't always happen as they're supposed to; a fact, I presume, you know only too well yourself. It appears that Connie has been having some kind of assignations with Senan; I did rather suspect that this might happen. Not necessarily with Senan, but I thought it might happen with somebody. Desmond has now discovered and is, of course, distraught. Connie seems to be bearing up well in the circumstances. She was embarrassed with me, but I've told her not to be, that old doesn't always mean brittle. I feel sorry for Desmond, of course, but in truth I've always thought that he didn't love enough, and perhaps this will be a good thing for him. Perhaps he will now realise that thinking that we deserve luck is, in fact, a contradiction. You have to take bets too and risk losing; you have to lose. I'm going for a drink with him tonight. All usual timetables have been suspended.

I hope that getting the books won't be too much trouble. Look forward to hearing from you soon.

Bernard

PS. When having my drink with Desmond last night, I said that I was writing to you and he told me to tell you that there was no need now to reply to him. I presume you know what this means.

11

In a place where most people – if they suffer from their pasts, that is, if they haven't grown above them – suffer from seeing a lack of love between parents, Desmond would have been considered unique. If asked, that's what neighbours would have said; so too would his mother and father. Or would they? Did his now departed mother and Bernard feel a niggling doubt about their capacity to include him, to satisfy his ravenous need to be the centre of attention? Or did they think that that need had only become unreasonably hungry because he had felt excluded?

That's what Desmond felt as a child. He suffered because his parents were happy with each other. They didn't need him. Many a person would have thought this a peculiar, even an amusing, state. They would have dismissed his feelings as unnecessary; they would have swiped them away with a wave of their hands, and there might have been a trace of contempt in the wave. But a child feels what it feels. And then does with it what it can. If Desmond had had a brother or a sister things might have been different. He longed for that, created scenarios around the impossible, wished there was someone he could look at, the way Moira and Bernard looked at each other. But he didn't want sympathy; he wanted to be so striking that they would have to stop talking to each other and gaze at him instead. He tried to be remarkable at school, but even when he got to the top of his class, and stayed there, all they did was think he was wonderful, be glad, and do nothing. It may have even brought them closer in their happiness.

When he left Waterford to go to college he believed that he wasn't missed. His relationships were dogged by lack of simple practice. But someday he would meet someone who would see him in his entirety and he thought that he would treat that person well. In fact, what he would do is, he would put that person where his parents had been and get from her what had been missed. That someone was Connie. In truth, during their first week, she was sometimes struck by his coldness but was sure that she could make a hole in it. In the first month she examined his face sometimes and thought that he seemed as if he was either going to smile or sneeze. He would do neither. But Connie was captivated by this detached, busy lecturer and doubts were begrudging nuisances. Indeed, it was as a teacher that he had finally got a satisfactory amount of attention. So when they married he had two horses to back, so to speak.

In college Desmond had discovered how good he was, how consistently he could do his work well, and how well he could also teach others. He wished he'd known before; no matter that Moira and Bernard had said so often. He chose to believe that they had never noticed. He decided on a career as a lecturer early on, and had found out what was required within a matter of days. That's what he would be; he never considered that being was anything other than the job a person did. He kept his secrets neat and safe, he marked them off as reasons for failure or disappointment, but he was careful in the way that he checked them, as a dog is when it makes a dash from the roadside at a car. He held his parents responsible for an inordinate amount of his own failings. He could have married someone else other than Connie, but with Connie there would be less pressure. This way he would be cock of the heap, so to put it, although he believed that thought to be a little indelicate.

The wedding puzzled him. That day was one of the few times that he felt something lacking in himself, and it wasn't something he could blame on anyone else. In fact, he was thinking that he didn't really blame his parents for anything, but he had to have some reason for the waves of emptiness that made up his mind at times, and after all, his parents had always been there. He didn't like the first night of his honeymoon – well, maybe he liked it a little, but there were nervous peculiarities attached to it. Surprisingly, for this time, Desmond had not had fully consummated sex before this night; to be honest he'd never been that pushed. He was afraid that he might not know what to do, but in the event Connie seemed to move effortlessly from one moment to the next. Unlike how other men might feel, Desmond did not mind this in the least. He was grateful to her and when he woke in the morning felt the greatest love for another person that he'd ever experienced. He went quietly to the bathroom and ran himself a full bath, using the hotel foam-bath. Lying there, he feared that this had been the best part of his honeymoon so far; he was really enjoying soaking in the warm water. How could that be? Look what he'd just felt for Connie a moment ago. There was a shower too and he put it on full, pulled the plug and sat back in the bath, letting the water stream over his head and face, bending his neck, letting it run down his back as the other water left the bath. If anyone could see him now – he looked as if he was cowering in the corner of the tub. After he had dried himself and assured himself that breakfast would cure this nervous-ness, he went quietly back to the room and dressed. He was glad when the knock came to the door with breakfast because he had been dithering as to whether to waken Connie or not; a few times he'd gone to her side and wondered if he should. Now he had a reason. He took the breakfast tray to her bed and woke her. She seemed surprised that he was dressed. He was glad that they had stayed in the hotel where the reception had been held and where many of the guests had also stayed; now they could join them. If Connie was disappointed, she was a good actor.

In time this part of their life improved and Desmond began to thoroughly enjoy night-times. His coming was often sharp and needy; many times Connie heard pleading in his low whisperings and it was not what she had expected. In the first months different things happened; they bought a house and his parents visited. He liked Connie for the way she talked to them, normal, as if they weren't anybody's mother and father. He envied her ease. In her parents' house he counted the hours until he would be at home, wondering if this chitchat of Connie's was really a necessary part of living. If they left now they would be in time for a drink in some pub where he would know people, and could tell funny stories about their weekend; not because he was expected to, but because it would bring him back into a life where he had control. His first language was being in the middle talking out.

When Connie got pregnant he presumed he was delighted. Why wouldn't he be? Wasn't everybody? She seemed pleased. When the idea of twins was first raised he felt neither less nor more pleasure. When this was confirmed he suffered from his first worry: surely they would cause a lot of extra work? But Connie didn't seem to be too worried. During the last month, when she kept saying that she was fed up, he felt that, really, he should say that so was he, but for some reason decided not to. Often he said things and Connie got hurt or angry. Why should she? He could just as easily not have said them; a person didn't always say what they thought. Certainly he didn't. It was easier not to. He hated the way in the last month she tried to haul him into her pregnancy. One morning after he had tried to distance himself she collapsed into tears and looked awful, a woman so big crying in the corner of the sofa. He had said, 'I wonder if I'd had siblings would they all have been as bad at this as I am.' It was an admission, and of course it let him off the hook. Connie nearly smiled. 'Who ever talks of siblings?' she sniffed. On his way driving to work, he said aloud, although he had only meant to think it, 'My wife cries a lot.' He did not for one moment feel any blame attached to him.

Although overwhelmed with an inexplicable pleasure after the birth, that those tiny little things that kicked in perfect time with each other and that tried to open their eyes were now his children; he felt his innocence was being emptied out of him. He drew back; he was expected to become a man before he had been given time to be a child. If Desmond had said any of these thoughts out loud to someone they would have advised him soundly, while restraining themselves from catching him by the scruff of the neck. But what others might have thought Desmond should feel is beside any point. He could not help himself falling into a solid void. But luckily, he had his profession and could spend every day among people who needed this much, and not more, from him, competence, skill. They also got a gregarious humour that he rarely displayed at home.

He had thought that at least that was that over, and things, vague things, could only improve. But then Connie got pregnant again and he seemed to take that as a personal insult. He began to stay longer than was absolutely necessary at college in the evenings, and also to have drinks with colleagues after work. It surprised him to find just how many others did this, married men like himself, fathers, and students. The pubs were warm and suitably lit. He changed drinking places so he would not become known as too regular. One of his new places was the Theatre Bar where the young ones thought they were going to grow into shit-hot very soon. The level of sincerity was minor enough and this pub became his favourite retreat because he had nothing to do with theatre. The painters who thought that they would be shit-hot, in other words, his students, could sometimes exhaust him. Connie rarely complained; you had to give that to her.

Nobody knew how Desmond felt; how slap-bang up against the wall he was. It took him some time to notice that Connie had changed and he was annoyed at not being able to pin-point how long ago it might have been. Days, weeks perhaps? She had loosened up in quite a shocking way; she seemed to have bought new clothes, or was that an old skirt resurrected? Resurrected like her old self, she was acting as if these last few years had not happened. Every time he tried to speak to her, a child materialised. And by the time he could work his way back up to it again (how out of practice they were) the conversation, or Connie herself, would be somewhere else. The changed Connie disconcerted him; he had got used to the other one, become accustomed to the shift that had occurred, post-twins. Now she was slippery, running away from him, he'd swear, when he was about to ask questions. He tried going out for a meal with her but found that at the end of the evening they had managed to talk of children, job prospects, the government even, for God's sake. He felt vaguely irritated by her, all the time. Or scared. And then he began to seriously wonder if she could be having an affair. He knew that was ridiculous, he himself had been tempted only once. Connie would never ... the children would suffer. He never believed the stories of milk and delivery men.

He wrote to Fergal and it was a difficult letter because he wasn't very fond of Fergal. But that was only natural; no man liked the men who were there before, not that Fergal had ever been there, actually. Connie had assured him of this and he believed her. A man and woman couldn't have been so friendly if they had ever, he was sure of that. In a way the letter could have been a humiliation, but he chose to see it as him taking control, and that was a relief. How had Fergal and her ever got so close; how come he knew no women like Connie? He remembered Fergal at his mother's funeral, him and the other neighbours, nice of them, he supposed, but odd though. He wouldn't go to one of their mother's funerals; he supposed they must have been there for him because of Connie. It got more removed from his mother by the minute, the closer he examined it. And that's another thing, how had his father ended up living down the street from them; how had that happened? Not that it really bothered him; he mainly ignored it or went for a drink with him more often than he would have, that was all. He had never missed his mother. He had, of course, been a little shocked by the suddenness of her death, a little in awe of the exactness of his emotions. During the wake he had felt himself conversing into unreality. He was surprised at how aware of himself he was, but he never actually missed her. How could he have? Anyway, Bernard would do all the missing of her that she could possibly need. It must have been Connie who persuaded him to come live beside them; she would care like that. And now he was making glass (I ask you) and she had taken up night-classes. Maybe it was someone from there? Although there had been a party and he couldn't remember any men from the classes. Connie was like that, always women. Except for Fergal. The party had been Connie's idea and he had dreaded it. The neighbours were included and neighbours could dampen an evening. Helena and Kevin, while they were good company, gave out an air of judgement. He wasn't that fond of them. In the end he'd gone for a few drinks first and it hadn't been a bad party at all.

Desmond went home one day at lunch time. He would never be able to explain why, and why he had looked in the window rather than opening the door. In the kitchen he saw Connie and some man, a strange man. They were having tea, but there was more to it than that; he could feel it out on the street. He was pleased with himself, delighted that he hadn't stormed in, made a show of himself. During the afternoon he lived through every minute of each hour and cancelled his class. Who could the man be? It was that prisoner fellow, had to be. He was out, that's who it was. Well, I can tell you one thing, he thought uncontrollably, she'll not get one penny from me. I'll starve her and those children if she's gone to bed with someone else. That would soon bring her to heel, her and those children. Unfit mother she was, what kind of a mother did she think she was, cheating on her husband? How had they done it? Niceties, of course, would not get in the way with a man like him; he would have a different approach to sex. That must probably be a relief after himself, he thought wryly. He could imagine this man, with one hand on Connie's nipple and the other working its way into her pants within the flash of a kiss. She'd love that. This was very hard on him; he was falling in on himself the more he imagined. But of course she might get tired of that. That was optimism prompting him.

Now that he was sure, he had to say he was as shocked as he was hurt. One never really thought of mothers as being in the running, so to speak. One assumed that their heads were filled with other things. Thoughts of revenge flooded into him, submerging sorrow. Revenge was active; he'd been suffering now for three whole hours and couldn't bear much more of it. He would go home, he would confront her and see how she would try to wriggle out of it. But he couldn't wait. Where had all his venom come from? It must be her fault. He left for home early; he would be home by five o'clock, for the first time in two years. The traffic was slow going up Rathmines Road. How he was noticing things this evening, new shops, but there were always new shops on this road, tearing the insides out of places they had just got used to, new façades, then the same again. Change, change, change. He was home at ten past five; Connie was surprised.

Boy, did she drop those children when he confronted her. But to his amazement – he had quite bluntly asked her if she was having an affair – she calmly answered 'yes', and then said, 'I've been meaning to tell you.'

'Really,' he said. 'And when had you been meaning to tell me?' He nearly added, 'pray'.

'When I got around to it,' she said.

'Oh dear,' he said, with a voice that surprised him, because it was still his own, even if it had a hard tremor in it, hard as a rock. 'I must get around to fixing that door; I must tell my husband that I'm having an affair; gee, I almost forgot.'

'Stop that,' she said, and he amazed himself because he did.

The next few hours were spent trawling over the last few years; they got rid of an awful lot of time per minute. Connie put the children to bed as the recriminations matched each other; she hoped they would remember none of it. She contemplated looking for a baby-sitter: 'This is an emergency, I need to fight it out with my husband.' But she was afraid to go into a public place with him. Desmond couldn't quite believe what was happening. She complained, actually complained, about him looking in the window. She said it made a voyeur of him; that seemed to upset her in some extraordinary way he simply could not understand. She said that she thought the marriage was over.

'Don't be ridiculous,' he said. 'You have three children; where would you go?'

'Just because I've got three children, and have "nowhere to go", as you put it, doesn't mean that our marriage is not over.'

The children went to sleep. Desmond and Connie continued. He drifted sometimes, it was funny how words were all you were left with in the end, and the same words could be used in a different setting and wouldn't draw up feelings in you at all. Funny how much could be said in fifteen minutes; how much of the unbearable uttered, taboo topics slashed through. Good Lord, was it only nine o'clock? They were tired.

In the morning Desmond felt awkward – there had been a lot

of harm done, but he had to admit that some of what she said was right. Some things remained clearer than others: she had accused him of reading Marx whilst she was reading books about why it took different lengths of time for a man and a woman to be aroused, and the psychology of it. It wasn't Marx actually, but she had a point; he certainly hadn't been reading anything to do with the matters associated with the relationships between people. Certainly not. There had been times last night when he had thought of saying, 'Excuse me, I'm going for a walk.' It was a marvellous thing that some men did – go to a shop for cigarettes and never come back. But he didn't smoke. And what consternation it would cause, what slow agony and grief. Unrecoverable from, he would suspect. No, that was never necessary. Surely a conversation could be had; surely time spent deserved at least one conversation. Well, that's what they were having now. Some conversation! He would never have known that so much frustration could have been settling inside Connie, inside anyone, ready to explode. Odd that. They had breakfast quietly; there was a great distance between them, yet at the same time that distance was in itself like a shy intimacy. Who was this other person? The children swung their legs in unison under the table, looking from one to the other. He wasn't sure if they normally did that. That thing about words that he had been thinking about last night, what was it? He had sometimes, not habitually, probably only a few times, wondered how a person would say that they were leaving, presuming they weren't going to be a cigarette runaway. I suppose they just said it. But words are only meaningful insofar as they describe action. Of course Connie would say that words used to describe feelings are every bit as important, but then she would. What was she saying now? Was she saying that she was leaving? Heaven help him; he didn't know.

Desmond left for work; he didn't kiss Connie or anything like that. He felt an excitement. At work, he wondered if he wasn't a little mad. Maybe it would be good if Connie left; although he'd have to leave first, set himself up, then when Connie had got a flat they could sell the house. He would, of course, see the children. They were fine words: 'see the children'. Women said they had children; men said that they took their children for a walk, or that they took them to wherever, or if they weren't living with the mother any more, they saw them. But women had children. Connie was right about language; it showed up an awful lot. He tried to remember how he had got here to this particular day but for the life of him he couldn't.

12

Dear Connie,

I think about you nearly all the time these days and weeks. I feel that there is a terrible turmoil going on for you, and that these are times when you need me and I'm not there. Please do write soon and tell me if there is anything I can do. How about you and the children coming over here to me? Funny how we always call your offspring 'the children', never by their names. Life proceeds as normal here; I've taken up no new pursuits. I've changed departments in my job and don't like the new section as much as the last. Work is nearer to what I was doing at home, but would you believe it, I think we were more efficient and on top of it in Dublin? Unusual that. I still go to 'Ireland', as I call it, on a Thursday night – everyone there is already discussing Christmas plans. Remember the people who made you feel guilty if you discussed cars or holidays or any luxury? Well, here you cannot discuss going 'home' except around people you know to have a green card. I think they're mad to stay under those conditions; one would definitely be better off on the dole. But it's easy for me, they say.

I feel like an old hand now. I get as rude as the best of them and find myself saying, 'This is New York – what do you expect?'

People say that all the time when they've just been rude, or done something awful, like take your taxi. Grow up, get bad manners, you're in New York. But then on Sundays I walk around, I come across streets that could be streets off Palmerston Road and I feel easy. And when Monday comes and I battle my way into the office against a tide of hope and noise, I know for certain that I'm alive. I slip into the museums and art galleries still on a regular basis. So I can keep in mind always that I am a visitor, that I arrived goggle-eyed, not so long ago, that I really don't know all that much.

So, Connie, this is just to say that I'm thinking of you all the time, and really will do anything I can that might help. I'm sure I could get you a book. There's a book for everything. There's a new one out here guaranteed to get you over any trauma in eight weeks. Any. So write soon.

Fergal

To Fergal from Connie

Dear Fergal,

I'm not in the mood for writing letters, or else I'm feeling that I should write page upon page, but for the moment I'm just letting you know that I got yours. I suppose I can't write because a letter is made from some sense of order; well, at least the writers convince themselves that there is an order, even a chaotic one, whereas with me now I'm not sure what will happen from one minute to the next. Neither with myself (and although that's scary it's also delicious) nor with Desmond. I will do my best to explain to him, to take the rap, to re-explain and to be kind, but not forever. I do not know exactly if we're going to split up, to part ways, but I suspect that's what will happen, for a while anyway. Of course all this might change tomorrow. So send me a book about waiting for change!

Thank you for the invitation. Funny, I'm getting asked

everywhere these days. And although it's pleasant, it is also infuriating and exasperating. How can you ask me if I'd like to go there when you know that's impossible? I have no money, and would not get permission either. Yes, you can bet if I suggested even going on a holiday to the Isle of Man for three days at the moment, Desmond would suddenly become the most dedicated father imaginable, wouldn't be able to do without his children for a second. I could cry with the feeling that I have of being trapped. I have learned that I am not myself at all, that once I had children I became the property of their father. Oh dear, I had better not go down this line of thought. Maybe that's why you asked me, because you know it to be impossible.

I think my children are called 'children' by people because they haven't as yet reached that specific character that gets a person named. They have for me, of course, and in private with them I would never not call them by name, and in my head I would never think of them collectively. Even the twins.

I'm sorry if the change in your office is not so good. Is change not always good? That's not a statement; I really do not know.

Connie

Dear Connie,

By way of introduction, this cannot be anything other than a strange letter but I must write to you at least once. I will tell you simply what happened to me since I left. And what I am doing. And I can only hope that you will do the same – write to me, I mean – but if you cannot, or don't want to, or find it too upsetting or confusing, then so be it.

So here I am, having accomplished my first month and already I'm used to it, in a way. Psychologically it's perfect, because I can take my last years apart little by little and arrive at some compromise with myself. It helps that the place has a look of the sixties; not all of it, just some aspects. So I can imagine myself back in time before. And then I can piece things together.

As I told you, things were getting awkward between my brother and sister-in-law and myself. I was finding being out and on the streets very difficult. Everything had speeded up, I thought, but maybe memory had just failed me. Here is slower, sedate, mannerly. My brother was providing me with money, plus I had the dole. All in all, not a satisfactory solution; although he was providing food, I was spending a lot of money. I found that I couldn't tackle the bus, so I had to take taxis if I was so lost that I couldn't walk. Lost, that is, as I went looking for the work that, frankly, eluded me, as if the suggestion of me getting a job was laughing in my face! Then there was the little matter of the two of them together. Frankly, I think I was driving them nuts. I got on fine with each one separately but when they were together my presence hung on them like a particularly heavy cold. They didn't see me as noticing this, forgetting that my last school had taught me everything there is to know about privacy, everything there is to know about the differences between two people talking and three people talking. The first is close, the second is a meeting. I didn't only learn these things from the process of survival within such tight confines, I also learned them from fiction. That, of course, I would never have read if I'd lived my normal life. My brother certainly lived a normal life. I knew him little because he had visited me only once. These things you forgive, of course, because of people's jobs and neighbours; sometimes a brother in Portlaoise can make things very difficult. And in Ireland we're used to cutting off our own so it can be accomplished. Few, if any, of his friends knew of my existence so there were only certain places I could go with him. One was to a small party, excuse me, dinner party, where the hostess got roaring drunk and started singing chorus songs. She left the room and returned dressed for the part, trailing a large umbrella. Things took a nasty turn when she started making up the words and jabbing at her husband's penis with the umbrella. He was drunk too. The suggestion was that he wasn't up to it. I'm amazed he didn't hit her. Her brother said to me that I might be able to help her, because surely I too was in need of satisfying. I'm amazed I didn't hit him. Her parents were mortified, naturally. I was offended that my brother would bring me there, but you see, there were so few places where I could be shown publicly, and apparently this was one of them; that did little for the recovery of my ego.

But that party was good, because the shock of it drove me into blind action. I spoke with my brother the next morning; a fact I don't think he appreciated because, I suspect, he had a terrible hangover. But if I had left it until the next day, efforts would have been made by them to cover up, to doubt the awfulness, to wish away the taste. So the solution was that he would give me his contacts' names here, who would set me up with a job teaching English, and thus I would somehow come back into life again. I did try to get in touch, as you will have gathered by the three peculiar phone calls. After the third time I thought I had better not push your luck too far. But I will fill you in now, not just because you might want to know, but because I want to tell you.

On my way here I spent a full week with another friend of my brother's outside London. That's where I was when I dropped you the hasty postcard. He needed a lot of gardening done and I'm still good at that, even better than I used to be, because I made great patches in my head when I was in the quare place. The reason for this week was to give my brother time to fix things up here. The reason for the haste was that I knew better than he that if I stayed another minute with him we would never speak again. I have to say this for him; he's the most efficient employment exchange I ever saw in action, spurned on, I suspect, by his desire to be rid of me.

The gardening was great; my first chance to get my hands in the earth again, but the man! He yapped away in my ear incessantly, like a week-old pig. He traded on his second-generation Irishness to outsiders, although he knew little of Ireland's history and less of its complexities. On and on and on he went. Every single thing that is said by any person reminds him of something else, even before the sentence has been finished. Why do some people feel that everything must have a double, a treble, elsewhere? He runs a sort of guesthouse, well, a guesthouse really, not a sort of. On my second day a visitor arrived and he took the two of us on a tour of his town, Reading. I ask you, as if I need to be there. No offence to Reading, of course, but what does it conjure up? We did a whiz job on all that was on offer while he dizzied us with one stupid question after another, to each of us, and one stupid conversation after another from his store of prepared lines. 'One can destroy by having too many questions or answers,' I heard myself saying, honest, right down to the 'one'. But if I worried, as I was saying it, that my offence might be too extreme, there was no fear, he carried on unscathed. 'Look at the lushness of that . . . you can feel the fluidity of . . . it reminds me of . . . na na na na na nah.' And I'm behaving like a madman, turning my head and actually muttering behind my hand, 'It doesn't fucking have to remind you of anything.' And pretending that I've got a cough.

The final straw nearly came when we and the visiting Welshman took a train journey into the country. You may ask why I didn't stay in the garden. The answer is I was at his disposal and he wanted me there, as a board against which to throw his inanities. Breakfast was as normal, an endless gorge of projectile stories of his past and his parents, dead five centuries, etc., and me trying to be as rude as possible. For God's sake, I was writing postcards at the breakfast table, who ever heard of anyone sending a postcard from Reading? And I had no one to send postcards to! Except yourself. I was just writing them. I was thinking of the sheer awfulness of one more breakfast with this pipsqueak. I tried to follow 'pipsqueak', which had just drifted into my head, and although perfect in some ways, it wasn't quite enough. I was thinking too that there could be three, four, even five more of these mornings to be got through. But I managed, as usual, my training standing me in good stead. Just about, because awful as have been some of my breakfasts, none were ever as long as these. We got on the train, I wondering if the sights out our window might shut him up, but it only served to put speed on him. I tried my new methods of being rude, then tried ignoring him, although I had to interrupt one particularly wild 'fact' about the relationship between Scotland and Ireland. I got up and went to the snack car and had a whiskey, at eleven o'clock in the morning! I knew that I was near breaking point, and was worried that the whiskey might make me worse. I thought that perhaps I was going mad, truly mad, that maybe this man was not saying all those things at all, that I was imagining them. For the first time in years I felt like crying, truly felt like saying, 'I cannot take any more. Why should I have to?' but the thought of breaking down on an English train soon sorted me out. When we got to the town we went for a swim. Now here was another new beginning. I plunged in, terrified by the fear that I would have forgotten. I was paralysed with the pleasure of the first sensation. Jesus Christ, if your man didn't swim up beside me, practically on top of me. I dived down and swam away as fast as I could. When I came up he was there again, ready to talk, I have no doubt. But I dived again – he could not swim under water – and steered my course as unpredictably as possible in order to lose him. As I went down I got the word to describe him, but when I came up again I was too impressed by myself in the water to remember.

I had a drink with him that night, it was the one way I could bear him, partly because I spend my time concentrating on myself when I drink, because I'm afraid of this new unremembered feeling of drunkenness. When I woke in the morning, of course, I dreaded it again. But the phone call came, and all was ready for me to pick up my ticket and come here. I felt, once I knew that I was leaving, that maybe he wasn't that bad, that the whole thing was just an incapacity on my part to mix with the ordinary. But as the plane took off I thought – remember, I know types well – that I had spent time, too much of it, with the best and the worst, so I do know. I was so glad that I hadn't succumbed to the desire to ring my old London friends. Friends? That would not have been a good idea; after all, I'm making a new life. Will I always be running from someone, do you think? My brother, our Reading friend, my old acquaintances? The plane above the clouds was good.

And then I was here. A new chance. I thanked my brother. I was working within two days and the independence is a blessing beyond belief. Money is a strange thing; what it buys you is a particular basic freedom. To do whatever, have a bed to lie in, buy your own tea. And wonderfully, here I could do only those things to begin with, people are not consumed with shopping and having things. In Dublin I was shocked at the number of shops and the intensity of the shoppers. I really did see it as quite mad. The other thing that struck me was that the customers seemed to have become all-important. I could not remember that as being the case when I was last there. Here you have to wait if the two women in the post office are talking across the hatches to each other. As is only right, and you might also hear something of importance. I spent the first week getting my bearings, finding buses, metros, being surprised when I woke each morning by how much I knew already, looking at my phrase book and starting the process of learning this new language, this most isolating of tongues. In Ireland we're surrounded by the sea; here they're surrounded by alien language. I got lost a lot in the beginning, but finally found the bridges over the Danube and now feel as if I'm local. I even look local, until I speak. I can put about twelve sentences together and already have the trace of a heavy accent when I speak in English.

I spend a lot of my free time in the sad cafés, dark smoky places that comfort me greatly. I walk around the museums and they soothe me because the lighting in them is deeply subdued. Too much of Edison hypes us up. And sometimes I telephone people who have given me their phone numbers. This can take a lot of time. I have to prevaricate and worry and get into sweats. Then when it's done, and an arrangement made, I either feel great, grown up, or panicked. I can look forward to a night in company or I can be dazed, not knowing how I will talk to another stranger. But it usually works out, although people are never as I think they will be. I remember my sister-in-law describing her search for a boyfriend who would be just right. She knew the Elvis songs by heart, and expected to find one of him in the next parish. I think of her sometimes, the fruitlessness of searching for something you never wanted in the first place until somebody convinced you that you needed it, even though they knew that there was no 'it'.

I have discovered the baths (not from monumental work on my part, of course, it would be hard not to know of them). I use them, the lolling about naked in the same hot water as dozens of strangers, as a means of washing away unpleasantness. But I see I'll get used to them and will soon forget to visit. I'm wearing down the pavements finding new things, passing on my way home the bridge where the two large lions have no tongues, teeth but no tongues. I've been told that the architect killed himself when the job was finished because he had forgotten the tongues, but I find that hard to believe, because surely someone would have noticed while they were being constructed. I think, maybe, he wanted them to be tongueless, but when people didn't like them he ended his life. Of course I'm supposed to believe what I'm told, but my nature doesn't do that easily. I watch the dancing sometimes, a great clattering affair akin to Irish sets for a few minutes, but then flashing out into much more complex innuendo, humour and loaded simplicity.

Mostly I've divided myself in two here: I question politics and I visit museums and art galleries. Examination of these two things will free me soon. There is always talk of war here and past wars. Makes us look like perfect pacifists. I had begun to think that the hatred of me and my kind – this, of course, is the only thing I have to worry about – is petty, when I think of what has happened, been done, by other men. Well, it's a long shot at comfort but I try it. These people are coldly pragmatic; well, some of them. One man said about their alliance with Germany in the Second World War, 'We were made.' Another said, 'For lost territories we went with Germany in the first war, but they lost, so we went with them again, sure that they would win, but they lost again. For lost territories, you understand.' Yes, indeed I do. There are a lot of murmurings about lost territories. How about letting them stay lost, I joked one night. No one laughed. I volunteer our mistakes, my own mistakes, to make it easier for admission of wrong. I feel like the nice policeman, but they're not having any of it. And maybe they're right. Who am I to say?

Last week I said at work that I would go to the holocaust exhibition; exhibition seems such a shocking word to use. One of my co-workers began to explain the emerging political party system in Hungary – 'one party which is quite rich, mostly Jewish'. 'Really,' I said, shivering. 'Well, you know, they stick together.' Indeed they do, I thought, I wonder why. I went to the exhibition; maybe for my own sake I should not have. All those scared and lovely men and women in the healthy photographs. The unbearable knowledge of betrayal was already there in hindsight. At one point we had to walk through the trailer of a cattle truck, which was how many of the Jews were removed from this city. I shall never forget that. I left, knowing that we have within us a baseness never dreamed of by any species of animal. But then I shared a cell with a man who had lain shot beneath a British soldier who had poked his open wound with the top of his gun to get him to give information. I should have known.

And my trips to the museums? The past needs to be explained because we cannot understand it at the time. Of course there's a danger in the people we choose to explain it to us. In the Royal Palace of Buddha – how Europeans reconstruct meticulously after wars, giving a separate importance to the art of buildings – there are some marvellous gothic sculptures discovered in the early seventies. They are beautiful, precise and smashed, of course; they had already been partially destroyed before being used as filling in the Middle Ages. But parts of them have been lovingly reunited with other parts of them. They are remarkable; the stone smiles at you like a modern photograph. The cloaks would be the envy of any fashion designer; some of them still have little teeth. They could make you weep. The brochure tells you that Lázló Zolnay discovered them but, of course, does not tell you that he had been ignored, hounded, driven to drink. He had always insisted that the find was there; he was considered a crazy crank. And when they finally gave him a crew with which to dig, it consisted of miners and prisoners, no experts. He allowed the prisoners to go for drinks on their own; he told them that if they didn't come back he would be finished, dead, ruined. They all came back, every time. That bit tickles me. Would I have? The first man to hit a piece was a miner, his name meant 'lucky one'.

Statues are important here. A row will rage over statue as symbol. An old symbol of a mythical bird was stolen (used, rather) by a group of young Nazis; something like the way Cuchulainn gets passed around. Should the statue now be destroyed? Should the Liberation Monument be removed or is it sufficient to remove the Russian soldiers from around her feet?

Could we live without her now, that big towering glorious woman?

I'm sending you this little book of Margit Kovác's work, for all the letters and catalogues that you sent me. Now I know how hard it must have been for you to do all that, now that I've seen how busy your life is. How smug Salome looks with the head on the plate, no regrets in the corners of her mouth! Great colours. The book cannot really capture them all; there is not one, there are many, many Hungarian blues. Directly after the war she made light ceramic birds to cheer herself up. Her friends have jobs in the museum minding her work; I think they miss her.

But not all the museums are like this; some of them have too many three-legged milking stools. Yet I go to them, sometimes from loneliness for my first language. Hungarian truly is strange, as isolating as any sea or snow mass. The people feel it too; some of them are bitter, even though they pretend to be proud. We know those games. Often in the museums, I sidle up to tourists to see if I can hear English. Of course, some of the conversations aren't up to much; they're words said for the sake of filling up silence. The 'lushness of the embroidery'; 'they remind me of . . .' Not again, I want to scream: not another one. Perhaps I'm not able for people any more. So I go back to look at the mourning outfits of the girls. I wouldn't mind mourning if I could dress like that. Time for the pub, there are seventy-seven for every hospital bed, I have been told, but yes, the man who told me was drunk.

But sometimes I get very afraid. I don't know of what. I'm here because it's better, of that I'm sure. For everyone, and I hope that includes me. I don't know about you. I'm doing my own personal penance, learning to dream in another language. Some people claim that water has memory; that is why it can be used to heal. But if it does, then would it also not remember the bad things and so it could make a person even sicker?

Love,
Senan

PS. This PS is because I'm reluctant to finish in case you ask me to make this, in retrospect, the last letter. I can imagine you getting this; the postman will come after ten, you will see my writing, and I hope you will smile. But, of course, I'm not supposed to imagine you.

I'm terribly sorry that I did not get to speak to you on the telephone before I left. I am also sorry that your life is in turmoil but, and, I don't intend being facetious here, that can sometimes be good. Things which are healthy and right do not end in turmoil. It really would be lovely if you and the children could come here. All right, I will go now. Give my regards to Bernard if you think that would be OK.

To Senan from Connie

Dear Senan,

What an interesting letter; it made my day, I can tell you. I'm glad you didn't have to spend too long in England; your brother's friend sounds unbearable, poor man. I always feel sorry for people like him, once I go away from them, of course. Budapest has never been a place I've thought of, but now I will. In fact, I'm on my way hot-foot to the library. It feels strange writing to you again, now. Thank you for the book; it's such a lovely little thing in itself, and her letter makes it such a personal matter. It's funny, now, to think of me sending you catalogues and postcards and all that. I remember once going to the National Library to get postcards for you, so I went again one afternoon last week with the children, a tourist in my own city. I'd like to know more about art; if I did, perhaps I wouldn't find so many of the paintings boring. Maybe not boring — stern. And then when I move to the next room I cannot believe my eyes, it is so pleasing. So here are some more of the postcards, I'll use the rest.

I'm afraid that I cannot explain what is going on with me at the moment; immediately I arrive at a conclusion the opposite seems true. But I should tell you that I do not feel guilty, nor should you. I'm glad you're away but I'm not sorry about what happened.

Neither of us did each other any harm, and whatever harm was done to Desmond had to be done. I would have had great difficulty in confronting him; in fact, I could never have done it without the confidence I gained from being reminded that I am attractive, well, attractive enough. The experience with you, the giving from me and what you took back, fortified me against the bad things that have happened and the bad things to come. I don't wish to elaborate; it's all in the gruesome messiness of examining what appears to be a mutually misunderstood marriage. I grit my teeth. It's a beautiful day.

Last week in the gallery I watched a group of convent schoolgirls walking around on a class tour. I thought I would see bad things there, that they would traipse, but no, they were cheerful and seemed to be enjoying themselves. It gave me hope. Yes, it is a sunny day. Well, there is little else I can say; I'm not sure if I see any point in us continuing sending letters to each other, but then maybe there is. Let's see. How long do you think you need to stay in your personal purgatory? I'm really not so sure that you should feel quite so guilty – people do get caught up in things. And you didn't do worse, or did you? Sometimes I wonder. But I don't want to know. I know what you are now and that's fine by me. I, of course, cannot imagine you receiving this letter and that makes us different. I would have to change my life, change my house for you to be in the same position. Now, there's a thought. But if I do not know where you live, or what your street looks like, or where your nearest shop is, or what kind of bread you eat, I do remember your face, your lovely, lovely eyes, your boney, thin fingers that liked to be drumming, and your lips that were often cold.

Yours,
Connie

PS. Of all the impossible possibilities in the world, going to Budapest is the last on the list; no offence.

Dear Connie,

Your letter made me sad, but yes, it is a lovely day here too, blue skies that are vast and still shocking to me. Not just because of here, but because I'm 'out', as they say. I do not think that I will stay away forever; at least I hope I don't have to. I'll know if and when it is right to return. About guilt: you should know that each individual deals with it in an entirely unique and ever-changing way. Some, of course, don't have it, are convinced of the rightness of everything they did, the greatest of men those, usually. But others think that because they had a conversation with someone ten years ago that they set the scene for their death, because a conversation can change a person, and so chose their friends and their habits, their walking home time – you can imagine. I do not intend to feel guilty, but I like being here where I can put my war, both the one I belonged to, and my personal one, into a framework. I'm learning, although perhaps I've had enough of that.

I'll write soon again, I think, if that's all right with you. I liked your children. And now I see you smiling; if I ever praised your children you blushed as if they were still a part of your own body. Nice.

My love to you. And thanks,
Senan

Dear Connie,

I've made up my mind – I'm going home, or coming home. I'm very aware of the fact that something odd and peculiar is happening to you, something good and something bad, and I want to be there. If I amn't there now, then I can have no part of this history of yours, so I have put things in motion. I've given in my notice in my apartment and job and I've even begun to pack. Today I'm writing to the tenants, but I won't ask them to leave until they are ready; it would not be fair. I feel wonderful about the idea; I will deal with the reality of a job when I get there. After all, who is to choose which people must be banished, jobless, to another place and which ones can stay? You have no idea how I look forward to seeing you.

> Lots of love,
> Fergal

Dear Bernard,

As Connie will have told you, I'm on my way back. I will spend one day looking for books and that will include yours. If there is anything specific to do with glass that you would like, do let me know. Must rush.

> Fergal

Dear Fergal,

I am so, so glad. Weights seem to have dropped from all around me, from places that I hadn't noticed were being dragged down. I took the children to Sandymount beach today. I looked out to Dún Laoghaire and could think of nothing but you, and how I've missed you, and how good it will be to have you back. Even if I never saw you, I would prefer you to be near, to be reachable. The beach looked good, vast warhorse that it is, giving out bits of hope to all who walk along it. It must be the stretch of water in this island that has most work to do. Of course, when you arrive, if your tenants haven't left, you can stay here, only a minute amount of reorganisation, and, of course, I'd love it. Desmond is in and out, here and not here, little discussion takes place, and there is an air of something about to happen around the place. Maybe you won't be able to bear it. Hope you can.

      Love,
         Connie

13

It was funny this morning bringing Connie to the airport. Desmond offered to baby-sit and Connie said no, that she had organised one of the tenants to do it and he could go on to work as she expected she would have breakfast with Fergal before they came back. All this was said in front of me, and Connie was so definite about it, a new woman, I have to say. I could see Desmond floundering for the right response; I almost felt sorry for him. I did, in fact, feel sorry for him, while I was standing in the kitchen, but as soon as we'd closed the doors of the taxi, I thought my comeuppance thoughts again. He's behaved rather badly, dragging Connie's family into it, among other things. 'Bastard,' I said. 'Slimy little prick,' Kevin, who never swears, said. And I suspect that that is only the tip of the iceberg. I don't ask Connie directly what is going on; I have never thought it a good idea to know if your neighbours love each other. I allow her to say what needs to be said, and leave the rest unprobed, because I know how dangerous memories can be. Someone tells a bad joke, an uncertain, off-the-mark joke, one they have their own doubts about, but let it slip off the tongue, anyway; I never forget that joke and never really forgive the person. So I leave it up to her to tell me what she must. She is brave. Yes, it's a different bravery from jumping into the river to rescue the drowning; it's more like going into the water in the first place without being able to swim. A passenger told me once (I really do prefer to think of people as passengers, I've decided) that he knew a man who wouldn't borrow a book from anyone in case he got a disease. Precisely. Connie's not that person. And of course I also think her brave because I simply cannot imagine how anyone could rear three children, all the time, teach them, love, soften their natures, talk to them, and not go mad. I looked at her in the taxi this morning and realised we were cut from the opposite ends of the cloth. I couldn't do it; I had to hold myself stiff for a moment in case I shivered.

We arrived at the airport nervously. I could feel that Connie was walking in some sort of vacuum, that she was burying moments of her life with every step we took nearer to Arrivals. She was beaming. She had brought a packet of cigarettes with her and I didn't remark on them, because I know that she hasn't smoked for years, and I knew that they symbolised something, but I didn't want to know what it was. We chatted about things, then forgot them immediately. I looked at the people waiting; I'm always interested in the fraughtness and the pent-up emotions that are being kept under wraps in this place, mothers removing themselves from the rest of the company so they can take deep breaths and wipe their eyes against all the missing they have felt. Fergal walked out looking embarrassed but happy and he waved at me but it was Connie that he strode towards. I could feel that the distance, as they moved to meet each other, was an expectant time rather than space and belonged to a history that would never be the same again. They kissed and looked to others like lovers, I suspect; like people claiming what was theirs.

Phew! I excused myself as I had to board. Was I glad to be leaving! How often have I been grateful for my job, the chance to leave and to leave things be. They settle themselves better in my absence. Some people are not like this: my dear husband Kevin, for instance, who refuses every year to take up the chance to spend Christmas in New York. He feels that something might happen in Dublin which would need him. My Kevin. I prefer the sideline, when people die, for instance; I'm glad I haven't known them. Not like others for whom tragedy is like a hot bath.

I am much better in the air where the mêlée of egos is suspended, so I boarded my flight and prepared myself to meet today's passengers.

14

To Senan from Bernard

Dear Senan,

Hope you're well. Will write properly soon. I've been thinking that you should not hesitate to come back if you feel that that's what you should do. The glass is coming along great. Connie's friend Fergal came home today.

Regards,
Bernard